TOES

IN

SAND

w w goss

Disclaimer
Toes in Sand is a work of fiction. Names, characters, places, and incidents either are products of the author's imagination or are used fictitiously. Any resemblance to actual persons, living or dead, events, or locales is entirely coincidental.

Other works by the author:

How I Learned French or Certain Events in the Life of Otto Pulaski

Red Monkey

Clave

Acknowledgements

Thank you, Marie, my wonderful wife, for not yawning or giving me a hard time every time I said, "I'm finished with *Toes*."

I am grateful to the people of Manzanita and neighboring Nehalem and Wheeler. These are communities where kindness is in abundance. Frank, thank you for the umpire story.

During breaks between rounds with *Toes*, I read David Foster Wallace's *Infinite Jest*. What a liberating work!

I am grateful to Holly Lörincz, a writer's rock.

The history of Manzanita was at my fingertips in the excellent *At the Foot of the Mountain*, researched and written by Jane Comerford and designed by Giuseppe Lipari, published by Dragonfly Press.

Jay Zebrowski, my longtime friend and post-publication proofreading cleanup hitter, thank you.

Exeunt Omar; Enter Magnus

Omar Adil Papadopoulos prepared to disembark. Not as Omar Adil Papadopoulos but as Magnus Krum. He wanted to feel it heavy in his bones, the new name. Instead, his heart fluttered at the newness of it. At the top of the steps, the hesitant Omar-now-Magnus looked up and down the train platform as if he were about to cross a dangerous intersection. He took a step, stumbled, and spilled onto the platform at Seattle's King Street Station.

"Coño, qué idiota!" The twenty-seven-year-old son of a Cuban immigrant mother and a Lebanese-Greek father, the young track star who ran a thirty-five-minute 10k, had made an uncoordinated ass of himself. He blamed the tumble on a distracted mind, cockeyed eyeglasses, and a simple misstep. The glasses he didn't need but wore anyway had landed undamaged on the grimy concrete.

He snatched up the glasses and—playing to an unseen audience—put them on with unnecessary vigor. The frame, a geek-black polymer composite, was an affectation, a talisman of sorts that he had adopted on a lark and used at his first serious tech-job interview. Even after landing the job, he found it reassuring to view the world from behind spotlessly clear lenses.

His hamstring ached from an old injury brought to life by twenty hours straight on the *Empire Builder* and, before that, a five-hour warmup on the *Wolverine* from Detroit to Chicago. Two days squeezed in the cheap seats on Amtrak. Two days on the run. Two days now that Omar-now-Magnus had left Detroit, his birthplace, family, friends, and job. Two days of jostled tracks and jostled regrets and the blurred rush of memories as quickly seen and lost as passing railroad crossings. Two days when maybe he had eaten and maybe he hadn't. Two days when he had half-thought about taking one-big-fucking-flying leap but didn't want to make a mess and anyway was chicken. "Guilty chicken." The words had a recipe ring to them.

His "luggage" was a black-and-white frayed-at-the-seams Nike daypack he'd had since junior high. The contents included spare glasses, laptop, Airpods, chargers, iFixit computer tool kit, Victorinox multi-tool in its black canvas pouch, Tri-Sport water bottle, Oral-B toothbrush and Smart Floss, patched adidas windbreaker hoodie (black-and-white), extra Costco t-shirt (black, in contrast to the white one he wore and to add variety to the wardrobe), a Black Diamond headlamp, and fifty-thousand cash. The stacked, rubber band bound bills weighed a hair over a pound and tucked neatly into a pair of two-liter dry bags, the kind with folded tops and used by river rafters. The bags broke from the tuxedo motif: one was neon pink, the other neon blue.

At a nondescript used-car lot a drenching schlep from the station, Magnus parleyed with the salesman and parted with fifteen-hundred dollars for a rusted '06 Subaru Outback (pearl white, L.L.Bean Edition with the seductive leather and wood gearshift knob and steering wheel). He gassed up mid-grade, flipped a coin—knowing that north, east, and west were not options—and headed south on Highway 101, thinking San Diego, maybe Mexico, the Shangri-La of fugitives and impoverished Americans scraping by on Social Security and dulling the pain of it all with cheap tequila. The fugitive had, in a moment of whimsy, considered Cuba, back to Habana to his mother's birthplace. Perversely, he feared he might lose his security clearance. Like that logic made any sense.

After four hours of butt-numbing and hamstring-throbbing driving through purgatorial fog and rain and crossing the dizzying breadth of the Columbia River, he busted into a headache bright sky at the Neahkahnie Mountain overlook and trailhead for Oswald West State Park. His phone showed him to be approximately a mile north of the coastal town of Manzanita, the "little apple."

Omar-now-Magnus took the improved weather as a good omen. He parked next to a distinctive, rocky promontory, exited the car, and took a deep breath. The salty, crisp air kissed his cheeks and filled his lungs. The would-be mariner spread arms Titanic wide and scanned the horizon for telling imperfections, a distant vessel or rocky hazard. On the side of the road the skyward yearning trees had been beaten into submission. The tops flagged east from incessant westerlies. Below, five-hundred feet or more, Manzanita's miles-long white-laced shoreline reached southward as graceful as a ballerina's arm and, at its furthest extent, touched a glimmering haze loitering above the bay. Above, a faded sliver of moon pressed flat against the starless sky.

His attention migrated from moon to phone to google maps and identified the terminus of the beach to be the inlet to Nehalem Bay, an organ-shaped body of water one could easily imagine as a living thing that swelled and contracted with tide, currents, and river's flood.

Subi and Magnus—outcasts in common—had come to an arrangement. She had shown him hers, and he had shown her his. She had gone first. At the used car dealer, Magnus had popped the hood, borrowed a creeper, and tenderly inspected her abused underside. He listened, an audience of one, for a skipped note in the three-liter, horizontally-opposed-six-cylinder engine's audition. He had visually detected seeping head gaskets, leaky valve cover gaskets, another leak at the rear main seal, smudgy blow-back on the oil cooler, seeping transmission cooler hoses and clamps, torn CV axle boots (both sides), and a steering rack leak (both ends). The car had a new battery, but badly corroded terminals. A ten-minute drive in traffic, negotiating washboards and potholes, accelerating and braking, added to Subi's bio. She wasn't up for a HIIT class, but had a couple burpees left in her. Magnus imagined Subi fearing rejection when he, as the prospective buyer, relayed to the used car salesman, an unfeeling-for-things-mechanical man, that to justify the asking price the following would need to be repaired: lower A-arms, front sway bar end links, bushings, end-links, rear wheel bearings (an especially unpleasant sound and fix) and backing plates. Magnus got pushback on the backing plates, although the salesman clearly did not know what backing plates were even after Magnus, gesturing like an ASL novitiate, demonstrated that it was practically impossible to access the bearings without destroying the backing plates. Any decent mechanic knew that. The used-car salesman dropped the price a grand and, to Subi's relief and the prospect of a future with someone who cared, a deal was struck.

Magnus, on his part, needed to talk, to verbalize and reflect. He voiced words to work out the stiffness in his vocal cords and he sang. He shared with Subi a list of things needing fixing in *his* life. And then, undermining the authenticity of these confessions, practiced dialogs wherein he introduced himself under his assumed identity, its fabricated background and the fictitious self's likes and dislikes.

The car-human conversation petered out as Magnus wove down the hill, turned right at Laneda Avenue toward Manzanita proper and, soon after the flashing *Slow 20 mph* sign, slowed to fifteen and watched dog walkers, kids armed with pails and shovels, underdressed tourists, and shuffling retirees enacting life-on-the-coast stories along a movie-set main street that curved rightward and downward toward shore and waves that rose taller and spoke louder as he approached. At Ocean Road, a street parallel to the beach, he nestled Subi onto a pull-off banked by window-high beach grass. Omar-now-Magnus closed his eyes and listened to the surf, the ruffle-shuffle of the grasses, and the off-key squeaks-and-ticks étude as Subi's engine cooled.

A motorbike zipped by. Omar-now-Magnus opened the door and stepped into the arms of a warm west breeze that tousled his messy mop of hair in the manner of an affectionate uncle. A wave full of attitude heaved itself at the shore and landed with a thwomp. He had never been close to the ocean, he had never known its draw or its expanse. Beach goers, more pale than tan, wore sunhats held in place with a crooked arm or a clasped chinstrap. No one swam. He hadn't considered why no one was in the water, the question less important than the compulsion to physically inhabit this place this moment, to be *here*, without question or reservation. He ignored the omens—the lost kite overhead, the half-eaten carcass of a gull—and walked on, halving the distance between Subi and the sea.

Shoes and socks came off. He stripped off his tee and exposed his willowy frame. Omar-now-Magnus squeezed and released sand between his toes and uttered the words "Toes in sand." Subi seemed safe enough, but he locked her anyway and then tossed the car fob in one shoe and his glasses in the other.

His body came alive. Toes bunched and spread, abs tightened and released, quads and calf muscles lengthened and contracted. Arms hung loosely at his sides and shook the way they did before a sprint. The stirrings of an athlete. A couple of deep breaths. The idea came in a flash: in goes Omar Adil Papadopoulos, out comes Magnus Krum—a baptism at sea, a rite of passage, a trial by ordeal, a test of courage. He would emerge annealed and transformed. At any rate, that's what he thought.

To the north, boulders lay strewn across the shore. Up from there, toward where an hour earlier he had stopped, the road slit the flank of Neahkahnie mountain. A blood-red van traveled along the road, appearing intermittently between clumps of trees before and after the rocky point where he had stopped and first seen the place where he now stood. The toy-sized bridge spanned a shaded, dangerous, vertical draw; a black dot marked the tunnel into which the van vanished.

The boulder-free shore to the south bordered rumpled hillocks of sea-grass-covered dunes and jagged D-Day accumulations of driftwood. Cow-pie size toupées of seaweed dotted the shore as if flung willy-nilly from the headless horseman's saddlebags. Two sets of horse tracks crisscrossed the sand. A gull screamed at the sky.

Omar-now-Magnus vowed that the inhabitants of Manzanita, the people of this city that was a nearly invisible dot on the map, would never know the nervous young man whose marriage hopes had dried up like an unwatered house plant; the man whose promising career with IBM's cybersecurity group had become a sideshow as he'd done penance for years by hosting a transfer pricing scam for shrewd Uncle Vinnie. They would never expect, of course, the Chaldean mob to come knocking and demand payback for a do-gooder prank that had gone south the moment he'd hit the Return key. Fuckups upon fuckups; flotsam from the storm, there for the sea to recollect and recollect.

Magnus: Carolina was my almost

Carolina was my almost ex, the woman I had almost married, the woman with whom I had almost moved to D.C. She and I had been competitive dance partners in high school and from my first class at the University of Michigan, Ann Abor, we had been an item. We belonged to MRun, the university's nationally ranked running club, and had spent endless hours training for our respective distances—half-marathon for me, four-hundred for her. Our relationship had been physical, some might say primitive: fuck, run, dance, eat, sleep, repeat. Within that apish, repetitive regimen and with little time for self-reflection, we did have fun. And we completed our respective degrees—European history for her, applied math and literature for me. Our routines had evolved into an emotional redoubt and had sheltered me from having to make decisions about, well, anything else.

Senior year, Carolina and I each made a list of what-to-do-when-we-grow-up. She whipped out her vision for our rosy future, and then, when I stalled, she whipped out mine, saving me the trouble. She could be generous like that.

My list begged for anything not about marriage, career, and the suburban afterlife. I added "buy a sailboat and rescue refugees at sea." Well done, I patted myself on the back.

We combined our lists (add ceremony here), then dated, signed, and printed two copies of the sacred document on vellum paper. Not real calfskin, of course, but that would have been a nice touch. I stowed my list in the back flap pocket of my raw-at-the-seams, Nike daypack, the same pack I'd slung over my shoulder throughout high school, and now, well into three-and-a-half years of college. Carolina had hers framed and glazed in museum quality glass that would protect the document from supernovas for two-hundred-thousand years.

"This is important," she announced. She proudly showed me the finished product. When she squeezed my hand, I thought we were going to prick pinkies and share blood.

Her list: Honors degree in History, Masters in International Affairs from Georgetown, marry me, Omar Adil Papadopoulos (she drew a heart after my name), Foreign Service, BLACK PASSPORT (I really want that!!), two years abroad (U.K. first choice), move to Washington, D.C, two children (boy and girl), cat.

Wow! How had "cat" made the list? I was allergic as fuck to cats and treated cats with the same indifference they treated me. Carolina was aware of this, but there it was in defiant Manx black and white script—Omar, condemned to a lifetime of itchy eyes and a stuffed nose.

Post graduation, Carolina moved to D.C. and checked the Georgetown University box on the W.T.D.W.W.G.U. list. She tantalized friends and family with hints about wedding plans. I stalled, using as my excuse a commitment to wrapping up things at Uncle Vinnie's company. I embellished the excuse, legitimately citing the necessity of completing a time-sensitive cyber defense project at IBM. My work need was real. The embellishment was that I said I hung in there because doing so would beef up my résumé when I hunted for the job in D.C. Carolina believed the IBM excuse.

IBM had hired me as an intern and soon added me to a cybersecurity team. My shockingly high-level security clearance prevented me from even hinting at what I was working on. Regarding the monkey business with Zio ("Uncle") Vinnie, any revelations about that would have put Carolina's future at risk by virtue of her knowledge about my criminal behavior. She probably would have turned me in—for my own good and the good of our relationship.

That ersatz vellum with my future on it dogged me from Ann Arbor to Detroit where it migrated from my daypack to the wall above my desk and socialized with a dozen neatly organized Post-it notes about chores and bills. During the Carolina-Omar hiatus, after she had left for Georgetown and beyond, I didn't date and treated social media as always, a habit only slightly less heinous than heroin. I worked hard and read stuff, lots of stuff.

I lobbed reads from the Safeway checkout stand into my shopping cart. Covid came and went, and I rolled with it. I was not a discriminating reader, though every so often, I cycled back to Shakespeare and Cervantes. I read works in English, Spanish, and Italian—my native and near-native languages, and mustered sufficient high-school French to muscle through random selections from Ernaux, Camus, and, oddly, a worn edition of Chekhov's complete works translated into French. The French I misunderstood more than I understood.

Carolina and I spoke with each other once a week, then once a month, then when we had a chance.

Despite my single life, or maybe because of it, people reached out to me. I listened to old classmates, work colleagues, relatives, neighbors, and people I danced with at Mom's salsa gatherings. In exchange for their good reaching-outs, I offered little of my own. I learned about their relationships with their partners, male and/or female, and who was cheating with whom and why. Even insider trading tips and which horse to bet on. To some, these things mattered. To me, not so much.

The end of our relationship—not the actual end, but its open declaration—was precipitated by a random event. The Twins—my friends and work colleagues Harry and Charlie, white as all get out but fluent in Mandarin and raised by Chinese parents—had run into Carolina at a hacker convention in D.C. She told them she had been seeing other guys. I figured the data point drop had been intentional.

Soon after, I phoned Carolina to inform her I wouldn't be moving to D.C. and wasn't ready for marriage. I braced for tears, a guilt trip, or anger.

"Oh, it's you," she answered.

"We should talk."

"Tried that, you know. Called. Emailed."

"Yeah, well. Work."

"I was in Tbilisi after Georgetown. And London. I told you."

"You ghosted me."

"Bullshit, you ghosted me!"

"Carolina . . ." Her name Velcro-ed off my tongue. I don't know why I apologized, but I did. No, I knew why. Our train wreck hadn't been because her train had been moving too fast. Nope. My train had never left the station. Relative, it was relative. "Hey, I'm sorry."

"That ship sailed, Omar." This confused me. I was still thinking about trains. "I don't even care enough to tell you you're a heartless dick . . . Wait, I take that back. You're a heartless dick! Don't call again."

She hung up.

A month later, I got an email. She must have hit "Send All." The engagement announcement included a photo of Carolina and a man with red curly hair, tortoiseshell glasses, and a promising future. The happy couple held hands in front of a banyan tree at a Blue Hawaii beach from the old Elvis flick.

I stared at the photo, feeling a vague disconnect from things that should have mattered, things I couldn't quite touch. Maybe that's how we, how people were, boxed in cubicles of our own making, marking time and oblivious to the vacuity of our lives, believing that one's story cubicle, a chimerical construct of chance, suffering, and raw instincts and inculcated habits, was something one controlled, or that it mattered. I was never a believer. Not stories about God and country, not stories about career and raising a family of good little consumers. Yet, there was no way to avoid it. I was one of them, in my little box: I worked hard, I did most things I did well; I ran. The running was good.

Hero: I do NOT want

"Mom, I do NOT want to talk about 'it'!"

I leaned on the porch rail. The cold metal drained warmth from my breasts. The rail was a sturdy stainless affair that I'd traversed forward and back a million times when my parents weren't around. I never did a flip—forward or back—off the rail. I could have stuck the landing and rolled, but the ten-foot runway to the blackberries was too tight and the slope was wicked steep. There's shredding, and shredding! Both draw blood; it's a question of style and volume.

Fog crawled over the shore and wiggled up the shallow draw leading to our place—well, technically, Uncle Theo's place—a two-story, yawn-worthy home perched on a flattened notch in the hillside and about two-hundred-and-fifty feet above the beach proper. Overhead, a barn swallow parabolaed into a nest under the eave. I flattened a mosquito sucking blood from my forearm. I had a lot going on, better things to do than chit-chat with Mom about my fuckups. I changed the subject. That was my best strategy.

"Super view, huh. Can't believe Uncle Theo's letting us just stay here." The "it" had been a poor choice. It floated in the air. Maybe a swallow would eat it. I moved on to limit the damage. "Bet he misses the beach."

"Dear brother said no parties."

That was a non sequitur. Mom spread the wool blanket across her knees, smoothing it across the settee.

"You and Dad *are* party animals."

We both knew what Dear Brother had been referring to.

"He remembers a certain someone else's party."

That was years ago, a rare holiday visit to the States. My friends and I had made a ramp and trashed a few plants. Theo, though, he was a fastidious gardener and had had a fit. I mean, get a life, Uncle Theo. This is Oregon; shit grows here.

"Yeah, Mom, I know."

"I always thought you would outgrow this parkour business."

"Ain't happening."

Mom didn't get it. To her, parkour was a childish hobby or sport. For my friends in D.C., amici at the International School in Firenze, and schoolmates at ETH, Zürich, parkour had been at the heart of our community, what made us a community. That's changing, of course, or evolving, as the once life-style choice became a recognized sport and people commercialized the crap out of it.

Mom sipped her vodka martini—it was always vodka, never gin. I wondered for the hundredth time why she and her spook friends drank vodka. Mind-numbing quantities of vodka, mostly straight. It was so the James Bond stereotype. The vodka martini was this indelible spy meme, especially in D.C.

"I saved your butt." Mom, the interrogator, was back on game.

"Mom—" I turned to face her but kept my hands on the railing. I could hop over it, pick up the trail through the blackberries and vanish. She was reading the tell in my white-knuckled grip.

"Okay, okay. I apologize! We will not talk about the kidnapping."

"Attempted kidnapping," I corrected, afterward realizing that the statement had been a self-defeating re-engagement in the exact conversation I had been trying to avoid. I went back to studying the fog's progress, sad that Mom wouldn't see the green flash tonight because of the clouds. There were only so many green flashes left in her life. That made them extra special.

Mom swirled the martini and whatever it was she was thinking about. That brain of hers never stopped. Even now. She was sick; they gave her six months to live. The "they" was an army of physicians and techs. So many it took a conscious effort to keep the names straight. Mom wasn't vague about death. She circled her personal D-day on the calendar with fat red Sharpie. She was going to sue the fucking doctor if she lived a day longer. Mom stuck to schedules. Our family was stubborn that way.

"Your not supposed to drink," I nagged, proving the point.

With unexpected and dramatic flair, as if a decision of great import had been made, she placed her drink on the side table, softened her voice, and patted the seat of the settee. "Come, sit by me. I want to tell you something."

The settee seat was freezing cold. Mom lifted the blanket and I nestled against her boney hip, willing the heat from my body to warm hers. My body was a veritable atomic power plant. I put an arm around her to draw her close. She reached across me to the bottle of Stoli and didn't just add to, but filled her glass to the brim.

"I want to tell you two things. The first is about the first time you were kidnapped."

"What? Seriously, Mom." I thought she was making this up to get back to *the* kidnapping, the one I didn't want to talk about and that wasn't really a kidnapping.

Mom followed the flight of a swallow. The bird sensed it was being tracked and took evasive maneuvers. Any creature Mom followed should do that if it knew what was good for them.

"The day you were born was cause for much celebration, a new national holiday—Resistance and Liberation Day—for the people of Lebanon."

The dramatic introduction got my attention—the lady could tell a story. I tucked the edges of the blanket under and around our legs, thinking somewhere there must be cushions for the settee. I couldn't imagine pansy Uncle Theo out here freezing his soft ass. The sun ducked behind the clouds without fanfare. Mom's eyes fixed on the spot where the sun had vanished. She was replaying in her head what had transpired on that day long ago. She had a killer good memory, a necessity in her line of work. Me too.

"Hezbollah celebrated Israel's withdrawal with gunfire, speeches, and public demonstrations, and glee over the rout of Israel's proxy, the South Lebanese Army. On your birthday, May twenty-five, the turn of the millennium, two brave Israeli soldiers packed a pregnant, thirty-three-year-old me in an armored vehicle and we fled toward the border. We were ambushed en route. My water broke and your birth, my child, became imminent. The Hezbollah slaughtered these young, handsome, brave soldiers, but—I wish I knew more about this part of the story. I don't. One Hezbollah fighter recognized me and brought me to his home where the women in his family managed my delivery. The same fighter—his name was Nabil, I remember now—a week later, successfully exchanged you and me for his brother, a captive at an Israeli detention center."

"Why on Earth were you there? You were majorly pregnant!" Now I wanted the whole story.

"Well, at the time I had been what we called a "Housekeeper," slang for someone left behind to clean up messes left by the CIA and whomever—the whomever in this case being the South Lebanese Army."

"But you were pregnant!"

"Eight months, sweetie." She drank a lusty swallow, not a sip. "We were tough in those days. But you're right. Technically, in my "condition," I absolutely should not have been in the field. I simply was in the wrong place at the wrong time and, you know, you never say no to an op."

This I understood. Mom was a big "op" dog at the agency. She hadn't gotten where she had in that select, misogynist, and viciously competitive organization by saying no. She had hinted at things she shouldn't have done, seldom elaborating, and was firmly of the opinion that a woman had to be twice as badass as a man.

And she was. One night, driving home on a four-lane highway, we saw a burning car pulled over on the other side of the road. The flames were coming from inside the car. Mom drove over the medium curbs and pulled up behind the car. She told me to close my eyes. I don't remember how old I was, but I peeked. Someone was in the car, stuck inside. I saw his arms flailing and his head twisting around. Mom called in the location on 911. She was running up the car, carrying a blanket—my backseat blanket—intending to pull the poor bastard out. The gas tank or something exploded. She darted from one side of the car to the other, trying to get to the guy. I remember the burns on her hands.

Others arrived—a trucker with a mostly useless fire extinguisher, then a highway patrol car. It took both the trucker and officer to hold her back. She was in a funk for a week. Not as much from the accident —this was my opinion—but from the memories it brought back, memories that, ephemeral as memories were, had hit her harder than watching some guy being burned alive in a car.

"Eight months?"

"That's why you're named Hero. You were a three-pound preemie. I could hold you in the palm of my hand. You were a feisty little thing!"

"Mom, I'm six-feet and weigh a hundred-forty." I hadn't thought about this often, but I was all about big bones and muscle. I thought my parents came over on the Mayflower. Where there should have been cross-country skis mounted over the fireplace and cabinet full of ski-marathon medals and ribbons, there were antiques and family heirlooms and pictures of Mom and Dad at the tennis club. What's with my icy-grey-blue eyes and goldenrod hair?

"Funny how that happens."

I smelled it coming. "Yeah, funny."

Mom leaned into me, her face close to mine. "Between us," she whispered. "It's time you knew."

"Knew what?" I played along, suspecting what. I closed my eyes and dreaded the words to come.

"Your dad—you know he loves you, really loves you—but he is not your biological father."

"I figured." I thought she would react to my not reacting. She didn't, so I continued. "But what the fuck? I'm twenty-four and now you get around to telling me!" I pushed her away, not hard though. I didn't want to hurt her. God, she was frail.

"Mom. You know, you're a fucking vault. What else don't I know? Who is my father?"

"He is."

"No, my natural father, for Christ's sake!"

I was pissed at her speaking down to me. It hurt, but I didn't want to let on that it hurt. "Does Dad know?"

"Of course, he knows."

She slugged down what remained in her glass.

"So, who is it? Or was it?" My head was spinning. I thought about my short, balding, slightly pudgy, and nearsighted father. No Norse god, better actually, a damned good man. I loved Dad.

I couldn't tell if Mom was faking or lying, she was a trained for both. She feigned, or maybe she really was embarrassed. "I'm not sure."

"Jesus!" That was it. I got up, went inside to get a glass of wine and went to my room to cry or scream, or hate myself that I should even care. "Fuck."

A few minutes later Mom joined me. She'd given me time to cool off. "Okay. He's dead. I never knew his actual name—that's what I meant. He was in the military."

Mom held me. I didn't resist because I was net grateful. A little truth, I thought. Thank you.

"Did you love him?"

I'd never seen Mom cry. She wasn't the crying type, but there it was. In her eyes, even twenty-five years later, there it was—the need to cry.

She shut her eyes and squeezed them, maybe to hold back the flood or to bring back the memory.

"I did. I loved him so very, very much."

At Sea

The plane of frigid water numbed as it rose. He stood erect, like a revolutionary soldier in linear formation. Waves slapped his chest and shoulders and struck hard at the throat. His arms flew upward and his footing gave way. Before him, the taut surface water swirled and then sucked him out to sea. He backstepped futilely, as if he were moonwalking the wrong direction.

In goes Omar, and out comes Magnus, a symbolic lark. That's what this meet-and-greet with the big, bad ocean was supposed to be. That was before his calf cramped and before he went under.

A riptide could drag a swimmer away from shore at eight feet per second. Why did he remember a useless piece of trivia but not what the fuck to do about it, the riptide? Two arms and the one functional leg flailed. He saw himself in the maw of oblivion. Less poetically—Magnus reflected—he was going to fucking drown.

Death would be swift. Panic would mask the fear and discomfort. But that wasn't what was happening. He was witnessing in some detail his own rather painful demise.

The pounding surf cudgeled her voice. He held his breath and listened. When he twisted toward the voice, a wave slammed his body into the sea floor. A thousand pounds of sea water played him like a piper and expelled the functional residue of air from his lungs.

Then, a miracle: A hand from above grabbed his upper arm and yanked him to the surface. She—his rescuer was a woman—towed him sideways, parallel to the beach, repositioning one arm around his chest and using her head to keep his head above water.

"You . . . gonna fucking kill yourself!" The words came in bursts between arm strokes and short, hard kicks.

The headlock made it impossible to speak. Acid and bile crawled up his throat and dribbled from the corner of his mouth.

A woman's voice again: "Shit!"

He gave up trying to understand the words. He gave up trying to understand the world and drifted into a numbed state. The baying dogs of memory went dumb.

Her nails dug into his bony ribcage. One last bit of wrenching, done with gusto, hoisted his skinny ass out of the current. As with the water that had risen to engulf him, he sensed the water's circumference retreat. She had won the tug-of-war, and he, a spectator curious in the watching of it, eyes wide mad and staring into the dazzling visual cacophony of light and blue-white foam and froth, realized that he had tried, as if he were a child, insane as it sounded, to see if he could breathe water.

* * * *

He was home, riding in the back seat of the car, his aunt and uncle up front. He remembered Vinnie insisted tia Alejandra drive at night. And he remembered that unlike many men, Vinnie DiMaso had never lied about his vision, which was cataract bad; or his height, five-ten; or his weight, two hundred on the nose. He never pretended that he had understood something when he hadn't, and he never put on tough guy airs because he really was a tough guy. The man enjoyed respect from his hometown mob because he himself was always, always respectful of everybody, from the mob capo to the homeless guy on the street. Omar missed Vinnie.

In three hours give or take—still in his dream within a dream—he would be home in Detroit. Mom would have been back for three days and would have recycled the empty tins and bottles, collected his father's work papers and put them in tidy stacks in his office, and scrubbed the shower floor with toxic cleansers and a wire brush. She had been in Miami for the better part of a year, watching her mother, Omar's abuela, waste away. Neither a funeral nor a memorial service had commemorated his abuela's life, leaving him with a last memory of a scratchy phone call, an unfinished conversation, and the feeling that he had been cheated out of something important. Crumbs were all that remained—las migas de la vida.

He recalled that the odometer on Vinnie's car, a 2010 Buick Enclave, had quit working after a hundred-and-twenty thousand miles. For years, the odometer had made a barely audible clicking sound and then one day the click stopped—like his abuela's heart. He had a sharp —as in painful—memory of riding in the Enclave, listening and wishing for the odometer's click, even though he knew it had stopped.

Both here and in his dream, the sun was falling away. He wanted to scrunch up in the narrow bench seat in the back of Vinnie's Enclave, inhale its familiar odor, and be disinterested in the landscape and equally disinterested in the conversation two rows forward, save noting and giggling at the playful deposit of a Spanish word or two in the Cubanized Italian his aunt used with Vinnie.

Out of nowhere, his remembrance leapt to his mom's sopa Tarasca: chicken, roast tomatoes, roast tortillas, pureed pinto beans, and chipotles. He had had a real home, reacting as if this realization had just come to him, and he had been deeply loved.

* * * *

"I'm hungry."

Magnus gagged on the words. Salt water and bile stung his nose and throat, trachea and bronchi. The rescuer rolled him onto hands and knees. He vomited. She supported and deftly manipulated his body. A wave washed over them. She slipped her arms around him to hold him steady, and then with heavy exhales lugged his body foot by foot toward higher ground. His head hung on his shoulders and looked back at two squiggly tracks in the sand. The forgotten leg with the cramp flopped to the side and twitched.

Their halting progress ended where the wet sand met dry. A straw-colored shelf of her hair stuck to his face. Still breathing heavily, she let go and landed on her butt, then jerked upright to extend her arms as far as they would go and shook them. She spread her legs and stretched and shook them the way a gymnast might. Her chest heaved and stilled as the cadence and volume of her breathing resumed a normal level. When sufficiently recovered, she propped herself up on her elbows and stared at Magnus. The expression was that of a woman who had matter-of-factly managed a difficult situation and had to wrap things up and get on with more important matters. She wasn't exactly impatient, but neither was she thrilled to be there.

He spoke his first words to her. "Thank you." That was all he could think to say. "Seriously. Thank you."

Magnus—water in his ears muffled the sound—thought he heard, "You're a pain in the ass."

She was younger than he, early twenties. And not the two-hundred-pound Amazon he had imagined, but about his height and muscled. To be fair, it took little to have more meat on the bone than he had. The reconnaissance paused at her face.

He couldn't ignore the uncanny similarity of their physiognomies—the way the cheekbone met the eye, the jut of the jaw and hint of a dimple, the slight leftward deviation of the angular nose. If any single feature were to be swapped between them, the resulting visage would be indistinguishable from its original. If standing side-by-side, a bystander would take them for brother and sister, for at least having a shared ancestry.

There was one extraordinary exception, an exception that would be the first thing that anyone meeting his rescuer for the first time would fixate upon. Her eyes might as well have been the eyes of a different species. To observe them was to observe the surface of a glacier; the blue or grey—depending upon angle and light—was wintry and feral. Wintry eyes, he settled on wintry. Abyssal, numinous, coruscating. A stunning contrast to his own loamy, warm, brown-green. A different season entirely.

She knelt beside him and used the sleeve of her t-shirt to wipe vomit from his mouth. Patiently, using those same firm hands but with a gentle touch, she wiped his face and around the eyes with the balled-up hem of her shirttail. Bits of throw-up clung to beaded braids dangling double the length of her the boyishly short hair. He noted her shifting her weight, her hands opening and closing to find heat between those moments she attended him. The wet tee tented across her breasts rose and fell with each motion and breath. She saw him notice and seemed not to care.

Magnus mumbled something unintelligible.

His caretaker, job done, switched her attention to her braids. She squeezed water and vomit away with her thumb and index finger, sliding over the beads, and slowing when she got to the woven hair. "Gross."

Post *gross*, a change in demeanor. The warrior withdrew; she trembled. Magnus, too, shuddered. Gradually—everything moved in slo-mo—her mouth relaxed; parted lips quit the pressed, thin appearance that had been the symbol of her determination. A wide smile breached her face, then relaxed. He imagined a fledging testing its wings by extending them to the limit and back. She was happy *for* him, and for herself, that he was alive and that she had saved his life.

Throughout this transformation, from the initial chaos of his rescue and to its denouement, he had noted everything about her, a record to file and never forget. He got goose bumps when her breath crossed his flesh. Or maybe he was just cold.

Most unexpected—being in this dazed state—was that he was aroused. How could a half-drowned man suddenly go there? Magnus ordered himself to chill.

Her hand rested on his shoulder and squeezed it and shook him.

"Hey you. Anybody home?"

He was embarrassed and had looked away. He lifted his head and saw her press the back of her index finger to one nostril at a time, clearing first the nostril with the ring in it and then the ringless nostril. She jiggled her nose between her fingers. Laugh lines exploded out of the corners of her eyes. The wintry eyes brought back a memory of a husky that had once threatened him. He started.

"I don't bite," she laughed. "Are you frightened?" She put her hand on his back to comfort him. The hand's warmth filled the space between his scapulae and calmed him. From cat-cow pose, he regulated his breathing. Two children, seven- or eight-years-olds, watched; no one else paid attention. The rescue had come and gone without fanfare.

Seawater and bile welled up in the throat. He swallowed.

"Got a name?" she asked.

Magnus remained disoriented. He shut his eyes to slow the spinning, but that made it worse.

"Yeah, well," she continued, "point of information, mister. When you see a flat section of water where waves are breaking on both sides, that's maybe a rip current. And it can take you out to sea, a long way out to sea. If you're caught in a rip tide, swim parallel to the shore." She motioned the direction of doing so with her hands. "Swim hard and you'll probably be okay. I mean, I've been there. And surfed here. You know, people don't really swim here. Not without a board and wetsuit or some kind of flotation. The surf's too rough and it's fucking cold, even mid-summer."

"Never been in the ocean."

"Never would have guessed."

She softened the deadpan sarcasm slightly. "You'll be okay. That was dumb, or suicidal."

"Not exclusive," he joked. "I couldn't *NOT* go in."

"No more swimming today, please. I gotta job."

"I had to see what it was like."

"The Hamlet act?"

"I'm not crazy."

"Fuckall had me fooled." She definitely didn't buy it. "You know the first thing you said when I fished you out?"

Magnus shook his head no.

" 'I'm hungry!' Now that's crazy! Right?"

Magnus faked cheerful. "Right."

She cracked a smile that could have been his own. Was he seeing himself? He hadn't put on a smile that big in a long time. They laughed together, though for different reasons.

"Loco, yes. But I am a little hungry."

She gave him one last check-over, head to toe, lingering longer at his waist.

"I got to run. Late for work. And I gotta change, thank you. I waitress at the Big Wave. Food's good. If" she winked, "you really are hungry. Or there's the Farmer's Market. You can get something fast there."

With difficulty, Magnus rose. He used her shoulder and balanced on one leg and gently rubbed and shook out the one that had cramped. He was determined to show self-control.

"You got a name?" she asked again.

The innocent question gave rise to a dissociative fugue, a disorientation within which he was once again distantly self-aware, a kind of madness that he prayed would dissipate.

He answered honestly. "Tough question."

She let that sink in and didn't challenge the nonsense of it. She had sensed that he hadn't intended the response to sound cute.

"Tough question, yeah." She moved to the side and let him stand on his own. "Give that water-logged noggin a rest." As an afterthought, she added, "And you really should eat. You're fuck-all skinny. Do you need money?"

The money offer made Magnus laugh. "Money? I'm okay. Really am. Thanks again. Swimming in money, money coming out my ears." Stupid, he thought. What a stupid thing to say. He was chasing normal but it kept slipping away.

She cocked her head to the side. The eyebrows huddled in faux disbelief. "Sure," she laughed. "Well, see ya 'round." Her head turned back to him as she walked away. "No more drama Mr. Money-coming-out-the-ears."

Would he be *'round* in Manzanita? *Why not, why not be 'round in Manzanita?*

His eyes followed her. She jogged up the rise to the road and threw a leg over the tan cushion-seat of a black Vespa scooter. He watched her don a helmet and drive off, her hair a golden fringe, braids flying willy-nilly.

A puzzled Magnus muttered to himself. "Hamlet Act?"

Magnus: Post the breakup

Post the breakup with Carolina and as I wound down my obligation to Zio Vinnie, I moved to Detroit's Mexicantown, commuting as needed to IBM in Ann Arbor. The move gave me a chance to see more of my parents. I observed, listened, took their love for granted—that's what children do—and assessed their marriage to be, as many marriages are, a mix of affection and indifference.

My father, Aristotle, "Ari" for short, was a by-the-books lawyer who made respectable money, got uncomplicated tipsy after work, and enjoyed the game from his La-Z-boy. The wrinkled XXL suits clothed a man whose linebacker physique had softened over the years and whose compassion had outlasted cynicism, a rare victory among the lawyer set. He was honest to a fault and Vinnie, the mobster brother-in-law, was his closest friend.

Ari never chased women and refused to tell me about how he and Mom met. Whatever the story was and whatever had shamed him into silence remained a mystery.

He golfed, but his first love was baseball. He had wanted to be an umpire. Even in fifth grade, he was big and loud. A grade school scrap seeded the idea. Two kids had argued over a called pitch, so Ari volunteered to call the strikes and balls, foul and fair hits, who was safe and who was out. He had good eyes, was fair, and though he had few player skills, he loved the game. A booming voice helped. He umpired through high school and college. After graduation, two paths beckoned: umpire trade school with its lengthy apprenticeship or law. A scholarship to law school decided for him. It was a good fit. The man always had the rules of the game down cold and enforced them with confidence on the diamond and in the courtroom. Law was grayer than baseball, but both demanded fairness.

Once, after Ari had had a few, I asked him why he had loved umpiring. He told me a story about a Little League game. A new kid was at bat. Ari called two strikes. The kid acted discouraged, lowered his bat, and stared at Ari. Dad asked, "What's wrong?" The kid pleaded in a small voice, "Do you have to say strike so loud?" My dad, heart of gold, replied, "Yes, because everybody on the field's gotta hear." Then he told the kid to not worry. "Keep your eye on the ball and swing like the dickens at the next pitch." The kid took a big swing at that pitch. It was the first time he had connected in a Little League at-bat. He grounded out, but the kid smiled all day. Ari loved giving people a fair chance.

My mother, Mari, was a different animal. She taught English as a second language. On weekends when Ari whacked little white golf balls into the welkin or when the Tigers played and he nursed beers with buddies in bars draped in big-screen TVs, Mari (she also went by Maria or Pepita) sang at salsa clubs and taught Latin dance at the Lithuanian Hall.

When she sang, it was impossible to turn away. On stage, every cell in her body screamed watch me, check out my Celia Cruz bata cubana, my dress of red polyester satin with ruffled sleeves trimmed in gold ribbon. She sang with such presence, even at home, even with a dirty, knotted up-do and baggy sweats and vacuuming the kitchen floor, that if you closed your eyes her voice filled your heart with soft ocean air, and lantern light, and the odor of stringy chicken, beans, and rice, and the dulcet swish of palm fronds, waves and the uninhibited galumphing of a child's barefoot heels on wooden floorboards. People loved her and she loved more than a few of them back, both men and women.

No son wants to know about his mother's dalliances. As far as I knew, Mari concealed her flings from everyone but me. But what do I know? I got a kiss on the forehead and a "Don't tell" in the ear. Her outgoing, warm behavior covered up negative consequences. I assumed she did what all good mothers did. Mari always came home to Ari, and she loved him and me more than anything in the world.

Mari was Cuban, therefore she danced. I did too. I didn't come across as Latino and spoke English without an accent, but the dancing was in my blood. There's an old video of Mari pushing a stroller and stopping in front of the bongo player. He put a drumstick in my hand and I wailed on the cowbell. The house cheered. Another film, a scratchy Super-8, showed Mari pregnant and belting out a Los Van Van number. She had one hand on the mic and the other on her swollen belly, every molecule of her—and yours truly inside—swaying side-to-side to the clave.

I couldn't remember when I hadn't danced, when I hadn't performed and lived with both the admiration and isolation that came with performing. Dance, similar to mathematics, required structured. The sequence of movements in three-dimensional space followed rules to which I conformed. I executed moves smoothly, tracing and expressing rhythm and melody, interpreting feedback—joy, sadness, excitement, whatever—from my partner. Ego was not part of the equation.

Mom and Dad, the dancer and the umpire, deceit and fairness, and, of course, love-filled days, months, and years. I was both nurtured and somehow left out.

Hero: Mom was wrong

Mom was wrong. The first time I was "kidnapped" I was less than an infant. Wouldn't that have made the act more like a child abduction? She, being an adult and an undercover combatant, had been a prisoner. Again, not someone who had been kidnapped. But that's splitting hairs. The second kidnapping wasn't a kidnapping either, but Mom called it that because the affair entailed an extraction—my extraction.

I was twenty-three. Dad was still living in Rome, a geographic comprise after I'd completed my IB in Firenze and bachelor's degrees in philosophy and architecture at ETH Zürich. I was in year two in the Architecture Master's program at ETH when it happened. Not in Zürich. Nobody would have the balls to go after an American in Zürich.

At a Swiss parkour fest I'd made a friend, this dumb, fearless Sicilian guy named Luca. We'd both competed. I ended up about where I always did, in the middle of the pack. He finished dead last. Luca loved high-ball, no failsafe rail-running on bridges and overpasses, the ones where one slip and you're a goner. He'd run tube rails barefoot because he had gecko toes and bonobo arches. Because Luca was a bighearted galoot—a ninety kilo, scary bold, hairy Sicilian teddy bear—and because the soles of his feet were freaky curved, simple parkour moves like jumps, neos, and vaults challenged him. Didn't matter. He was charming and enjoyed a solid rep. More important, Luca and I were becoming an item. We hadn't hooked up yet, but the signs were there and our friends treated us as if we had passed the finish line. When he invited a few of us to hang with him for a weekend at his hometown in Ragusa, Sicily, everyone said yes. Luca informed us that he had some business to attend to, but would be free most of the weekend. I was hoping the business was me.

Ragusa province was on the southern coast and its capital sat plopped atop a limestone prominence tucked in between two deep valleys, Cava San Leonardo and Cava Santa Domenica. The city, a UNESCO World Heritage Site, was home to Baroque palaces and churches that I wanted to study and sketch. My friends, with Luca as tour guide, were more excited about viewing the place from up high, "flowing" from tiled roof to tiled roof and crisscrossing the città in any compass bearing with no need to ground out. It was traceur paradise. Terraces galore and parapets wrapped rooftops spilled down the hillside, a lava made of Lego blocks. Within the raised sections and gaps (merlons and crenets, in architecture speak) the inhabitants hung laundry, stored things, and gardened. Families dined alfresco and were protected from the elements by wooden, vined, or canopied pergolas. The Valle dei Ponti divided the old town, Ragusa Ibla, and high town, Ragusa Superiore. Luca had earned his parkour chops on the four bridges that spanned the ravine. Pop-out blocks studded the arches of the forty-meter-tall, hundred-fifty-year-old Ponte dei Cappuccini, making the surface ideal for climbing, wall flips, launches, all kinds of movement. The pedestrian-only bridge had been Luca's personal playground. He could wrap his prehensile toes around the column corners and hang no hands. I failed this trick when I tried.

We crashed at Luca's place in Ragusa Superiore and spent two laid back days exploring a string of rooftop lines and free-running near the neighborhood piazza. In the afternoon, when tiles sizzled, we drove to the coast. At my favorite beach, Calamosche, when Luca and I were alone, he proposed a rendezvous à deux. He would tell the group he had family obligations, and I would announce a guaranteed-to-bore sketching expedition. Secretly, we would meet at an apartment he knew in the old town, Ragusa Ibla. Luca gave me directions, describing a creepy sounding place on the second floor (third story US) of a crumbly, uninhabited building. The authorities had boarded up and condemned the structure. Access, he had explained, was via a short climb—easy for a traceuse—to a balcony with shuttered but unlocked doors. The door to the apartment was easy to find. The unit had a big eye painted on the door. I should have said no when he told me about the eye.

Someplace Not Detroit

With zombie deliberation Magnus poked and pulled until his half-dry tee fell into place with the tag where it was supposed to be at the back of the neck. He blew away the sand on the lenses of his glasses and felt better after he'd put them on and checked for clarity. He emptied the sand from his sneakers and stepped into them without bothering to pull up the heels. Socks ended up in his pockets and gave his pants chipmunk cheeks as he slog-waddled uphill to Subi. A handful of people on the road had followed the rescue drama. A kindly man, a dog-walker who cradled his long-haired whatever breed in his arms, asked Magnus if he was okay. Magnus nodded and thanked him.

He wasn't okay. He was depressed, crashing, and confused. And needed sleep, days of sleep. And food, mountains of food. Depressed people need both.

Subi's sheet-metal cocoon muffled the sound of the pounding surf; the tinted windows hid him from gawkers. He drove up Manzanita Avenue—the street paralleled Laneda—until foot traffic blocked his progress. In Detroit, these pedestrians would have been roadkill. *Relax*, Magnus told himself, and failed when he tried yoga breathing—unwilling to do the weird stick out your tongue double-exhale part. His lungs ached and the back of his throat was raw. The damned calf twitched the exact same time that Subi's oil pressure light flickered. Daydreaming or dazed—either way not good—Magnus slammed on the brakes unnecessarily hard when a child in oversized flip-flops twirled and whirled into the street in front of Subi. The little guy spun in circles, head down, trying to make himself dizzy. When he could twirl no more, he stopped, smiled, and tipsy waved at Magnus. A Bernie joined him and plopped down in the middle of the road.

Magnus thought about the meaning of it all. *Manzanita, I hear ya.*

He turned right and parked on a cross street between Manzanita Avenue and Laneda. Subi's nose pointed toward a sign that read *Holder Vacation Rentals—On the Oregon Coast since 2010*. An arrow on the sign pointed to a two-story, clapboard-sided mid-nineteen hundreds office building, that took up a couple of prime street lots. In the front yard a flagpole flew weathered US and Oregon State flags. The glass case beside the sidewalk posted sales and rental information, including an ad for a townhouse on 1st Street. The townhouse was one of the few places offering long-term rental.

Too tired to rehearse the story he would spin, Magnus walked pack in hand in the front door and asked the receptionist if the townhouse was available. His wet, beat-up appearance got him a sympathetic, "Please, honey, take a load off. Water? Coffee?" She and Magnus exchanged smiles at the irony of water being offered to a man soaked to the bone. "I'm Meredith. What can I do for you?"

"The townhouse available?"

She handed him a rental form that required a dizzying amount of information, another form with the security deposit terms, and the last form, a monthly payment agreement. According to the forms, the unit was available for eleven months. "Dear, can I get you a towel?"

Magnus scanned the documents. "Tell you what," Magnus spoke as he read. "How about I pay cash upfront for eleven months, plus double the security deposit? You make a copy of my license—here's my cell—and we do the rest of this application business later, after you give me the keys and I go change and get a bite." He helped himself to a pen from the jar on her desk and wrote his number on the nearby pad. She spread out the papers. As if in a stage performance, he wrote the unpracticed signature, amazed at the foreign viny thing that emerged and left its mark on the paper.

She winked at him. "Pricey cabana." In case he didn't get the reference, she added, "A place on the beach where you change clothes."

"With, I hope, a hot shower," he winked back.

"There's that." She held up a jug full of lollipops. "Sugar?"

He noticed the mini fridge. "Got a Coke?"

She batted the eyelash a second time, the same eye. "For you." She rolled over to the fridge, fished out a can of Coke, and handed it to him, lingering as their fingers touched. "We surely do."

He held the can between thumb and second finger, popped the tab, and swigged more than he should have. Magnus wiped his chin with the back of his wrist and belched. A sugar and caffeine hard-on was what it was, jock-erotic stuff.

The door to the back office swung open and a handsome man with cowboy boots and a rugged cowboy jaw stepped forward to greet Magnus. He ignored Magnus's sodden state and the droplet of Coke hanging from his chin. Before the door closed behind his greeter, Magnus glimpsed an older man in a wheelchair and sitting at a desk. Their features identified the two men as father and son. The son, Lee Holder, introduced himself and welcomed Magnus to Manzanita. He'd overheard the conversation with Meredith.

"Cash is fine. We take wet or dry," he quipped, proud of himself for resisting the temptation to inquire about Magnus's disheveled condition and unabashed in his prioritization of money over propriety.

He read the name on the application and watched as Magnus peeled off hundreds and placed them on the receptionist's desk. "You talk my language, Mr. Krum." He wished Magnus well and went on about how lucky Magnus had been to find a long-term rental. He mentioned that the other townhouses attached to the one Magnus had rented were short-term rentals owned by himself and—with a nod to the back room—his father, whom he respectfully referred to as *Mister* Shortley Holder.

Magnus turned to the receptionist. "Food recommendation?"

She was about to suggest her place, but backed off when Lee Holder answered for her.

"Right now, your best bet for no-frills food is the Farmer's Market. Right around the corner on Manzanita. Or, if you want sit-down, the Offshore Grill. A lot of locals go to the San Dune. And Trio Loco. Up the hill's Big Wave."

"I saw people walking to the Market. Thanks."

In committing to the yearlong rental, and presumably to a year of living in Manzanita under his new identity, Magnus had acted without pre-thought. His near drowning notwithstanding, he trusted his gut. He trusted it when he did math proofs, wrote code, hunted foreign poseurs trying to hack U.S. business and government IT systems, and when he improvised dance moves.

Magnus, weighted down by his assumed identity and soggy clothes, hungry and sleep-deprived, travel weary, and emotionally spent, was determined to survive. The runner in him, Coke-infused, had made it to—if not the finish line—a place to rest up for the next leg, whatever the hell it entailed.

He had found what he had been seeking—someplace not-Detroit.

Magnus: I parked the car

I parked the car a few blocks from the Detroit Institute of Arts. Charlie, one of the Twins, would pick it up later. I knew Mom's schedule and that she would be at the Institute tagging along on a school trip to translate for Spanish-speaking fifth graders.

Detroit's Art Institute is huge, over a half-million square feet of galleries. She had picked a specific painting in a specific gallery for our meeting. I recommended the Diego Rivera room, one of my favorites, but she objected because of people traffic. Mom chose *Judith and Her Maidservant with the Head of Holofernes*.

She noticed me as I approached, but didn't look at me. I drew close enough to brush her shoulders. We stared at the six-foot by four-foot tableau. I wanted to hug her, but didn't want to draw attention to our meeting. She turned. Her eyes, those rich, coffee dark, oculi, were a portal to a host of urgent questions. She couldn't turn away and embraced me.

"I'm okay, Mom."

"You are so not okay, mijo." She pushed us an inch apart, her hands squeezed my forearms. I smelled yerba mate on her breath.

I shifted my gaze to the painting. "Caravaggio?" It's what I would guess about any Italian oil with that distinctive theater lighting, a spotlight illuminating the faces and hands of a painting's subjects.

"Artemisia Lomi Gentileschi, a woman painter, born the same decade Shakespeare wrote so many plays." Mom did that, always finding a context one could relate to.

"Last year, you know, I read a lot of Shakespeare. I want to read every word. I want to start over, Mom. With Shakespeare."

Mom stayed on topic. "Su papá taught her. And Caravaggio influenced his work and Artemisia's. Dime, what does this painting say to you?"

I wasn't in the mood for this, but she was my mother. "She just cut off some old guy's head. But there's no remorse or regret. Both of the women are really calm. Freaky calm. And Judith is dressed up as if she had a date with this guy and then lopped off his head."

"Sí! And the hand? What about her hand? See the shadow."

I studied Judith's hand, completely forgetting the urgency and purpose of the meeting with my mother.

"She's blocking the light from the candle to see better. See, the shadow covers her eye."

Mom waited, and I thought about why Judith would block out the candle. "They heard something, something in the dark. They're scared. She's trying to see what made the noise. That's the expression on their faces and bodies. Scared to death they're gonna get caught. I can relate."

"They did what they thought was right, Magnus. Like you. I love you. Your father loves you."

"I know, Mom."

"You're a smart boy."

We stood in silence for a minute. Mom spoke first.

"I forget the whole story, a bible story. Trouble then, trouble now." She sighed a pit-of-the-belly sigh and took my hand. Her hand was freezing. "Qué te pasa? Zio Vinnie said you were in not big, but not little trouble. He gave you money. You took it."

"I screwed up. You know, when I helped Rafael and his friends get Green Cards."

"Dios mío, I am so sorry. I know, I know. It is my—"

I interrupted. I wanted to get through this with as little drama as possible. My train left in an hour. The walk to the Amtrak station took twenty minutes.

"Cálmate!" I rarely used that tone of voice with my mother. Her hand was shaking. "Not your fault. It's all on me, Mom. I didn't think about what I was doing. I love you and I'll be back soon."

"Your father will help! He is abogado!"

"Sure, sure. Not today, though. Maybe later. Please tell him I love him and that I hope I haven't made trouble for him. I'll keep in touch." I handed her a burner phone I had pre-programmed. "Texts will be from a señor Krum. So you know I'm okay."

She wanted to argue, to say more, to ask about the name. I put a finger to my lips. A group of visitors led by a museum docent were walking our way.

"Prométeme." She spoke as much with her eyes as her voice.

"Te juro."

I whispered the words again and bent over and placed my chin, then cheek, on the top of her head, smelling the eucalyptus shampoo she used. I longed for the home I was about to leave, and for something new and unexpected, a curiosity about the uncharted journey ahead.

Hero: We were eye-to-eye

We were eye-to-eye, me and the eye.

Luca had been wrong about the place being locked. Under a red triangular sign with an exclamation point in the middle were the words "attenzione struttura pericolante." A sign nailed to a dilapidated wood fence warned trespassers in large caps, DIVIETO DI ACCESSO. Given the cautionary signage, it surprised me to find the entry door ajar. I entered, noticing first—as architects do—the light, its many gradations and the causes of those gradations. Where windows remained, dust and grime coated the glass and diffused and thinned the light's intensity. Rays shimmered and motes of dust gave the illusion of mass.

This building had a story to tell. The limestone stairs, shaped in the classic Italian manner, fit one's natural step. Who had worn in these gentle foot-worn hollows? Characters out of Lampedusa's *The Leopard*? The walls seemed textured by the echoes of their footsteps. The old stairway and its lacey Tuscan railing predated the exterior facade, a facade that could have been used for Hollywood horror set. What was Luca thinking? This was so not a place for a romantic tryst, no fucking way. What was he thinking?

With my index finger I traced the outline of the black, brush-painted eye, and felt the texture of the dry, splintery wood. I shivered but should not have been cold. I'd just doubled-stepped up three flights of stairs and on the way here I'd basked in the heat as the Sicilian sun as it peeled back the shadows from city streets. Yes, the creepy eye marked my destination. Freaky. Below the eye someone had painted a smiley face with a toothy, crooked maw and witch's pointed hat. The sign invited self-doubt and fear, a mocking "Enter if you dare." Well, screw you! Parkour girl ain't spooked by mystic bullshit.

A painful and sickening groan came from inside the room. I started, then eased the door open and froze. Luca was duct-taped to a tall-backed, wooden kitchen chair. Tape covered his mouth, and his beautiful, easygoing, galoot body, hung listlessly encased in horizontal bands of more silver tape. Vertical rivulets of blood dribbled from his head and one ear and had dried and darkened to a deep cherry color. He resembled a morbid Christmas package wrapped in a plaid of silver and red. He saw me. I'd never seen pure fear. There was fear for me, the most fear I'd ever seen a human being express. And this was Luca, my friend and lover to be who could slack without a safety net a hundred feet off the deck. Fuck. One eye had swollen shut. The gaze from the good eye flitted back and forth between me and a large-enough-to-jump-through, narrower-than-tall window. The glass was gone save a few pieces at the corners and top.

I ran to Luca and held him. In an adjacent bathroom mirror I glimpsed the face and torso of a well-dressed, handsome, clean-shaven, forty-something man who was bent over slightly, inspecting something held in his hands. He cocked his head to the side and up, as if he had just shaved and was checking to see if he'd missed a spot. I quickly looked away. He hadn't seen me, but he must have heard my approach.

Luca shook his head no and frantically moved his good eye back to the window. I fumbled with the slippery, bloody tape covering his mouth. Finally, he conceded and accepted that I wasn't going anywhere. His head, his entire body, shuddered. He struggled to fix his gaze on me, trying to still the tremors. I noticed, as I gently peeled back the tape, that Luca had pissed in his pants. I was standing in a puddle of urine, filth, and blood. A silver strip of tape jiggled like drool from one corner of his mouth.

An ugly garland of green-brown bruises ringed his throat. Luca spoke in whispered puffs of air from the back of his throat. "Go now, now! Two meters. T' amo." He managed a crooked, painful smile and wink with his good eye. He was tough, brave, and kind. In that second, I loved him more than anything or anybody I had ever loved.

A hatless carabiniere stepped out from a room that had once been a kitchen. He was big, big enough that his shoulders brushed the sides of the doorway. The man's long torso and short legs clashed with the svelte, proportioned intention of his uniform. Bulging, hairy, pineapple arms poked out of the short sleeves. Tree-stump thighs threatened the seams of pant legs that gathered in folds at the ankle. He was a cop, yes, but so not Italian. No Italian sbirro would so disrespect his attire. I pegged him as a Slav. Something about him telegraphed weightlifter. If so, he would be strong, quick, and limber. I'd competed with weightlifters. They ranked right under gymnasts and ballerinas in flexibility, and maybe tops for fast-twitch, explosive power and strength. My brain went from one-hundred percent I love you Luca to one-hundred percent this big guy could catch me and kill me.

In one hand the chunky fingers and thumb wrapped around a sack, a kilo of something—heroin, coke, no idea except it probably wasn't a bed pillow full of barley corn. In the other hand, he held a knife, the handle swallowed by his massive fist. The knife had a narrow, curved blade, one that would be good for filleting fish. Powdery bits of whatever was in the bag stuck to the tip of the knife. I eased my pack off my shoulder and set it gently and soundlessly on the floor, avoiding the wet, then wiped the soles of my shoes on the cuffs of my baggy, parkour pants. Traceurs knew how to run from the cops. It was a rite of passage. Traction mattered.

This sbirro acted self-assured, unruffled by my arrival. He moved calmly between me and the door through which I had entered, the only access to the stairwell and the only exit from the apartment. He soundlessly closed the door, mimicking the gentle care that I had taken with my pack. We were both moving in slow motion. The other man, the "looker" that I had seen before in the mirror, quickly closed the door to the bathroom, leaving it open a crack so he could listen. I shifted my weight. Sbirro did the same. My heart pounded in sync with Luca's shallow, labored breathing. We could have been on the Nature Channel, Sbirro and Hero, the dance of hunter and prey, one of those shorts the viewer can't leave until after its predictable, grisly conclusion.

I stood in front of Luca and leaned forward. My face just touched his. Patches of blood on his body and clothes had caked and dried. How long had he been here? He'd been beaten and tortured. I held back the tears because I needed to see clearly. And I acknowledged that I had understood what he had been trying to say. My hunter—had we known each other for years?—stepped a foot to the side, a pawn move, enough to counter a dash to the door. The asshole grinned. I knew why, the way every woman knows why an asshole grins like that.

A noise from the bathroom disrupted the stasis, that suspended state of attraction and repulsion that had kept Sbirro and me apart. He turned his head toward the bathroom and I took the shot. I bolted for the window, thinking about a two-meter jump. Trust Luca, I told myself. Focus. Should be a piece of cake.

Luca, his voice a screaming whisper, yelled. "Pippa!" The insult; it meant "hand job." I heard the sickening "shunk" of the blade going into Luca's chest. I heard a gasp escape his lungs, taking his life with it, and then visualized his dying breath drying my tears and lifting me across the jump.

The sill looked solid and a two-meter launch over a three-story drop was something I'd done before. The landing was iffy. There was no way Luca could have explained that I'd have to touch down on planks of wood strapped to steel scaffolding strung across the entire side of the adjacent building. Italian workers, bless their hearts, did scaffolding well. As part of my architectural studies, hard-hatted yours truly had hands-on inspected a dozen restoration sites.

The landing for the ten-foot vertical drop was two thick wooden planks. If the planks could support a couple of pot-bellied masons and a wheelbarrow of mud, they could hold Hero. I jumped and stuck a ski-jumper landing with one leg in front of the other to spread the impact over the two boards. As I squatted to absorb the shock, my phone squirted out of my back pocket. I couldn't grab for it because I needed both hands on the wall in case my foot slipped or a board flipped. The phone tumbled in the air like a wounded bird and landed, intact, in a pile of construction dirt and debris. My hands wrapped the top of the chest-high wall. To vault the wall, I visualized being on a diving board and sprung upward. The interior drop on the other side was two feet. Tubes of extra scaffolding, cement blocks, and wood boards complicated the roll-out. My ankle caught between two blocks and twisted. I was a traceuse, so I sucked it up and remembered that one time, during a stunt, Tom Cruise twisted an ankle and kept running. If he could do it, then I sure as hell could.

I was sitting there in pseudo lotus pose and examining my ankle, when the Sbirro exploded out of the shadowed window and flew toward the scaffolding. Shards of broken glass spun in the air, caught the light, and flashed intermittently as they floated to the ground. The scaffolding shuddered, a board cracked, but the son-of-a-bitch made it. Muscled hands flopped over the top of the wall. Sbirro's associate, the clean-shaven guy, stood in the shadows, framed by the window and too far back to be recognized. He watched us and adjusted his collar and twirled a cufflink or something. I had already memorized his face and vowed that if I ever had the chance, I would kill him. That simple.

I'd never thought that I could kill somebody. But I'd never been so terrified or so angry.

Two meters off, my predator scrambled to regain his footing. A plank cut loose and pinwheeled groundward, singing out when it collided with the metal bracing. I listened and watched as Sbirro searched for something to push off of, gave up, and braced his arms to heave himself over the wall. Frantic that I would not be able to outrun him because of the ankle, I searched around for something with which to defend myself. I grabbed a short section of pipe—the equivalent of a five-foot long, twenty-pound baseball bat. Multiple scenarios played out in my head. In all of them except one, I lost. I used the pipe as a crutch and stood up and hobbled toward the wall. My assailant's eyes bulged as he watched me bring the makeshift bludgeon to his skull. The first blow glanced off his head owing to an imperfect swing and a quick head flinch. The guy had fast reflexes. He tried to block the second blow, swatting it away, but missed. It must have dazed him, because he failed to avoid the third blow, and the fourth, and then I lost count. I wanted to reduce his skull to crushed bone and brain matter. When the frenzied beating stopped, he was still there, his head like a smashed pumpkin and hands flattened to a pulpy goo of bone and tendon. I used the end of the pipe to scrape free the sticky flesh from the top of the wall. People had gathered in the street below and watched. They screamed when the lifeless slab of flesh flopped awkwardly from one level of scaffolding to the next, and with great finality, kissed the ground like a gargantuan Fiorentino steak.

The Looker, more revenant than real, watched from the shadows. I had eagle eyes. Odds were I could see him better than he could see me. I peeked over the edge. A stupid mistake because the voyeurs below had phones at the ready and were chasing after their fifteen minutes of fame or a way to monetize the incident. Assholes! Had they not understood that this guy had murdered my friend, and that I had been next in line? I threw the pipe at the crowd and watched them scatter. The ankle screamed. I screamed at myself—if Tom Cruise could run with a bum ankle, I sure as fuck could. Anger was the only emotion I had left.

I vanished in the crenellated maze of roofs and walls and chimneys.

"I'm Magnus, ma'am, Magnus Krum."

The ensuing pause was so long Magnus thought she had forgotten that he was standing in front of her. The woman had to be in her late seventies or early eighties. A ceramic woman, fragile and strong, shaped by experience, flawed to perfection, skin a thin glaze. An obelisk with salt-pepper hair—hair like his abuela's. There the resemblance ended. His abuela had had a honey-silk complexion, a cushioned, pear-shaped tummy and giving breasts.

"Yes. Well, I am pleased to meet you, young man."

Distracted and thinking about how he never minded waiting for his abuela to speak, he had totally forgotten where he was. "Ma'am?"

Her arm reached out, the fingers fall-dry sycamore leaves at the end of a branch. When he failed to take her hand, she took her seat again, twice reviewing a list of names on a clipboard on the green-surfaced, fold-up picnic table. The breeze licked at the paper. A frown from the woman told the papers to settle down.

"Magnus—"

"Yes, ma'am," He shot back. That was the third "Ma'am."

"May I call you Magnus?"

"Of course." The lips pursed, but he didn't say the "M" word.

"I do not see your name. You did register in advance."

Was that a statement or a question?

"Is that Crumb, as in the word *breadcrumb*?"

"K. R. U. M." He corrected the spelling, feeling solid this time about dropping the ma'am.

Krum found its place on the list. The neat, confident handwriting suggested hours of penmanship exercises. She was of a generation that wrote longhand.

The sign hanging from the table at which she sat read: "Serve Your Community. Volunteer for *WeDrive!*" That made sense. A small town wouldn't be profitable for Uber or Lyft, much less an actual cab company.

A river rock the size of a child's fist secured quarter-sheet flyers from the wind. These fliers were identical to one that he had seen posted on the bulletin board at Holders' offices.

On foot, in part to dry out and in part to work off the sugar and caffeine rush, he'd taken a winding route back to the Farmer's Market, wandering several blocks up and down Laneda, noting the usual small-town touristy array of gift shops, ice cream and pizza parlors, restaurants with odd hours that were impossible to keep straight, the requisite Mexican dive, real estate and rental offices, a library and arts center, the Wonder Garden (beautiful), bus stop, police station, city services agencies, a slew of bed and breakfasts and motels, and, of singular importance, what appeared to be an excellent coffee shop—the Manzanita News. Missing, he noted, was a decent bakery. Every small town should have its own bakery.

Making the best of his newly adopted home would mean getting out in the community and avoiding his natural tendency to gray-stone the world.

"I presume you are new to Manzanita," she stated—again not a question—and handed him a clipboard, this one with a Bic pen trapped in the spring clip. "I know most folks here."

Nodding yes, he added, not convincingly, "Hope to stay. If I can find work." He sat down on a folding chair at the end of the table and scanned over the one-page form. The questions were innocent enough —if you were innocent. His responses would be lies.

Name. Indeed, Magnus Krum was a real name. Someone out there had worn the name since birth, passed away at a relatively young age, but would have been close to Magnus's age had he survived. New Magnus had a credible credit history, a construct of his IBM cohorts and supported by documents sourced from a Chinese supplier. The driver's license was good enough to use to apply for a new one in his adopted state of residence. Magnus liked his adopted name.

Address. That, he reflected, would be the actual brand-new address at 404 First Street.

Occupation. Easy. He didn't have to lie and wrote "IT Consultant" in the blank space. He had rock star IT chops, and although he couldn't provide references or admit to having hacked Chinese computers as part of a team at IBM and funded by the NSA, he certainly knew enough to manage any common IT task.

License and Vehicle. He scribbled the info from his phony Michigan license. At auto make and model, he went for detail. Detail adds credibility. Subaru Outback, 2006, L.L.Bean edition.

Contact Information. The email address was new, as was the pre-pay burner mobile number.

He struck out at *Local References.*

"Ma'am, I'm not from here and don't have a local reference."

Their eyes met. She was decoding the neurons and glia in his brain. "So, why are you here?"

This woman expected the truth.

A half-truth surfaced. "I don't know why. I had to stop somewhere." Then, "Why do you live here?" He had asked politely, trying to make the comment not sound as cheeky as the words per se.

That struck an unexpected chord. His sixth sense kicked in and told him when someone had something to hide and wanted to tell him about it. Omar had been everybody's safe space. The old woman finessed the urge to confide. What he perceived was subtle, like a change in air pressure. "I watch the waves come and go, the shadows and the light. What do you make of that?"

The poetic dodge warranted an intelligent response. "Uh-huh."

"At any rate, you seem a nice young man—"

A Venn diagram—man, nice, and young—flashed in his head.

"—and I shall need a ride home after the market. Then, you see, you shall have a reference."

"True," he laughed. He'd composed himself since the bit about the sea, when he'd failed to find anything appropriate to say. The still foggy Magnus rebounded: "But what if I'm not?"

"My assessment is at least two-thirds correct." She was being playful. "As for the *nice.* I suppose you might not be. A charmer, perhaps, but also perhaps, a despicable *misfit!*" She cocked her head to the side and once again met Magnus eye-to-eye, acting as if she had only one good eye. Maybe she did. "Well, I hope not! Ah, I forgot to ask: Is your automobile nearby, close to the market?"

Something about the words *automobile* and *misfit* registered in his brain. "I'll bring the car around and park over there." He pointed toward the market's grassy parking lot. "This is really kind of you. What time?"

"Give me a half hour. No, forty-five minutes. I want to buy a half-flat of strawberries—although it's not quite the season for them—and a jar of pickles, and . . . basil. Yes, I mustn't forget basil." The good eye followed something behind him—two swallows scribbling kanji in the sky.

For the next thirty minutes, Magnus mingled in a crowd of a hundred plus people circulating a round and between three rows of vendors. Gayly colored canopies shaded the vendors and their wares, fruits, and vegetables from the late afternoon sun. Eventually, he joined a group seated at fold-up chairs around a makeshift stage where a trio of grey-haired, grey-bearded musicians performed. A young woman, introduced as a daughter of the keyboard player, added vocals to some whiny country number. The song resonated with the older crowd. A couple vets—their hats identifying them as such—rocked their heads side to side. Weed was in the air. Stage left, a woman with a tambourine and tie-dyed sundress danced barefoot with two towheaded children. Everyone was happy and safe.

The halcyon scene had a contrary effect on Magnus. As minutes ticked by, the unease grew. *Magnus*, he told himself, *you need to eat.*

He rose, marched over to the nearest food stall, and ordered a lemonade and a crab taco. "Caught this morning." A young woman ladled pieces of crab and fixings on the grill. The crab was delicious and the first he had ever eaten. In Detroit, crab was a scary ice cube of bleached mystery meat produced by indentured workers at health-code-violating aquaculture factories in Indonesia. The stand's tortillas weren't bad, not as good as his mom's tillas, but a major improvement over the commercial product.

A line of people had formed in front of a stall selling smoked salmon. Half the people in the line wore straw sun hats. Magnus made a mental note to learn about straw hats and get one so he would fit in. Or maybe those were the weekend tourists. He didn't mind being pegged as a tourist.

Salmon man's wife leaned over a cooler of fish. A sign read: "Coho, Fresh Today." Two large filets remained. A customer pointed. She grabbed a filet by the tail and flat-slapped it on a white polyethylene board crisscrossed with cuts and dotted with bits of ruby flesh and nacreous fish scales. The edge of a curved knife traversed the filet until the buyer said stop. There, the scimitar blade rose and fell, parting the tough, scaly skin and pink-orange flesh. Nearby, the woman's child, maybe seven, played with ice cubes in a stainless-steel bucket.

Magnus wondered about the wisdom of the distracted child and the proximity of the deadly blade. *I had almost died.*

"Magnus, hello! There you are!" The old woman hailed him from the behind the back of the salmon stall.

"Time?" He spoke over the head of the fish-slicing wife, making eye contact first so that he wouldn't startle her.

His passenger-to-be nodded yes and extended two arms, each bearing a canvas bag. The larger bag bulged from the half-flat of strawberries. She was ready to go.

Her bony, outstretched arms handed over the bags.

"Where was it you parked?"

Magnus tilted his head toward Subi and then guided her there. He loaded her bags, letting the tailgate rest on his head because the struts that supported the tailgate had no gas left in them. Standing beside him, his passenger carefully replaced strawberries that had spilled over the rims of their green cardboard containers.

He had intended to get the door for her, but she beat him to it and got in on her own.

"Where to?"

"Not far. Take Laneda toward the beach, right on Third Street, a block and a half. Three-six-five Third."

The new volunteer driver drove with caution, abiding tourists who would cross the street, change their minds, and then wander off in a different direction; he minded unleashed dogs and unleashed children. She pointed when they arrived. "This is it."

Subi rolled to a stop in front of a modest home with yellow clapboard siding. A trellis bordered the entrance, a rosebush on one side and a voluptuous purple rhododendron on the other. The knee-high, white picket fence imprisoned a garden in need of thinning. A half-hidden-by-weeds driftwood board, the address hand-painted on it, hung sideways from a single nail.

She was first to the front door. With canvas totes in hand, he trundled behind, passing the opened gate, up a creaky step, and then squeezing by his rider as she held the screen door open.

"Where to, ma'am."

She took the bags from him and then introduced herself. "My name is Estelle Angel. It is not Stella, so do not call me Stella." With some effort, Estelle Angel—not "Stella"—marched the totes to the kitchen, elbowed aside a couple of books and placed the strawberry flat on the tabletop and the other bag on an adjacent chair. "I do not care for that *Miz* business either," she continued. "*Miss* Angel is fine, and so is

Estelle—though I *am* old enough to be your grandmother."

"No way, not at all." Magnus checked out the room. "Miss Angel, you have a lot of books. I mean, you *really* have a lot of books! Wow!"

Books piled upon books, upright books, books on their sides, clusters of books with their spines facing the wall. It was nearly impossible to find a barren patch of wall space. Stacks of books—tall stacks, short stacks, some tidy, some twisted—covered side tables, foot tables, end tables, chests, bureaus, footstools and ottomans. He wound his way through the room, a Godzilla wandering the streets of New York. Who the hell had time to read all this? The centerpiece of the room, a white leather and a birch plywood Eames chair and matching footstool, angled toward a paned window framed on the outside by a rose trellis. Symmetrically opposite the Eames chair, opposite in terms of both style and location, was a worn, green leather armchair. Beyond the trellis, blood orange poppies and sea grasses shaped like inverted whisk brooms sprung from the ground.

"Was that *flattery*, young man? That unpleasant device favored by two kinds of people: those who have something to hide and those who want something from you!"

"Flannery! Flannery O'Connor." He seized on the serendipitous opportunity for connection.

"Excellent, Magnus." The smile was unforced; her eyes sparkled. "I am genuinely impressed."

He had made up for the "Uh-huh." She took Magnus's hands. Her face was that of a schoolteacher, surprised and pleased to see a lackluster student rally. Or maybe she wanted him to be still, the way a teacher would hold a child's attention.

"Yes, *A Good Man is Hard to Find*, by Flannery O'Connor. You've read her short stories? At times, dark. But, my God, what a gifted writer."

"Yup! I remember the story. It's the only one I've read by O'Conner, the one about a family that spends the day together, driving around and listening to the grandma's stories. Then they're all murdered by an escaped convict who calls himself *The Misfit*. Miss Angel, I promise I will *not* shoot you!"

"You better not! If you do, I shall *not* be your reference. Or, for that matter, anybody's!"

"Understood, ma'am." He stood at attention, acknowledging a commanding officer. "Miss Angel, I mean."

"Good," she laughed, "And I'm not a petty, self-serving old bat like that woman in the story!"

She laughed at something unshared and then opened the door for Magnus to leave. She wasn't, however, prepared to dismiss him. Not quite.

"I suspect you're an interesting man, Magnus Krum. And I think you come from an interesting family and that we shall become friends. And someday, you will tell me the truth about who you really are, and your family." She dredged up a quote from *A Good Man is Hard to Find*. " 'These days you don't know who to trust.' Do you remember Red Sammy Butts?"

Magnus shook his head no. He waited.

"Yes, well why should you? But, Magnus Krum, I choose to think the best of you—though I don't know quite why I should—and, who knows, perhaps someday I shall—" She picked a book from the top of a stack of books, turned it around, and replaced it on the stack. "—It doesn't matter."

Such was their last exchange. Magnus was exhausted. He headed off to inspect his new place, thinking about what she had said, and thinking, not for the first time, not for the tenth time, but maybe for the thousandth time that day, about his family and about how selfish and thoughtless he had been.

Magnus: Zio Vinnie was

Zio Vinnie was a nimble, though at times distracted, man. He hadn't expected the front door to be unlocked and tripped over the transom, stumbling into his office and cursing in Italian as his Muji travel thermos escaped, bounced on the floor, and rolled toward me.

"Whaddya doing here?"

As he spoke, Vinnie inspected his clothing for coffee stains. The ironed, white short-sleeve shirt, khaki slacks, and olive-hued windbreaker passed.

I moved to pick up the thermos, but he scooped it up first, inspecting the carpet as he did so. He showed it to me, proud of the little thermos that could.

"You been here all night? What the fuck?"

I'd often asked myself the same question. Why the fuck was I, Omar Adil Papadopoulos, a degreed University of Michigan graduate with five years of work experience as an intern and employee at IBM's NSA-funded cybersecurity department, not somewhere better than his Uncle Vinnie DiMaso's nondescript, downtown Detroit office at eight o'clock Monday morning?

"Server upgrade. No distractions. Reinstalled stuff." Vinnie didn't want details. I skipped those with him and with myself. Half the reason I was here was because I had nothing better to do. And work was important. Getting things right mattered to me.

I sipped at the dregs of an espresso long gone cold and had this flash that the deeper explanation for my presence here was equally long gone cold. I was making bank, though. And money, as everyone knew, justified just about anything.

Vinnie didn't want tech talk. Neither did I. And neither of us wanted to revisit that other explanation for my being here, namely, that my family owed Vinnie. I had given Vinnie three years of weekends and a month of days off from my job at IBM. Recently—recent being two months ago—Vinnie had announced that I'd done plenty and that I should get the hell out of his hair and get a life. The not-so-subtle advice implied that Vinnie knew that my hanging around was a pathetic excuse for nothing better going on in my desiccated life. It was true. He knew it and I knew it.

We never openly discussed the why my family owed Vinnie. This was the norm, the omertà among members of family Papadopoulos and family DiMaso. Our families even hid shit that was utterly unimportant, an example being when Zio Vinnie had once gotten two speeding tickets within the space of ten minutes. The second time was a different cop. The officer asked him when was the last time he'd gotten a ticket? Vinnie grinned. "Five minutes ago!" The indignant cop responded, "You think this is funny?" to which Vinnie and his three mobster passengers completely cracked up. The outburst freaked the cop and he drew his gun. This, of course, the four men found riotously hilarious. When Zio Vinnie finally told the story to us—us being the Adil Papadopoulos clan—he laughed so hard he cried. You know, families should share that kind of funny shit right away, not months later.

I was an anomaly, a retention valve, the outsider with whom one could take exception to the code of omertà. Data flowed only one direction. People—not only family members, but all kinds of people— told me private, delicate, explosive, embarrassing, frightening, worrisome things. My DNA waved an invisible white flag saying that here was someone you could tell your darkest secrets to. I wasn't particularly warm or protective, and I never gave advice or judged. Talking to Omar was as risky as talking to the fucking wall. Here was the soft-spoken guy with glasses, a weirdly epicene loner, a math nerd who hacked computers, a neatnik who was twenty-seven but with the delicate facial hair of a seventeen-year-old, and a ringer for his mom when she taught salsa. So, again, why had I been here all night?

Zio Vinnie's wife, Aunt Alejandra, had been the first to tell the story. Being Cuban, she preferred the Spanish Tia Alejandra. The story I'd been told was that quiet Zio Vinnie, as a young buck and acting alone, had quietly "disappeared" a hit man who had planned to kill my grandmother and her two daughters. That's my sweet abuela, whom I loved dearly; my mom, Mari; her sister, Tia Alejandra. The intended femicide was in retaliation for fucking up a cartel deal made by the then young, lovely, aspiring and drug-abusing Alejandra Guerra, Vinnie's wife-to-be. Separately, again for my ears only, Vinnie had told a similar story. Each version had been told in confidence, and, mostly, the stories jibed.

My immediate family may or may not have known all the details, but we owed Zio Vinnie. We owed him big time and I was making good on the debt by using my techie skills to help Vinnie set up his personal and very illegal IRA.

"Janette," Vinnie squinted at the seventeen-dollar F-91W Casio watch he had purchased at Sears not long after the invention of the automobile, "she comes in at eight."

"I know, I know. I'm wrapping up."

"You got a gal yet?"

"Zio, non ora, per favore."

"Get a gal, kid. You ain't getting younger. I mean. While it still works." Vinnie made an obscene gesture with his hips and almost dropped his mug again.

"I got the picture." I smiled. "Not pretty."

Vinnie was full of high-octane advice in the mornings. I wished he would stop jumping around.

"My eyes are shitty. Don't get old. Dat's another thing." He half-groaned, half-grinned, and used a handkerchief to blot what might have been a coffee spot on the carpet. "And get some sleep. And mabbeeee get a real job. Your Zio Vinnie can pay for a bookkeeper and . . . whatever."

"I have a real job. And it's tech support."

I knew better than Vinnie what he could afford. And I knew that the end of my internship in white-collar crime with Vinnie was imminent. "A couple more days, that's it."

Conflating Italian and Spanish, Vinnie asked, "Bene, dimmi más."

I summarized: "We got seven years of clean data—backed up and reconciled. If there's an audit, the auditors will find deductions you missed. That'll be a disincentive to dig deeper."

Vinnie grunted satisfaction.

"And" I continued, "I'm double-checking the other thing."

We never talked aloud in the office about the other thing. It was a silly precaution. As an IBM paid-for-hire hacker, I knew what the Feds could do. But I humored Vinnie.

"I thought," Vinnie settled into the leather recliner at his desk, spinning around and speaking when he faced me, "you said . . . the other thing . . . was done?"

"It is. But I wanted to let it marinate. Then, you know, one more time."

The next revolution he caught my eye. "Smart."

"Not smart," I replied to the back of his head. Smart implied I should do more with my life. "Humans screw up. I think Pope said that."

Another cycle. "Not you kid, not you."

One last rotation, faster, speaking away this time and me wondering about the Doppler shift. "Why'd the Pope say that? I like the Pope. He's one of us, from Chicago or somethin'."

Vinnie's computer system was as clean as I could make it. I had planned for and presumed Vinnie was okay with shutting down the other thing. He knew I'd move on. And he would move on. There was no one else he would trust. He'd been hinting for a year and I'd been planning my exit for almost as long. His office records showed no connection between the foreign bank account I'd set up for Vinnie and his little import business. I'd similarly sanitized my own, smaller account. Vinnie's "savings" we had converted into gold bullion and tucked away in a safe deposit box in Zug, Switzerland. Lovely place, Zug. I'd seen pictures.

I'd set up the bones of the cash shunt years ago when I was at Ann Arbor and still an intern at IBM. The transfer pricing structure, built from the ground up and reinforced to withstand the scrutiny of IT and accounting professionals, was only possible because of help from my long-time hacking cohorts, the Twins. The brothers, my closest friends through high school and university, were now full-time employees at IBM, doing what they did best, but legit and, like me, funded by government contracts.

That the Twins were "brothers" had not always been the case. Charlie had been assigned female at birth. At puberty's onset she chose to identify as male. She, when "she" became a "he," s(he) swapped her birth name, Charlotte, for Charlie. That Charlie was transgender had never been an issue. We had always been close friends.

The Twins enjoyed a serious rep from having successfully hacked an impenetrable NSA server. In an uncharacteristic spurt of patriotism, they informed a paranoid NSA about the hack and promptly landed jobs as contract government hackers. I tagged along. Ironically, our petty criminal past gave us dark web "street" cred. I figured if I got caught doing what I was doing for Vinnie, there was an even chance the authorities would ignore it.

Vinnie's business imported and sold Italian paper wares—including colored toilet paper, which was experiencing a resurgence since its peak in popularity in the 50s. Shit brown was a hot seller.

As with any respectable, touristic item from Italy, a percentage of the goods were manufactured in China and rebranded as Italian. I had taken advantage of this universal practice and skimmed a little off each transaction. The technical word for this is "defalcation." The off-the-top cash funded a retirement account for Vinnie. Moderation ruled the operation. The total take, ten million plus or minus, was enough for Vinnie to wind down the defalcation scam and not lose sleep. Vinnie's wife, my Tia Alejandra, thought Vinnie had a sparrow-sized Swiss nest egg. My parents, Ari and Mari, knew nothing about it.

Vinnie went to excruciating pains to hide the skimming operation from his mob associates. Had the mob crowd known, they would have muscled in. But Vinnie resisted all forms of attention. He cultivated an image as a dim, risk-averse, petty crook. With his legitimate earnings, he funded loan sharks and bankrolled a pin-ball-machine vendor. These profits were reinvested in small cash operations: a carwash, two laundromats, a bar, and a picayune investment with a Native American partner in a small casino. "I like that Injun," he complimented and offended.

Vinnie had wanted to dive into cryptocurrencies. I explained that there would always be a record of every transaction. After that, he agreed to stick with old-school money-laundering. The Twins had told me, and this was years ago, that IBM could successfully trace any so-called anonymous cryptocurrency transaction—it was simply a matter of compute. IBM played it close to the vest, revealing nothing to the public or the Feds.

Financial schemes like Vinnie's usually failed because of people, not process. Spending disproportionate to one's means was the universal red flag. My uncle, content with his beloved seventeen-dollar F-91W Casio, would never make that mistake. Born and raised in Lucca to a family of modest means, he clung to that humble image. He also clung to an unrefined Tuscan Italian tainted by association with Sicilianu friends and his Spanish-speaking wife. The linguistic output was pico de gallo on pasta.

In sum, the imperfections in Vinnie's life were camouflage. He performed his act, and I performed mine—a behavioral similarity that raised questions only a paternity test would answer.

Shrewd Vinnie was family. Did I want to help Vinnie? No, not really. Did I care about the money? No, not at all. Did I give a shit about the NSA and Chinese hackers? Fuck no. I did what I did because it was in front of me, the way you might avoid shit on the sidewalk en route from point A to point B, from birth to death. There's something existential in that.

Hero: Mom worked in

Mom worked in the Operations Directorate of the CIA, a job that required an uncommon amount of hutzpah and total dedication. Those were the terms. She accepted them and we accepted them—Dad, because he loved her, and me, because that's just the way it was. I grew up in the manner of an army brat; places I called home included Djibouti, Berlin, Mexico City, Washington D.C., Rome, Florence (Firenze), and Zürich. Since Leonard Wheelwright had trained as both an emergency medicine physician and a medical informaticist, he could work anywhere. He practiced hands-on medicine at George Washington University Hospital and leveraged his informatics training to work with various NGOs in Rome. I became a First Responder, encouraged by Dad to pursue a medical career. Mom pressed me to find a career that wasn't messy. She never defined "messy," but was passionate about art—hence, the high school years in Firenze where I received my International Baccalaureate, and then my enrollment in the architecture program at ETH (Eidgenössische Technische Hochschule), Zürich. Dad maintained a home base for us in Rome while I did my studies. Professionally, he did whatever he could find that accommodated my schooling needs and Mom's clandestine work. Some of that "whatever" took him to Jordan, Iraq, and Afghanistan.

Her work entailed personal risks and risks for her family. The family risks she sedulously managed and foresaw every bad thing that could happen to her little girl. There was always a family protocol if something happened to her, or her and Dad, or me. I loved it.

For a twelve-year-old, spy-craft training was all a game, a sort of AP hide-and-seek. By the time I was a teen I had trained in detection avoidance, a variety of communication techniques, and basic information gathering. Mom even threw in a smattering of martial arts.

I wasn't gung-ho on the fighting aspect—neither was she—but I enjoyed tumbling and that was what got me into parkour. Then parkour became a passion.

Many of the skills I learned from Mom were mental games: remembering how I got from point A to point B, memorizing or making a mental map of anyplace I was, riding in a tram or taxi with my eye's closed and describing where we were by sounds around us. I don't think Mom knew any regular kids' games. We had so much fun! We'd dress up in disguises when it wasn't Halloween. Memory, she lectured, was more important than anything else. This I was naturally good at. So, seeking admiration and attention, I wowed Mom and others by taking on challenging roles in kids' theatre, counting cards or city blocks, describing by memory and in great detail places we had visited. I wasn't special, and anybody could do what I did if they trained for it. I learned how to maintain cars, build things, and fix the jury-rigged wiring in our fifteenth-century Rome apartment. This physical fiddling around with the practical added to my interest in architecture.

Dad, poor Dad, was good at the medical stuff but a hazard around a breaker box. He needed help when the power went out or our beat-up Fiat wouldn't start. He watched when Mom and I fixed things, bemused, loving and adoring his grease-smudged women.

The what-do-I-do-if-got-in-serious-shit plan was simple, and it was an option that, frankly, I had never needed until the incident with Luca. First, contact Dad. That was number one. I knew all their numbers, emails, etc. by heart. Second, contact Mom. She had a waterfall of numbers and series of categories that I could use to describe the severity of the crisis. By intention, the categories had silly code words that wouldn't draw attention and came from book names selected from the BBC's "2020 Favorite Children's Books of All Time." The name of a children's book was easy to slip into any note or conversation. *The Very Hungry Caterpillar* was the lowest level: say, someone stole my passport or phone. *Where the Wild Things Are* was the highest severity category. *Wild* was no joke—a half-dozen numbers, a couple safe house addresses (one in Rome, another in Paris), coded message protocols for social media, dead drops. Serious shit. Another special code was *The Cat in the Hat*, not part of the top ten but reserved for medical emergencies. Think rape or being flogged for skateboarding into the Ayatollah. Any emergency message I sent had to have a number associated with it that identified the number of people who needed help and if Mom or her buddies needed to be armed. And a location, of course, and a time frame. A *Wild* message meant extraction and physical intervention by Mom or her cadre.

Mom, my dear mother, had never followed proper spook-mother protocols. She had not lied to her family, at least I think not, about much of her work. She never pretended that she had a normal life or a normal job. Her insubordination should have cost Mom her job. This fate she had avoided because she was really fucking good at what she did, and because some higher-up had always covered her ass—I never learned who. Late in her career, when she had a desk job, her promotions outpaced those of rivals.

* * * *

My first screw-up had been leaving my pack behind and with it my money and ID. But hell, there's no time for packing when your life's on the line. The second big oops! was dropping my phone. I should have carried it some place more secure than a back pocket. Traceurs keep their pockets empty by habit and usually stashed all personal crap in a pack. Again, same excuse. I ran out of time pre-escape. The worst was giving bystanders the photo op when I leaned over the wall.

The emotional reaction to having killed Sbirro, and not just killed him but gruesomely, intentionally clubbed the bastard to death, had been to transform the memory of the experience into a radioactive abstraction that I shoved in a lead-lined box in my brain. Luca too got his own lead-lined coffin. I tried to do the same with my ankle and failed. It hurt like hell.

Luca was a category *Wild* event and Looker's next move was obvious. He would pin Luca's murder on me and leave my body in a dumpster. A half-dozen people had witnessed my beating Sbirro to death. There was no way the Polizia would believe that I had acted in self-defense. Every account of the affair would paint a target on my back. Yeah, this was *Where the Wild Things Are* for sure. I had few options. Returning to Luca's family place would be crazy. Looker and company obviously knew Luca and had been involved in some very shady shit with him.

I zig-zagged across a half-dozen rooftops, moving light on the weak ankle and searching for clotheslines hung with something to replace my bloodied tee and shorts. No luck until, along a quiet alleyway, I spotted an open Juliet balcony with a pair of men's khaki work pants and a blue, collared shirt, the same sky blue as the ones the carabiniere wore. I crawled on my backside, easing my way down the warm-to-the-butt, sloped tiles, and used a gutter to hang-drop the last four feet onto the half-balcony—hoping that Romeo wasn't home and that I wouldn't scream from pain when I hit the deck. Inside, a curtain hung across the window. I changed on the balcony, swimming in the too-big menswear, and stuffed my bloody clothes under the front of the shirt. Another easy hang and swing took me to the balcony below. Repeating the move, I reached ground level. An older couple walking arm-in-arm had seen my descent. My pained smile implored them to keep my what-could-only-have-been-a-tryst a secret.

The bloodied clothes found a dumpster. The next item I needed was a phone. My brain was on autopilot, in the zone and with the singular flow that freerunning entails. On the other side of a small piazza, beyond a miniature fountain and ficus tree at its center, three pre-teen girls strolled, laughed, and shared photographs or videos—whatever —on their phones. A half-dozen people milled about. None of them were the type to intervene, and anyway, I didn't have the time to care. The street wound downhill from the piazza. I borrowed an unlocked bike leaning against a shopfront, pedaled across the square, and came up behind and between the girls. One girl shook a fist, a fist holding an iPhone. I wrenched the phone from her hand and coasted down the hill, punching random apps to keep the phone from shutting down and needing a code to reopen. It was impossible to text while riding on cobblestones, so turned into an alleyway and stopped. My hands were shaking from the vibration and hauling ass down the hill. I opened apple maps, memorized where I was, and texted a message to Mom's number. All it said was Wild Things, the number 1, and Calamosche, and then left the phone on the ground in an obvious place, a place where it wouldn't get run over or damaged. I wanted the girl whose phone I had stolen to get her phone back, for my call to be traced by Mom, and for Mom's people to find the girl and then, hopefully, find me.

The road to Calamosche took an hour by car, probably close to three by bike. Peddle girl, I told myself. Ignore the ankle and peddle like your fucking life depends upon it.

The Holders

Miss Angel was as good as her word. The fire department office manager doubled as the dispatcher for *WeDrive!* He called twice the following week. Magnus cleaned Subi at the drive-through carwash in the neighboring town of Seaside, returned to Manzanita, and ferried a gentleman in his eighties from his home to the Nehalem Bay Health Center in Wheeler. Stickers on the tailgate of the Ford 150 parked in his rider's driveway broadcast its owner's politics: US Air Force Veteran; A Citizen with a GUN; What part of ILLEGAL immigration don't you understand; God, Guns, and TRUMP.

The volunteer work was just that—no compensation. On the return leg Magnus stopped at the local Shell station, part of a chain owned by Mario Andretti, or so he had been told but didn't quite believe. The attendant topped off the tank. Oregon allowed self-service, but many stations still had attendants. His rider, politics or no, offered to pay for gas.

The driving was purposeful, and Magnus enjoyed it. He had this theory that long commutes gave people purpose. Construction workers who lived in Portland or Tigard and drove two hours each way to job sites in Manzanita treated the driving as part of the job. They bemoaned the hours, but, he believed, found something meaningful in pushing a two-and-a-half-ton pickup ninety-five miles each way to the coast and back, the sun in tow on the aptly named Sunset Highway. Same with running and dancing. If the body moved spatially, the psyche tagged along. For Magnus, the movement dulled memories of the mess he had left behind in Detroit.

Manzanita, as was true of all Oregon coastal communities, struggled to find workers. Every restaurant and shop advertised for help: a sign in the window, a flyer on the bulletin board, or a sticky note on the tip jar. Employment needs, all service sector, ranged from long-term to seasonal, the latter because the summer population was a multiple of the off-season population. The high cost of food and housing, lack of public transportation, and age of the resident population added to the local labor shortage.

The typical resident was sixty, retired, but dialed into a host of non-work activities. This older set played golf and pickle ball, attended yoga and Pilates classes at the North County Recreation District center, and walked little white dogs on the beach. They vigorously participated in local politics and in weekly online exchanges. Public sales ads and event announcements were folksy: used barbeque, old Milwaukee table saw, dog stroller, garage sale, Hora del Cuento at the Library, Seal Rescue picnic, free bagged chicken poo fertilizer, antique Fiesta Ware (may or may not be radioactive), Sunday Grange Square dance, Last weekend—*Girl on a Train*—at Riverside Theater. A few news items intoned big city concerns: theft from storage shed in Neah-Kah-Nie Meadows, County Sheriff seeking info re abandoned vehicle on Highway 101, brush fire contained at Seaside RV Park. About once a month, an apocalyptic ranter vented at a city council meeting or on the long-running online website, *BBQ* (named after the founder, not the barbeque).

Locals volunteered at community farms, land trusts, library committees, art and theater groups, and support sessions for vets, men, and women. Many of these volunteers had been hire-powered executives from Portland-based Nike and Intel, or from Amazon and Microsoft in Seattle. These men and women took skills honed from years as leaders, technologists, and managers, and applied them to small town affairs with the same gusto they had shown in their former roles at Fortune 500 companies. The decision about what variety of squash to plant at the one-acre Alder Creek volunteer garden had the tone of a C-suite meeting.

A week and three more service drives into his new role, Magnus received a voicemail and recognized the voice as Lee Holder's. Lee had called on behalf of his father, Mr. Shortley Holder, whose name and face Magnus also recalled.

Lee answered the phone when Magnus returned the call and asked Lee where he heard about his driving for *WeDrive!*.

"The rich cat lady, old bat Stella Angel."

Magnus bottled up the antipathy he felt. *Play dumb, be apolitical. This is small town USA,* he told himself.

Lee gave the time and place for the pickup: a half-hour, Holder Vacation Rentals. They disconnected with no further confirmation of the details, no goodbyes, and with the word *asshole* left in the air on both sides of the conversation.

There was some confusion about the pickup point. The son had directed Magnus to Shortley Holder's office address. The residence was across the street from the office. Lee flagged down Magnus from the sidewalk. Holder senior was ready to go.

"About time. Careful with that chair, boy!" Shortley Holder introduced himself.

It took a minute for Magnus to figure out how to fold the wheelchair. Holder senior wasn't happy with the delay, nor with the way Magnus set the collapsed wheelchair in the back of Subi while struggling with the broken tailgate.

"Ain't got all day, y'know."

"Buckle up, sir," Magnus ordered.

"You worry 'bout yerself."

Holder's family, Magnus learned, hailed from somewhere in the southwest. Magnus wondered if the cowboy-jawed son, in his late thirties, shared his father's view of the world. He didn't share the accent.

Magnus had grown up in multi-lingual pot-pourri and had an ear for accents. He had thought about why some people kept their accents while others lost them. He didn't believe that those who kept an accent were incapable of adapting. The basis for his belief came from personal experience with his multinational colleagues at IBM, the ethnic hodge-podge of neighbors in Mexicantown, the Detroit dance community, and from the undeniable data point that humans routinely adopt non-native languages. Zio Vinnie and Tia Alejandra, he believed, clung to their Italian and Spanish accents to enhance their respective identities, lending color, distinctiveness, or maybe as an out, an excuse for mistakes and misunderstandings or behavioral oddities and offenses. The accents were a successful coping mechanism. To Magnus, clinging to accents suggested vulnerabilities. What, he wondered, were Holder's vulnerabilities?

Holder spiked Magnus's reflections. "You daydreamin'? Get a move on."

Wheeler was a ten-minute drive. The trip took fifteen because of road work. The female voice in his AirPods guided Magnus to the address Holder had provided, a small bakery café with seating for a dozen, including two canopied, outdoor picnic tables. An asphalt-shingled shed roof covered the stick-frame structure. Its translucent fiberglass awning projected from the roof and covered the main entrance and the hand-painted sign: *Panda Bakery*. White paned windows on the tallest side of the structure faced the road and the wide shallow bay that formed the signature feature of Wheeler and gave it claim to being a coastal crabbing destination.

Magnus parked Subi behind a mud-splattered, dual-rear-wheel pickup piled high with grounds debris and the burl of a once mighty cedar. Toolboxes flanked the truck bed like body armor and a bobble-head chihuahua on the dash begged for a treat.

Holder said nothing during the drive. He shoved Magnus's hand away when Magnus attempted to help with the transfer from the car to the wheelchair. Holder fussed about as he settled in. His movements were jerky and quick, those of a person who shoved and grated and fought with things he touched and met, movements sufficiently offensive that Magnus silently apologized to Subi as a muleskinner would to a pack horse forced to carry an imbalanced load.

Holder removed a folded letter from a leather satchel attached at the side of the wheelchair and placed it on his lap. He tried to wheel himself forward toward the entrance but was stymied by the three-quarter inch gravel. In a passive aggressive act, Magnus let him complain before stepping forward to help. No one is a hundred percent asshole, he told himself. He had been petty and made up for it by leaning forward and pulling Holder and wheelchair over the last yard and through a door held open by a Latina woman in her forties and wearing a loose fitting, floral print bata de casa.

"Where's that husband of yers? Yer married, ain't ya?"

Magnus caught oblique glances from two Latino men at a corner table, eating and not talking. They gave off a protective vibe.

"I'm sorry, I don't understand. Please, one minute." She raised a single finger, closed her eyes for a moment, and then gestured to someone in the open kitchen.

The husband, a stout man with a pencil mustache and widow's peak, left his station in front of the stove and wiped his hands on a dishtowel hanging from his apron ties. The aroma of freshly roasted peppers followed him and made Magnus ravenous and homesick. It was true, what he had read somewhere, that smells were the most enduring memories.

With no word of greeting or recognition between them, the husband took the sheet of paper that Holder offered. The pencil mustache twitched as he read the document. A finger traced the words and lingered on certain expressions as if to physically extract their meaning. All actors had frozen in place: the corner customers held silverware in a vertical configuration. Fork and knife flowers poked out of fleshy, fist-shaped vessels. Magnus stood as upright as their forks and knives. Husband and wife could have been two figurines on a wedding cake. The wife watched, immobile, dollish, moving only her eyelids. The letter in the husband's hand fluttered with the oscillations of the fan atop the counter of the pastry display case.

Holder broke the spell. "That there's an eee-viction notice. You got thirty days. 'Less you pay rent. Comprende?"

A girl in her late teens watched from behind the door to the kitchen pantry. Her expression asked if she should join her father and translate the document. Her father noticed and shook his head no. She frowned but didn't retreat.

"Yes, I understand," the father answered. "Why is rent two times before?"

"You people think I'm made of money, but I got 'spenses to pay; I got taxes to pay; I got repair bills to pay with no end in sight. You got a break b'fore." Holder fixed his gaze on the daughter. "She ain't been coming to work. It's a favor I'm doing you, giv'n her housework. She's not doing you a favor skippin' out. No notice neither. My boy's gotta do it. Or someone when she don't show."

Father and daughter glanced at each other. Magnus read nothing in the exchange.

"Mr. Holder, we fix the roof with our own money!"

"Mr. Señor Reyes, that's your business and your problem. The goin' rate's the goin' rate. End of story. Pay up or pack out. Thirty days. Comprende?" His eyes scanned the room and paused—this was the second time—when he saw the daughter. "Give ya time if she come back to work. I need that housecleaning. Otherwise, out by the end of the month. And take yer . . . with you."

Holder waved a hand with a dismissive gesture, likening the Reyes family to objects.

Reyes had understood Holder's demands, as had his wife and daughter. "Yes, I see. I will speak to Constanza, but—"

"Next time I'm comin' with the sheriff. Don't want nobody sleeping here neither. This here's a place of business, ya hear?"

Holder glared at Magnus and nodded toward the door. Magnus

couldn't turn away. "You're a dick!" he thought but didn't say it. He wanted to console Reyes—in Spanish—but held back. He watched Constanza and sensed that she wanted to speak with him.

Holder whacked Magnus on the thigh with the purse hanging off the arm of the wheelchair. He expected Magnus to jump, but got no reaction. Instead, Magnus took his time as he wheeled Holder back to the car. He helped him settle into the passenger seat and put the wheelchair in the back of Subi—this time with care that masked his anger.

"Damned immigrants," Holder muttered to himself.

Magnus searched Holder's bright, clear eyes for a spark of humanity and came up short. The man was a jerk, end of story. No, he told himself. No one was black and white. Somewhere in that bag of bones and flesh was a human being. That was the small-town story he'd been repeating to himself. You got to get along with everybody. Accommodate, not love. Think UN.

"Be right back," Magnus told Holder. "You want anything?"

Holder frowned. "Crap, no. Make it fast."

Inside the bakery the charged atmosphere had dissipated. People mingled and conversed in rapid Spanish. He understood every word but acted as if he only got the gist of what they were saying.

Magnus cornered Reyes and explained that he was a *WeDrive!* driver and that he wanted to help. He asked in English to see the eviction letter and if he could take a photo. Reyes agreed and held the document steady as Magnus explained that he would get back to him in a day or two. He tried to buy an empanada de fruta. Reyes's wife put one in a paper bag and wouldn't let him pay.

"I am Carmen," she introduced herself.

"Magnus, my name is Magnus Krum. Thank you, Carmen. That's very kind of you."

"Magnus." She took his wrist and tried out the name. "Magnus. Sometimes Constanza needs a ride to Manzanita, Magnus. Can you do this? Do we pay you?"

"*WeDrive!* is free. I'm a volunteer." He used the pen and pad on the counter and wrote down his number and the general number for *WeDrive!*. "Anytime. If I'm free, I'll do it. If not, there are other volunteers. They're all *nice* people."

One Hour Charge

Shortley Holder and Magnus arrived to chaos at *Holder Vacation Rentals*. Lee kicked over a mesh-metal wastebasket beside the desk. The toe of his boot left an indentation. He leaned over Meredith's desk and hammered the keyboard with his index finger. In a fit of pique, he picked up the monitor—still strung with power, mouse, and keyboard cords—and acted as if he were about to heave the lot across the room. Magnus caught the tail end of the tantrum and the tail of the still plugged-in power cord.

" . . . son-of-a-bitch computer!" Lee hollered.

"No, no, no!" Magnus yelled and put a hand in the air and waved him off.

Lee froze, then lowered the monitor and not so gently set it back on the desk. "Sorry, Meredith." His receptionist/admin had rolled away from the potential techno-carnage.

Magnus relaxed the pose he had assumed—that of being prepared to catch the monitor midair. He let out a boyish laugh and smiled and shook his head. The pent-up resentment at Holder senior's prior behavior fell away in the moment of Schadenfreude. Lee glared at him and twisted around, the message being that one more word and he might pitch the monitor at Magnus. He was a big guy, an intimidating guy.

The issue at hand, one with which Magnus was familiar, was the latest Windows incarnation of the Blue Screen of Death. Magnus recognized the symptoms the second he saw the display on the monitor.

"Let me help," he cheerily announced.

"You goin' to hustle up to Warrenton?" Shortley Holder asked. Probably the Best Buy in Warrenton was their go-to for IT.

The snooty tone of Holder's question made Magnus recalibrate the offer to help. He could fix their IT problem gratis, but now, since they were acting like assholes, he would charge them.

"I'm good at what I do." Magnus kept it straight, not smirking. "Real good. A hundred an hour. I can take care of it right now."

"Yeah, how do we know yer so damned good?"

"If it's not up and running by the end of the day, there's no charge. Unless it's a piece of hardware that needs to be replaced. I don't have parts."

"And if you screw it up?"

Magnus grinned. "I won't."

Lee had cooled off. "Right now, you say?"

"One hour's all I'm paying fer." The miserly Shortley Holder never disappointed. Continuing the passive aggressive theme, Magnus stopped addressing him as *Mister* Holder and went with just plain "Holder."

"I can fix this, Holder. But not in an hour."

"You fix it. I pay for one hour." Shortley snarled the word "hour," making it into "Aaahr."

"How many workstations do you have? Cloud server or local? Are they all like this?" A quick visual inspection tallied three PCs: reception, Shortley's office, Lee's office.

Lee answered. "These three and one with a big screen."

There was nothing with a big screen.

"It's upstairs," Lee explained.

Magnus had gotten up early to chauffeur Holder to Panda, too early to enjoy his usual AeroPress, toast and juice, the Times puzzle, weather, and the Detroit Free Press. He never checked social media until after noon, the latter always done minimally and anonymously.

"Try again." Magnus folded his arms. A showdown stance with Senior.

Shortley Holder glowered. His face took on a grotesque, grinch aspect. Eyebrows closed together, the upper lip thinned and hid behind a protuberant lower lip. He was a sixty-year-old infant whose pacifier had been taken away.

"Can I look . . ." Magnus spoke as he turned toward Meredith's computer. She had abandoned her swivel chair. Magnus grabbed it, sat down, and rolled up to the desk. He tapped a few keys and got the same result Lee had. The scrambled screen stared back at him. "If this thing reboots—which it may or may not do because the operating system is going to take its own sweet time to reset and there's not a damn thing you or I can do about it, and if you want your system working again, it's gonna take as long as it's gonna take."

The tightness in Holder senior's face gave way to resignation. "Well, we all got work to do. Fix the damned thing. How long?"

"Three hours, maybe less."

Senior nodded at Junior, waiting for confirmation. Meredith put a hand on her hip, amused, watching three stubborn men stare at each other.

"So?" Magnus was tired of quibbling. He swiveled around, stood up, and headed for the door.

Lee spat the words. "Hold on!"

Magnus turned Shortly Holder and got the okay. The man did so by pursing his lips and then retracting them, a repulsive air kiss with a faint smack.

"Right. So, couple three things . . ." Magnus ran through the usual checklist: What version of Windows? Were the computers on a network? What was going on right before it crashed? When was the last virus scan?

Lee approached and rummaged through a desk drawer. He unloaded a handful of manuals and other documentation on the desk next to the computer. Magnus leaned over the machine, depowered it, and restarted in safe mode. "Don't remember doing a virus scan. I think the system does that automatically. We didn't do anything new or different. It just crashed."

"While this thing reboots, I'm gonna run get a coffee at the News. When I get back, we'll have a better idea of what the problem is. I'll do software upgrades as needed, check for malware, and install an anti-virus program if necessary. Probably cost you between twenty and fifty a month, but worth it."

The News was less than a block away. There was no push back on the coffee front, nor on the software charges.

Holder senior moved uncomfortably close. Magnus picked up an unpleasant aroma. He had smelled it on the ride to Panda. The memory brought back the conversation between Reyes and Holder. Had missed something important in that conversation?

"We do business on the Internet. Very private business and I want no one snoopin' around, ya hear? Shortley Junior here'll be watchin' ya."

Lee was six-four. He shrugged and explained to Magnus in case he asked. "I'm not exactly short, so I go by Lee."

Holder senior's aftershave and body odor made Magnus lean away and not want to inhale. "I need your logins and a list of programs you regularly use—so I can upgrade to the appropriate versions."

A little rummaging in the desk's top drawer found an older generation USB thumb drive. Magnus inserted the stick into a slot in the PC. "Diagnostics download."

It was easy to lie to assholes. The lie was one of omission. He did not mention that once their computer was up and running, he would upload certain diagnostics tools and programs from his own site that would allow him to service the company network remotely and without access permissions from the Holders. He wasn't sure what had inspired him to break the consulting privacy convention. Maybe a little birdie said these guys might stiff you.

Lee unlocked a second desk drawer and fished out two sheets of paper, each with a list of passwords. The list on the top sheet was the usual: operating system, real estate broker programs, Office 365, Adobe, Gmail, and so on. Neatly printed next to each program was the application password. Holder had committed the rookie error of using the same password for multiple applications.

Magnus made a mental note to install a password manager to make life easier and more secure for the company. The second sheet, this one hand-written, listed a handful of VPN and other websites. Many of these he did not recognize. When Lee saw Magnus examining the second sheet, he snatched the paper out of his hands, folded it in thirds, and slipped it into the inside breast pocket of his jacket. "You won't need this."

"Do you have an admin? I mean, other than you."

"I'm it." He half-curtsied. "At your service."

The curtsy was gross. These guys were weird; the smells were getting to him, especially Lee's cologne. Magnus was hyper-sensitive to odors. He needed air but stayed on task. "Later, we should identify folders you want backed up."

Holder senior had lost interest and was punching numbers on his mobile. Lee orbited the desk as Magnus fiddled with the safe mode restart and switched to terminal mode.

Lee seemed to follow what was going on. "You back up everything first, right?" he asked.

"A file recovery folder, yes. Better if you've got an entirely separate drive."

Unexpectedly, Lee unearthed a drive out of the bottom drawer.

"Dad and I have an online business. Not real estate."

That was the second time. Magnus considered the standard lecture about how you should always be straight with your lawyer, doctor, and tech support. He didn't deliver the spiel because he didn't want to delay the latte.

"Yeah, sure. You can encrypt whatever, archive data to an online server. No mystery. Same as email."

"We use a Tor Browser."

That was a shocker. He had been talking down to these guys, but Lee asking about Tor suggested a higher level of computer savvy. Magnus tried to not overreact, but what the fuck did these yokels need Tor for? Maybe he was the one who was behind the times. People used The Onion Router browsers for anonymous communications— legitimate private transactions; buying and selling arms, drugs, porn; dissident political expression; a million other things. Onion routing hides users behind layers of encryption. Magnus's team at IBM inhabited the dark web night and day. His co-workers, the Twins, especially, were tenth-dan Tor users.

"Sure. No problem. Other programs I should know about?"

"Freenet."

He'd heard of Freenet. A solid peer-to-peer privacy program that had been around forever.

"Freenet is more user friendly than Tor. Runs faster and doesn't attract the attention Tor gets. I'd stick with Freenet, unless you're, maybe, selling arms in Africa."

Lee raised his eyebrows: he would think about the arms in Africa idea. "Freenet crashed yesterday—"

He cut Lee off, sensing the urgency behind the Holders' desire to find a fix asap. "Got it. I'll fix Freenet. And Tor. First, the News."

Lee ceased hovering and hung his jacket on the office coat rack. A corner of the page of logins, the ones he had hidden, poked out of the inside pocket. Magnus made a mental note: If the reception area cleared out for a minute, he would photograph the document.

Magnus girded himself for a tough day and headed for the News. En route, he thought about the last server upgrade he had worked on, the one for Zio Vinnie. He missed Vinnie; he missed family.

Magnus: One example

One example of my nephew-adoring aunt's overcompensating for the murder-inspiring transgressions of her past was my doorknocker—a weighty, solid brass, crucifixion piece that she had gifted me and which she claimed would provide holy protection from the devil and, more important, the Mexicantown mafia—both the Italian and Chaldean varieties. She had opted for the Chaldean Cross, the same overall shape as the Catholic True Cross, but wrapped in branches symbolizing the bond of the divine and the human.

At one a.m. Christ's brassy butt clap-clapped against the strike plate. The sound, preceded by stiletto heels clicking up the three front steps, identified my visitor. She pushed open the unlocked door. I scrambled to look for pants and remembered that I had tossed them in the dirty clothes in the closet. Underwear it was.

"Hi Mom."

"I had to come and tell you. He's so inCREDible!" Her face glowed. She let herself in my tiny but tidy apartment, doing so without warning or caring that I might be asleep, have a guest, or be sitting here working in my shorts—which I was. I turned aside from the coding project that filled the twin computer screens. An empty beer can had been sitting on the desk for two hours. A once full Safeway bag of taco chips lay crumpled next to a bowl with dried remains of guacamole dip streaking its sides. If I didn't run a 10k every day, I'd look like a fucking avocado.

Many Detroiters would feel uncomfortable after dark in Mexicantown, but not Mom. She was weird enough to blend in to Clark Park's stone soup of Latinos, Blacks, Whites, and Middle Easterners. Detroit's leftovers. I, too, made a conscious effort to fit in and helped kids with computer problems, spoke Spanish half the time, didn't mess with Chaldeans, and drummed once a month with a couple Black kids who were sick good musicians.

After a couple of keystrokes to exit my work, I asked the obvious question. "Who's incredible?"

"Rafael!" Mom texted as she talked. "You should wear pants when people come over."

"Yes, Mom. Who's Rafael?"

"Un momencito! You'll see, my darling."

I waited un momencito and again Christ's brassy butt clap-clapped. Shit, I thought, it's late and I had work due tomorrow.

"Puedo?" In one word, a soft, man's voice asked: Why am I here? And I'm sorry if I'm bothering you and this crazy woman dragged me here but I'd rather be home with my family. One word had said it all.

The door opened a little at a time, pushed by a worker who didn't want to upset whatever was on the other side. I saw his hands first, scarred flesh toughened by sun, lime, and stone; but fingernails scrubbed clean as a surgeon's.

"Rafael," she whispered, "is a mason." Ergo, the honest occupation implied, someone to be trusted. It was common knowledge that masons didn't do bad things to people.

Swept along with whatever Mari wanted, Rafael and I politely mucho gusto-ed each other. He was missing a top front tooth. An adjacent tooth bent toward the gap; the gap must have been there for years. Or maybe not, I'm no dentist. A bony, firm hand took my own, and didn't squeeze it overly hard the way insecure macho men did, but firm enough to say we're hombres. He was a slight man, forties maybe, several inches shorter than Mom and hard and lean.

A baggy shirt stuck to his collar and shoulder bones. A familiar body odor, that dog-just-come-in-from-the-rain, followed Mom and Rafael. Eau de dance. A stained crescent of drying sweat hung under each armpit on Rafael's shirt. No liquor smell, which meant he could be a real salsero. Real dancers were athletes; they drank very little or not at all. That's why a lot of salsa bars shuttered the doors after a couple of years in business. The better the music, the more real the dancers, the less booze got sold.

Rafael eyed my drums. "Toca congas!"

Mom answered, explaining my life history, all this in rapid-fire Cuban Spanish. I winced when she offered a demonstration. I declined. "Tengo que trabajar. Sorry, Mom."

Rafael was relieved. He was tired and probably had to work

tomorrow.

"Una canción, solo una," Mom insisted.

It wasn't a question, or I would have objected. She fussed with her phone, connecting by Bluetooth to the speakers in my place, and played Ke Lo Ke, a hard-driving Timba number. The neighbor upstairs worked nights. The neighbor next door was stone deaf.

My apartment, small and spartan, had almost no furniture. It did have a six-foot-tall mirror on one wall because I used the place for practice and for the rare private dance lesson. Mom's hand was a ghostly, marble white. So vulnerable in Rafael's. I rolled my chair and standup computer desk to the side. Good dancers can make do with surprisingly little real estate.

One minute in, I knew why Mom had been so excited about Rafael. Without a hint of doubt, without hesitation, he opened the dance with a dip and roll. Mom's upper body swayed a hundred-and-eighty degrees, bent backward with her head floating a foot above the floor. Glued crotch-to-crotch, Rafael stood above her as solid as the Colossus of Rhodes. Smart follows—and my mom was one of those—when dipped, always bent one leg under their center of gravity in case the lead slipped or let go. Rafael had earned unusual respect. She let him move her wherever and however he chose. He would not drop her. Rafael's sure and original footwork suggested that his dancing was home grown but not Cuban, maybe Puerto Rican, probably from some town with its own salsa vocabulary.

A lot of salsa leads figure they know how to dance if they dish out turn after turn. It's annoying as hell to follow and boring to watch. Rafael didn't need endless turns because he transformed the simple into something individual and dynamic, and very physical. Making a flashy move himself was not his thing. He didn't smile, but focused on his partner, always aware of her hands and putting or inviting them where they had to be, making the dance about her, about her feeling good, excited by the movement. The wind-down shifted into gentle Cuban old-school contra-tiempo "Son" that went on for several bars after the song ended. You heard whatever was playing in Rafael's head by watching them sway, pause, and sway again. They came to a stop in front of me. Little kids seeking approval. I clapped, meaning it.

"That was pretty great."

No puffiness from Rafael, no gloating, no showy anything. A simple, "Gracias. Tu madre baila bien."

Mom wiped her brow with the tail of her blouse, exposing a pale, middle-aged tummy and a red, frayed-edges brassiere. Blouse still in hand, she touched my shoulder and leaned closer. Still catching her breath, she whispered. "I promised Rafael you would help him."

She could have stated this in a normal tone of voice. What the whispering in English implied was that she was sorry that she had sprung this on me and really didn't want no for an answer.

I gave in to Rafael's soft eyes, the kindness in his face, and addressed him: "Okay. Qué puedo hacer por ti?"

Rafael waited for Mari to answer for him.

"He needs ID. A Green Card. And he can set you up with his cousin. She's really cute!" She took Rafael's hand. "Puede hacerlo?" Then, in my direction, a scolding finger in the air. "No girlfriend in what, forever? Are you gay and you won't tell your mother? She understands and loves you!"

"Jesus. I don't have time for this, Mom." The girlfriend lecture from my mother was humiliating.

Mari scowled. "You work for your uncle for years and you have nothing, honey, nothing to show for it. I ask for one little favor, and you don't have time?"

"I get paid by my uncle, Mom."

"So, I have to pay you now!"

"Jesus, okay, okay." I scribbled my mobile number on a yellow Post-it note and handed the note to a Rafael, embarrassed at being the center of a family argument. "Llámame mañana, como a las diez." I was busy tomorrow, but Mom would hold it over me the rest of my life if I didn't do something.

"Bueno. Gracias. Nos vemos a las diez, mañana!" He shot back a toothy smile, the first smile I'd seen on this kind man.

Child's play, I told myself. The Twins and I had never been caught, had never been held accountable for our hacking capers, and had never reacted with remorse or fear because we mostly hurt bad guys and the good guys didn't seem to care. If anything, we'd been consistently rewarded by the NSA types, shareholder driven IBMs, and crooked Uncle Vinnies of the world. We were insignificant cogs in a universe aswirl in crime and deception.

The hacks we worked—I did think of it as work—existed in a parallel, untouchable universe of code in which I, a keeper of secrets, had found a modicum of agency, autonomy, and identity.

My mother's flesh and blood world was complex, messy, and confusing. Raphael followed her as she departed. His silence and her click-click-click retreated together into the night.

Hero: Some time after

Some time after the bomb about my biological father not being Dad, I dug into records and tried to figure out where Mom was eight months before my untimely arrival. I asked her, of course, but she refused, playing the "classified" card. The reason didn't matter. She had said as much as she was going to say. I interpreted classified as meaning too painful to talk about. Mom didn't need more pain.

At first, I figured Norway or Sweden, or maybe the Netherlands. They make 'em big in the Netherlands. The average woman is five-seven. That's three inches taller than the average woman in the States. Alas, no luck, by about seven-thousand miles. Mom—possibly—had been visiting a CIA station in Key West, a joint force investigating Caribbean gun runners. I tried but never learned squat about the team members.

She and dad met soon after she had finished training at Camp Peary and when he had started a residency at Virginia Commonwealth University in Richmond. His story was that they met in a coffee shop and dated soon after. Mom's story was that she had been engaged in a covert training exercise off the Farm campus and picked up dad at some dive where he was having a mid-morning beer after a twelve-hour shift fighting to save a young girl's life. He lost the fight. Loaded with guilt and self-doubt, he was rethinking his commitment to medicine when Mom arrived in the picture, paid for a hotel room, smoked a big fatty with him, and gave him something else to think about. For her, the event had been a training exercise. She had given him a false name and a bucket of lies about ever seeing him again. After six months of dropping off the radar, the real Peggy showed up at his front door.

I cornered Dad last night. He was in a good mood because Peggy had had a couple of good days and they had gone out to dinner, even danced a little. When they got home, Mom was tired and headed to bed.

"Pops, what did you do when Mom was off on her trips?" Unlike Mom, Dad wasn't a professional liar.

"Nothing special. I worked. Busied myself with epidemiology research, plus, of course, my regular shifts in the ER."

"But you traveled too. You guys were in Rome together, before and after I got my IB in Firenze. And when I was little you guys were in Medellín and Djibouti and all kinds of places."

"Yes and no. The first five years she was away a lot. I focused on work. Remember our boat?"

" 'Jump!' How could I forget!" Jump was our twenty-four-foot J-Boat. She was in storage in Annapolis.

"D.C. was always home, in a way. And Peggy and I loved Rome. Then you were off to school in Florence. A big girl already! I stayed in Rome and Mom was stationed in Jordan. I worked with Médecins Sans Frontières—half administrative, half hands-on. And with an NGO that cared for African migrants escaping climate change and persecution. This is still a major concern."

I'd heard horror-filled stories about his work with Médecins Sans Frontières in Niger. Victims of gang violence and torture inundated the aid stations. Dad, somehow, never became jaded by these experiences. Nor did he talk about them. That's a kind of jaded, when I think about it.

"When you got into ETH, we decided to live in Rome. Be close to you and your friends."

He had been right about the stability of being in one place long enough to have friends. I wondered about Dad. He had close friends, but none that were nearby.

"Weren't you lonely?"

"Yes, at times, I was very lonely. Your Mom and I worked it out. She couldn't talk about her work and had to go wherever they sent her. I was on my own when she was gone. No rules. But it worked out."

"No rules! Explain to daughter, please. Daughter for whom there were lots of rules!"

"Less exciting than it sounds. Turns out your dad is a boring guy. But I did what I could with you. The single parent thing."

"I hated our camping trips. Pops, you're a great doctor but you kinda suck at camping."

He laughed, the same way he laughed at himself when he couldn't figure out how to set up the camp stove. "No excuses. Fortunately, you were there to save the day."

"And you'd always forget something, or your boots were too tight. Remember we camped in a ravine somewhere and it rained all frickin' night. The tent filled up with water and our bags got totally soaked!"

The memory elicited another lovely laugh. My father's laugh came straight from the heart.

"Oh God! I tried to find a self-serve laundry in the middle of the night in . . . I don't remember."

"All night laundries don't exist in Italy, Pops. At least where we were. You didn't believe me."

"I was good at pooping in the woods. I had the hygiene part down."

My turn to laugh. "That you did! The ICU in the woods drill."

He was always that easy to be with. Dad made few demands. He was always helpful. But he was human, and I wondered if that moral compass had ever drifted off the mark. If so, I decided that I didn't want to find out. I never again brought up the paternity issue or the "no rules."

I longed for a safe place where I belonged, and I bore a nostalgia for what I had never had—not a Hegelian historical memory, but something more down-to-earth: a corner-soda-shop owner who had known little Hero since she was in pigtails; a paper route where I had ridden my bike up and down familiar streets and where I'd memorized every pothole; a bestie I'd known since first grade. A place where I didn't have to look over shoulder and worry about being followed. A place where people weren't kidnapped or murdered.

Manzanita News

The queue at the News reached out the door and onto the patio. Magnus took his place, grateful for the quiet, natural setting. White-crowned Sparrows, Chestnut-backed Chickadees, and Spotted Towhees splashed in and drank from a water-filled, bubbling concavity atop a tall, concrete pedestal. Inch thick, impossibly green moss wrapped the base of the moat. A contorted paperbark maple wound around the eave to find sunlight. Mature japonica (Camellia japonica), holly, huckleberry, viburnum, andromeda (Pieris japonica), and Oregon grape—all evergreen shrubs except for the osoberry—wrapped the patio. Salal covered the ground; spruce and shore pines shaded the enclave.

She saw him first and greeted him. "Hi there! Didn't recognize you. You know, with your clothes and all."

Others in line checked out Magnus and smiled.

"Pants, I had pants!" He defended himself to the crowd overhearing the exchange, "I think."

He tried to remember what she had been wearing and drew a blank. Today, she wore black ninja pants adorned with brightly colored draw cords, some functional, some not. The top three or four inches of fabric folded over and lowered the waistline. Frayed cuffs dragged on the ground.

She raised her arms and put her hands on top of his shoulders. They stood in place, Magnus's arms vertically pinned to his sides and hers horizontal on his shoulders. She assessed him and he let her do it.

"Much better."

Magnus noticed her bared and toned abs. Her street wear was urban hip; not the standard in Manzanita. A mint-colored, cut-off tee was oversized. A man's tee with sleeves that reached the elbows and a wide neck that exposed one shoulder and a white camisole. Her hair was an in-between length, barely enough for a problematic ponytail that would come undone at the first toss of the head. Untied, the hair hung as straight as straw and the same color. A set of two beaded and twisted braids waggled to below her chin on each side of her head and framed her face. A nose ring—unnoticeable unless one looked closely, no visible tats, double studs in each ear.

She sipped her chai and flirted with him. "Forgot the pants in all the excitement."

He good-humoredly flashed her an okay-you-win face. The crowd enjoyed the back and forth.

"How's the arm?"

A purple-green bruise on his upper arm had made it difficult to sleep on that side. "Sore as hell."

"You're welcome. How's the ego?"

He laughed. "Sore as hell. I should buy. . . . Did I say thank you?"

As if making a point, she toasted him with her chai. "You did."

The line shuffled to the counter. The barista took his order: a triple oat milk latte.

"I'll get a table."

She took a seat in a dark green Adirondack chair, one of those plastic ones that are stacked outside of garden centers and come in a dozen colors. Her feet rested on a tree stump older than she was. She patted the arm of an adjacent chair and removed the pack she had put on the seat to reserve it.

"I meant it, the thank you" He was in earnest. "I really might have drowned."

"You might have, yes."

"I was stupid."

She removed her feet from the stump, making space for his coffee. He put the bagged empanada next to the coffee.

"If you don't know the water, it's easy to get in trouble. My Uncle Theo—he's come here forever—said that every year someone gets caught in a rip tide or sneaker waves and is swept out to sea." To illustrate the point, she waved the back of her hand through the air and accidentally bumped her cup, splashing hot Chai onto her hand. Magnus used his napkin to dry the spill. Neither of them spoke. Hero watched as he gently followed and patted dry the places where chai had flowed across her fingers and into the sinewy grooves between them, including the pronounced muscle between the thumb and index finger.

"Burn?" he asked.

"Not at all. Thanks."

Her cool-headed and unrushed manner calmed him. *Holder can wait.*

They sat together in quiet and watched the queue lengthen and shorten. They overheard talk coming from a men's support group at a nearby table. Magnus followed and enjoyed the antics of sparrows, towhees, and chickadees at the fountain.

"You see the eave, above the fountain?" She pointed with her drink hand.

"By the maple, yes."

"In Japanese architecture those big eaves are called 'Noki.' "

"Interesting. Good for rain or snow, ventilation, sun protection."

"Exactly. Most people don't think about the ventilation. The Noki covers a functional, sort of protective but invisible space. One needs to think in terms of the open space as much as physical structure. It's a key element of Japanese architecture."

". . ."

After another hiatus, she breached an invisible, emotional wall. "So, what's she like?"

Magnus removed the empanada, broke it in half, and offered a half to her. She accepted it without fuss and took a bite.

"Good." She wiped a crumb off her lip, then picked up the bag and read aloud the words on the hand-stamped label. *"Panda Bakery, Wheeler Oregon. Never been there. Have to try it."*

"The bakery may not be there long," Magnus explained, and then elaborated and recounted what had transpired that morning.

"You gotta be kidding. What a total asshole." Some in the men's group turned their heads. "Can you do anything about it?"

Magnus watched a chickadee ruffle its feathers, cleaning itself. He wondered how one could tell males and females apart.

"Actually, I can," he announced. "Why the hell not!"

He pulled out his phone. A quick search on the legality of the Holder's eviction notice suggested it would be illegal in Oregon. He then searched for Portland church organizations that helped immigrants with housing matters. He selected a group with a long history and excellent reviews. Hero leaned across to watch the screen of his phone. Her braids fell across his shoulder. Magnus waited for confirmation of the organization he had selected. She nodded okay. He wrote and sent a brief email summarizing the rent demand and included the photo of the eviction letter, thus handing off the responsibility to right Holder's unjust attempt to force the Reyes family to shutter the doors of their business and sole source of livelihood.

Magnus stepped away from the patio and called the Bakery. He left a message in English, informing the owners about what he had done. He included contact information for the church group and suggested the family fight the eviction and, as a backup plan, search for an alternative location. The voice recording device cut him off before he could add a last bit about Tillamook County services.

Pleased, he returned to his chair. "Mission accomplished."

"Well done!" Her eyes watched him from across the top of her chai. "Both the call and avoiding the question."

"What question?" Distracted by the ice-grey eyes, he really had forgotten.

"What's she like?"

"Who?" Magnus thought the reference was to the bakers' daughter. "Hard to tell. I mostly spoke with her parents."

"No!" Hero laughed, "the girlfriend." She tossed her head back and popped the last crumbly bit of empanada in her mouth. "The one who dumped you. And don't tell me I'm wrong."

Magnus reddened, yes, but also realized that the last week had been the first time in a long time that he had not thought about his ex-fiancée, Carolina.

"No girlfriend."

"Save that for other girls. Remember! I saved your butt. We're on a different level." Hero did that thing commandos do, pointing two fingers back and forth between his eyes and hers.

"Cross my heart." He went through the motions. "You don't believe me?"

"I half do," she half-smiled. "Now that you crossed your heart."

"Name's Krum. Magnus Krum."

"Like 'Bond, James Bond.' Except for the complete lack of self-confidence. Bond was totally, the ultimate in self-confidence. Très hot."

"It's Magnus. And Magnus is not a very exciting guy. Sorry."

"Hero." She lowered the pitch of her voice and aped his own. "Hero Wheelwright." She delivered the punchline quietly, tilting her head to the side. "I'm *very* exciting. And terribly self-confident."

Magnus returned the smile. She had omitted "hot." He knew better than to say it. "I believe you, Hero Wheelwright! I'm living, bruised, waterlogged proof of it!"

She moved her head side-to-side, pathos in the expression. "So, so true." Another pause. She stared at something—a bird or cloud, a branch. Her hair caught the light. He'd had the vision before—the light coming from behind her as she had lugged him ashore. He remembered feeling aroused. The memory stirred and warmed him. But then somewhere he'd read that a dying man's last thought was always of his mother. Gross, he thought, just gross. Mixing aroused and mother.

The sun edged out from behind a cloud. Needle-thick branches of spruce and pine shaped the light into blinding, halated patterns. Where the sun was absent, patches of blue floated like ornaments.

Hero's words washed away the unease. "Karma, balance of life, you know. It was me who needed to save somebody."

Magnus downed the last of the empanada. "I gotta get back to Holders'. Today, this morning." He nodded in the direction of their offices. "They're gonna have a fit if I don't return ten minutes ago."

"Keep in touch, Krum, Magnus Krum." She pulled out her phone and placed it over Magnus's Apple Watch. They exchanged contact info.

Again, he was taken aback by their facial similarity.

"I know." She recognized the same. "It's weird, huh."

"Yeah. Weird."

He turned to walk away.

She called out to him: "Her name?"

A wry smile, a twitch at first, worked its way across his face. "Carolina."

Hero raised her chai. He winked back at her and offered a half-bravo, half-goodbye.

Groove

Magnus had found his groove. Three times a week he jogged from his place in town to the jetty and back. The first week, he had worn sneakers one way and made the return run barefoot. By week three, the flesh on the soles of his feet had toughened up; he managed the nine miles without shoes. He wore a Patagonia running vest with slotted pockets for collapsible water bottles and carried a windbreaker and a waterproof pamphlet with photos of coastal marine animals and plants. Training and learning were purposeful and familiar routines.

On Tuesdays he "took tea" with Miss Angel. Magnus's reading background both appalled and impressed Miss Angel. The quantity impressed. The quality got a mixed review. Miss Angel was determined to fill the gaps in Magnus's hit-and-miss literary education.

Long retired from academe, she was surprisingly keen to take on a student, or at least take on Magnus as a student. She was lonely. And he was a good companion, a patient one. He didn't judge, he respected her privacy, knowledge, and intelligence. Too, he knew how to interact with people Miss Angel's age.

One afternoon, mid-discussion, she slipped into Spanish. Magnus had been so engrossed in their discussion that he hadn't noticed and had followed up with questions in Spanish, questions which, when he spoke too quickly, she struggled to understand. She never asked why or how he spoke the language, but afterward she included Spanish texts in their reading, introducing Magnus to a bawdy classic that pre-dated his beloved *Don Quijote.*

La Celestina, by Fernando de Rojas, followed the tragicomedy love affair between Calisto and Melibea, the business of it orchestrated by the hoary procuress Celestina. The bawdy tale, the speaking Spanish, and being able to speak his mind, brick by brick, brought normality to Magnus's life.

Miss Angel had insisted that Magnus always sit in a specific chair. The chair's worn, grey-at-the-edges green leather welcomed complete thoughts and detested sound bites. That chair was older than he by a factor of two. The seat had long accommodated someone who had been large boned and heavier than Magnus, someone who was absent but present, and whose aura observed Magnus's thoughts, not censoring his responses, but insisting that they met Miss Angel's standards. At times, Miss Angel would say little or nothing, lost in her own world. In this state, or those times when she hadn't slept well, the masseter muscle in her jaw relaxed and lips parted as if she were about to say something or fall asleep.

Magnus didn't know what had prompted him to mention it, but he did: "Mr. Holder referred to you as 'rich' Miss Angel."

Her eyebrows rose. She thrust her jaw forward, chin up, a tsk-tsk expression. "That's all? Little imagination, that man."

Magnus added: "Rich *cat* lady."

"That's an improvement!" She slapped her hand on her knee. "Well, so I am. Not literally, no cats. So what?"

He waited for more. People always said more if he waited, and he was curious about her opinion regarding Holder.

"You wish me to elaborate?"

He waited.

"Ah, the silent inquisitor. You're good at this, Magnus!"

She rose from her chair, paced aimlessly for a minute, and then resettled, legs crossed and arms on her lap exactly as they had been before she had stood up.

"My long-standing policy is to never discuss my sources of income. People behave oddly around those whom they believe are richer or poorer than they are. An understandable human trait, don't you think? Particularly, when there is—" She paused as if something overhead had distracted her. "—a significant wealth gap.

"Shortley Holder believes that I'm worth a great deal more than he is, and that really gets his goat." She found this funny, made a little fist in the air. "Between us—see, your strategy is working—I rather enjoy rubbing it in. To him, that is, not to everyone! Heaven forbid! The punchline, Magnus, is that I am a very, *very* successful writer. Sufficiently successful that if I were to publish under my *own* name, I would never have a moment's peace and quiet."

"That explains the home library. I'd expect writers to read and know a lot. Successful writers, that is."

Usually, Miss Angel's facial expressions were a still pond. His words, however, seemed to have stirred her. Wavy wrinkles on her forehead deepened, her eyes receded and aimed at Magnus's apparently naïve or misconceived observation.

"No. My God, no! For the most part writers are ignoramuses, charlatans and thieves, imposters and pretenders to knowledge! Their books and their characters are so much smarter than they are. Writers read, listen, and observe. They repeat and recast—like eager, little machines—what they've read, heard, and seen. Ninety percent of the eleven thousand books published every day could have been written by robots; in the future, they will be. Which is good—all those unemployed authors can do something more productive with their time! The ten percent—the writers that survive this—what some call a cognitive apocalypse—will be authors who truly, deeply engage in life's follies. *Live* and write, I say."

"Are these *your* books?" He pointed to books with the spines against the wall, and others, books without titles. Miss Angel beamed.

"I'd like to read one of your books. Do you write fiction or non-fiction?"

"Really, Magnus? You disappoint me."

"I do?" Her remark confused him.

"Surely, as a mathematician, you remember Russell's paradox. I don't approve of that overgrown, too-big-for-its-britches, all-exclusive 'OR.' "

She walked over to a shelf, selecting and examining one book, then another.

"Both, and neither." She answered.

"So many non-fiction works," Miss Angel went on, "are romans à clef in camouflage. Don't get me wrong, there is excellent reportage. But a well-told story trumps truth any day. In a way, the lies are a necessary part of the context, part of the hermeneutic circle of understanding."

Miss Angel left a hand on the chair as she walked around Magnus. It reminded Magnus of how he, as a dancer, would gently guide or assure a follow with his hand.

"Imagine, Magnus, that you, sitting quietly in this lovely, cozy green chair, were, at the end of the hour, going to die. This is revealed to you, quite suddenly! What would you think? What would you say? To whom would you say it? Someone I loved sat right where you are now. The chair has been empty since she died. There was so much we never had a chance to say—oh, how I regret those self-serving assumptions we made about each other, the things we took for granted. And how I so loved the endearing fabrications we shared. I so regret not asking questions. You see. That is the stuff of life."

Magnus asked. He asked before he realized how personal and potentially hurtful the question might be. "Were you lovers?"

The furrows in Miss Angel's brow softened, as did her tone. He barely heard the "Of course we were lovers."

It was as though, for a moment, she had become insubstantial, a wraith. That, or she had cast a spell over him. Then, suddenly reconstituted, she resumed the book search. On the fourth or fifth try, she found the book. "I swear, if you tell a soul that I wrote this, I shall —oh, I don't know what. I'm not good at threats."

"Understood. No, of course I won't."

The corners of her mouth turned up—only slightly—and her eyes assumed a playful aspect and sparkled. "We *are* good at keeping secrets, aren't we, Magnus."

"That a royal we?"

"Not on your life, *Magnus Krum*. Not on your life!" She pronounced his name as if it were a stage name and then laughed. She knew. Maybe not who he was, but certainly who he wasn't. And he was okay with that; it was a relief.

* * * *

Another weekly routine was the check-in with Mom and Dad and the Twins. Mom fed Magnus the same contentless story: everybody was good, Ari golfed on weekends, she had met yet another incredible dance partner. The report from the Twins, his cohorts in work and crime, was similarly bland. They monitored local Chaldean web traffic and had come up blank. Magnus had given them a temporary password to let them search Vinnie's files for red flags that would reveal any tampering with the account. There was zilch to report.

Despite the uneventful updates and the superficial normality of daily life in Manzanita, Magnus couldn't shake the angst. Living under a false identity ate away at him. Miss Angel fed the angst, ruminating about the nature of authentic existence in postmodern society, or, as she preferred to label it, post-postmodern society. That such abstractions had teeth, surprised him.

And then there were the recurring nightmares about Zaidu going after his family for the million Magnus had stolen and given away, and about Zaidu having reported him to the Detroit Police and Immigration and Customs Enforcement. Both organizations were hunting for O. A. Papadopoulos. He hoped Rafael and friends appreciated the Green Cards. Did Magnus regret what he had done? Yeah, big time.

And there was Hero. He was managing the relationship with Hero much as he had managed the relationship with Carolina, by avoiding her and filling his time with training, reading, and with work, building a reputation as an IT fix-it guy. He knew too well how to appear "busy."

Alder Creek

The mobile rattled on the bedside table and woke Magnus.

"Are you ghosting me?"

"Hero, hi. I was sleeping. What time is it?"

"Seven a.m. Get your butt out of bed!"

"No, not ghosting. What is today?"

"Saturday. Crap, Magnus, you know what day it is!"

"Hey, I was in this dream—"

Hero sighed. "I'm gonna get coffee and bagels at the News. Then pick you up. If you're free, I need a hand and it'd be nice to see you. Been forever. Cream cheese good?"

Magnus was too sleepy to argue. "Yeah, whatever. Plover patrol?"

That was the first thing he'd thought of. Between March fifteen to September fifteen, a three-mile section of the Manzanita beach was designated as a Western Snowy Plover nesting area. Signs along the beach announced that the Snowy Plover was an Oregon state and federally protected threatened species.

Two weeks prior, Magnus had tagged along with Hero and other members of the Oregon Bird Alliance to do a "wet sand survey." He had carried the weighty scope and tripod that the group used to identify nests and birds. The birders surveyed, picnicked, and made small talk. Hero and others educated Magnus about the Plover habitat and migration. He had tried to appear enthusiastic and, when asked personal questions, dodged them and talked about IT work. The only one-on-one engagement between Hero and Magnus had been when Hero challenged and completely humiliated Magnus in a cartwheel and handstand competition. "Parkour," a feisty Hero had announced. She called herself a *traceuse*. Still, it was better to flop at handstands than talk about Carolina.

Magnus, sleepy and lost in thought, forgot he was on the phone and jumped when Hero spoke. "Nope, farm work. LNCT. I told you. Remember?"

The memory rushed back. The Lower Nehalem Community Trust was an organization involved in conservation and land restoration. As part of a larger holding, the group managed a one-acre farm that grew crops for church and community food share programs. The work was something he could get behind and support and he'd said as much to Hero.

"We need muscle and I'm behind on hours."

"Meaning?"

"I'm supposed to volunteer three hours a week. I'm behind and today is composting, so the farm needs extra hands."

"You get the credit and I do the work. I see where this is going."

"Nice people volunteer at the farm. You get to meet a whole bunch of nice people."

"It's raining."

"Duh, we live in Oregon. I'll be there in a half-hour. Don't shower. You're gonna sweat."

"Yessum." His mind was back on cream cheese, thinking he was hungry and that he didn't want to wait. Hero disconnected as he threw off the duvet and headed to the kitchen to scramble three eggs, happy to take a day off from running in the rain.

LNCT, he knew, was a nexus for locals from Arch Cape to Rockaway Beach. For a guy who wanted acceptance, it would be politic to show up. On the other hand, he would feed a self-defeating cycle. The more Magnus lied, the more he wanted acceptance. But the more people that accepted him, the more he had to lie. *I'm screwed.* The return-to-Detroit option was too risky until Vinnie and Ari gave him the green light.

Before Hero arrived, he squeezed in breakfast and a shower, and dressed in Adidas brand farmer wear. She arrived as promised, driving a pickup with several recently sharpened shovels in the bed. They drove south on 101 and turned off the highway at a nondescript dirt road that led for a quarter mile past a handful of homesteads with well-groomed hedges and lawns, gloss-white plastic picket fences, and paved drives and walks. The settlement lacked the cozy, carefree, beach-home vibe that Magnus associated with Manzanita. Then again, he was too new to judge.

The dirt road ended at an entry blocked by a yellow nylon tow-strap slung in a gentle arc between two sturdy cedar posts. Hero hopped out. She leaned in through the driver's window, mischief in the eyes.

"I'm gonna show off!"

She walked up to the middle of the strap, carefully placed one foot on the strap, and stood up, waving arms and hands in short, precise movements to keep her balance. She walked in one direction and then did a 180-degree spin and walked in the other direction. Then, that not being enough, she did the same thing again in each direction but walking backwards. The grand finale was Hero, facing Magnus, balanced sideways and almost motionless. Magnus was appropriately amazed. Hero beamed, acting the gleeful and very adorable child. She hopped down and freed the strap at one end, let it drop to the ground and, in a few steps, returned and jumped back into the driver's seat. Beads of water on her slicker got everywhere. Water dripped from her face and hands and her hair, which she had not covered.

"It's a truck."

"It's a truck," Magnus agreed, adoring her.

"I miss parkour, sigh. That was trickier than it looked. The line's wet and greasy. Slick as snot." She snorted, appropriately.

"I can't imagine. Amazed! Really, Hero. Blown away."

Hero placed her left ankle across her right knee to show Magnus the sole of her shoe. "These are for boats. They're great for slacking in the wet."

His fingers ran across the sole and brushed her bare ankle. "Like siping for tires, similar cut and pattern."

They drove through a blossoming paradise. To the north was the orchard, to the south a stream and a foothill that Hero described as raptor heaven. Birders from afar traveled to the Alder Creek. Within the compound, a concrete patio inlaid with colorful mosaics and banked by flower- and herb-bearing planters gave the leg-weary a perfect vantage for wetland birding. Fat, waddling ducks wandered freely, begging for handouts, hunting snails, and trying to nuzzle their beaks under netting to get at tender shoots.

The farm was an Eden. Paths bordered by cranberry and chokeberry bushes guided visitors through an orchard of apple, lemon, plum, and quince trees. Red-orange poppies had populated a fenced-in native permaculture garden where colorful, hand-drawn labels identified flora. Several hoop-houses grew crops vulnerable to the weather: tomatoes, peppers, eggplant. Hundreds of pods of starter plants packed tables in the solar-heated greenhouse.

The centerpiece of the farm was a large, open-sided barn that was in need of repair. The barn housed a meeting area, rooms with carpentry and irrigation equipment, and storage areas for lumber and farming implements. Standing opposite the barn and greenhouse were a ramshackle, concrete-walled pen and a cement water reservoir, converted from prior uses for livestock and dairy manure storage. The water from the tank was not potable, as noted by signage at spigots at sinks and troughs.

Hero introduced Magnus to a group of volunteers. The group's leader had once commanded a division of Nike. She directed Magnus to do whatever Hero told him to do. Today, the job was to hack weeds and other unwanted brush into smaller pieces and wheelbarrow or tumbrel the green mulch to chest-high compost bins where the organic material decomposed over several weeks and would eventually become fertilizer.

Machetes in hand, Magnus followed Hero through one of the hoop houses. They stopped by four people trying to figure out how to use a multi-meter to measure voltage on a hot circuit for a to-be-installed on-demand hot-water unit. Magnus watched them fumble about and then interceded just in time to prevent them from completely frying the multi-meter. They had set it on resistance mode.

"You know how to do this stuff?" a woman asked.

"I do." His tone and confidence convinced.

"Well then, whoever you are, here's your job. Please install this darned thing so it works and doesn't electrocute anybody! Can you do that?"

A job that fit his skill set! Magnus was thrilled.

"I can. Manual, please." He extended his hand and another man, he had to have been eighty, grinned and presented him with a manual still wearing its plastic cover.

"I'll give a hand with plumbing. It's PEX, same as my trailer."

A woman passed him the multi-meter. He handed his machete to Hero. She winked and, with both machetes slung over her shoulder, headed out the door and to the nearby table-sized chopping block, a tree stump with more rings than years of anyone at the farm.

Over the next hour he wired up the water heater. The job turned out to be more of a pain than it should have been because the hoop house wiring was 220V and the water heater ran on 110V, meaning he had to add a junction box, restring the wire and tweak the connection at the breaker box.

Outside and a few yards distant, the sure, forceful swing of Hero's machete marked time. Flying debris ricocheted against the hoop-house's translucent plastic walls. Hero was strong and worked continuously, alternately chopping and muscling fifty-pound wheelbarrow loads to the compost bin. She swung equally well with either arm.

He was putting the last screw in a corner of the junction box when an unusually heavy thwack of the machete caught his attention. Another thwack and grunt followed. And another, more violent and desperate. Magnus ran to and pushed aside the plastic sheet hanging over the door. The last blow stuck the blade in the stump. Hero's head shook side-to-side as she tried and failed to wrench the blade free. She screamed something unintelligible, a scream of an animal trying to free itself from a trap. Wet hair stuck to her brow. Droplets of sweat, tears, and water flew from her chin and nose and lashes. White, blistered hands froze to the machete's handle.

The group leader, the take charge woman he had met earlier, strode toward Hero. Magnus cut her off and slipped under and through Hero's arms. He rose between her and the stump, wrapping his arms around her shoulders and back and holding her. The struggling ceased, the heaving subsided. Her head fell to his shoulder. They faced each other; foreheads touched.

His glasses slid down the ridge of his nose and came to a cockeyed stop. This made her smile, seeming curious in a mad sort of way. She stared into his eyes—the eyes minus the glasses—and wondered at something. He drew her tighter and cradled the nape of her neck, spreading his fingers through her hair. A beaded braid nestled in the web between his thumb and index finger. He pressed his forehead against hers and willed himself to be inside her head and able to vanquish the demons that were tormenting her.

Several well-intentioned co-workers approached. Magnus worried she might feel threatened. He lifted a palm to tell them to stay back.

Hero's hands shook as she released the machete. Steam rose off the handle. Her cramped and blistered fingers retained a gnarled, T-rex shape. She slumped into Magnus's arms. Her body stopped shaking, then spasmed and relaxed.

He guided her to a bench set in an island of mown grass about thirty yards from the hoop house but a universe away from farm activity. They sat. The rain had abated and a low-lying mist drifted over the wetland bottom. Patches of flattened grass, amorphous shallows where elk had bedded down, dotted the meadow. A red-winged blackbird vanished in the meadow grass and then reappeared to perch on the topmost branch of a nearby shrub. It repeated the maneuver several times, finding the same silhouette.

Condensation on Hero's cheeks, lips and eyelashes glistened. She was an incredibly lovely woman. Enisled by tall wetland grasses and mist, they sat in quiet stillness. Magnus said nothing, giving Hero time to think or not, to take in the pastoral setting or not, to smell and sense the things he smelled and sensed, or not.

Her gaze sought gaps in the mist and glimpsed what lay beyond the mottled shroud. She was seeking—he felt this—her story in this meadow's history. A sense of place, how she fit in a drama running thousands of years and loaded with signs of give and take between man and earth. Magnus sensed her yearning as sure as he felt the passage of time from tides, moon, and seasons. For the first time in a long time, the world was not about him and he was deeply, deeply at peace.

Hero squeezed his hand.

"It was too loud." She was referring to the howl of the air exchange fans used to regulate the temperature in the hoop house. "And the chopping was . . . I can't find the words."

"You don't have to find the words. We're going home. Okay?"

"Panic attack. I'm sorry. People must think I'm crazy. I'm not crazy —"

"Don't worry about them," Magnus cut her off. "They're your friends and they'll understand."

"Magnus. Remember what you said?"

He did. *I'm not crazy.* That's what he had told her after she had dragged him out of the rip tide.

She made eye contact. An embarrassed, apologetic, sorrowful grin surfaced. "I gotta retch."

He held her hair and hood out of the way as she slid off the bench and knelt on one knee and tried to vomit. Mostly, she gagged. She wiped her mouth with the back of her sleeve. "We're even," she laughed.

"People who aren't crazy throw up too, you know. Have you eaten?" He'd forgotten about breakfast and was still thinking about when she had rescued him. He had thrown up and then had told her he was hungry. Weird what people say when they're at their rawest.

"Just my bagel. I'm sorry. I'm really sorry."

"Sugar, basically. You need proper food and I've got a container of

Miss Angel's homemade chicken noodle soup in the fridge." He held up an open palm. "For a rainy day. Miss Angel warned me that living in Manzanita in winter was like living inside a carwash."

The carwash comment drew a hint of a smile.

"Magnus, you're a seriously sweet guy. Do you know that?" Hero wiped her chin.

More confused, he thought, than sweet. Protective, he thought to himself, and attracted to her but afraid of complications.

He pulled her elbow tight against his side to support her and share his warmth. Clumsily, side-by-side, they zig-zagged to the pickup. He took the driver's seat. She let him buckle her seat belt and took his hand. She was about to speak, then stopped. There was sadness in her eyes, a sadness that he had never imagined would be possible in eyes so wintry. He closed his eyes and rested his lips on her forehead, tasting sweat and fear. He smelled the odor of petrichor rising from the damp earth. There was pollen in her hair, and the aroma of tea tree from her shampoo. She must have showered in the morning, a million years ago.

Haven House

The next visit to the Panda Bakery was two weeks after Hero's breakdown at Alder Creek. Magnus had asked Hero if she wanted to join him. She had declined, needing to spend time with her mother. But, she qualified, she would see him later that afternoon.

Carmen Reyes had called Magnus directly, requesting a *WeDrive!* lift for her daughter. Magnus arrived with time to spare. Again, Carmen handed him a bag of bakery goodies. Constanza re-introduced herself and translated for her parents and Magnus. Understanding both the Spanish and English, Magnus appreciated how well the daughter interpreted both his words and those of her parents. Constanza claimed she was seventeen. Tall and mature for her age, she could pass for a year or two older. She added that she hoped to attend Neah-Kah-Nie High School in nearby Rockaway Beach in the fall and that she had been a science student in Chihuahua. She wanted to continue her science studies.

The slight disconnect in the conversation between Magnus and her parents reflected not so much a linguistic misunderstanding as it did a certain intentional filtering by Constanza. Hiding behind the young, outwardly demure Constanza, was a girl with a cocky confidence and a bit of an edge. Not a surprise, Magnus told himself, recalling his teenage years. He also trusted his dance instructor instincts. First impressions and what follows on the dance floor—the litmus test— may or may not comport. Magnus read the tells. Sometimes the red flag waved wildly, other times it gently fluttered. Either way, his policy had been to always be polite. He went for polite with Constanza.

"Do you like to bake?"

Her nose wrinkled; she shook her head. "I hate baking."

Okay, he thought, that was authentic. "So, what do you like to do?"

She answered directly. "School. Biology. And medicine."

"And for fun?"

Her turn to laugh. "Music. I like music and dancing." She spun around, the cocky side showing off, and extended an arm to display three Swiftie bracelets.

Dancing! In the Papadopoulos household, if anyone, be they nine or ninety, announced they wanted to dance, the family would hastily move furniture to the walls and fire up the tunes. Magnus wanted to ask—in Spanish, of course—that everyone in Panda do the same. The Zio Vinnie demon on his shoulder scolded him and told him to cool it, shut his mouth and listen. No scene, señor. The customers, probably not dancers, would think it was weird if he, a twenty-seven-year-old man, suddenly asked this young girl to dance.

"Have you seen her perform?"

"I didn't go to the big concerts. I wanted to. My uncle Félix gave these to me."

"Uncle" sounded a little old for a Swiftie? Whatever. Magnus didn't ask about the uncle.

"So, where are we going today?" Magnus asked.

"I'm going to the Haven House, in Manzanita. It is next to a golf course." She showed him the address on her iPhone, and he keyed it into his own. The house, a few blocks from Holder's office and the News, was at the end of a driveway off Dorcas and tucked in a thickly wooded enclave abutting the golf course. He remembered having seen a flyer at the Holders about three dwellings that shared a common parking area off of Dorcas. The rent was pricey and the units were only available as short-term rentals.

Constanza added, "I don't want to be late."

Magnus helped her carry and load cleaning supplies and her pack into the back of Subi. En route, he again took care to not speak Spanish. A silence fell between them, as it can between those who shelter behind linguistic differences. When Magnus broke the ice and asked about how things were going with the Holders, Constanza's answers drifted toward distrustful. She delivered a too pat report, the essence of which was that her father and Mr. Holder had come to an agreement and that the upcoming rent increase would be within guidelines suggested by rent control programs in other Oregon communities. This good news, Magnus presumed, had resulted from his having connected the Reyes family with the Portland church group. He thought it odd that the family had not mentioned it or thanked him.

The other news, not so heart-warming, was that Constanza had resumed working for the Holders, cleaning their office, Shortley's home across the street from the office, and the Haven House rentals.

When they arrived at the parking area, Magnus helped Constanza carry her cleaning supplies to a house with a cozy wraparound porch and oversized eaves. A moss covered walk under an arbor of spruce led to the front door. He waited until she had punched the code on the lockbox, extracted the key, and opened the door. Together, they deposited the cleaning supplies on the front porch.

"Do you need a ride back?"

"I am finished at two. My papà gets me. But he leaves work, so if you take me home, he would be happy. If it's not trouble to you."

"No trouble. Done. Text your father. See you at two."

Side Business

Magnus had underestimated how long his next driving job would take. He had promised Miss Angel that he would run her up to Astoria for an eye exam, thinking he could make it back to Manzanita before two to pick up Constanza. But he had cut it too close; it was after two as he turned off 101 to Laneda. The morning drizzle had turned into a soft, spring shower, a ubiquitous weather pattern that passed unnoticed to a coastal Oregonian but would make most people scramble for a raincoat or umbrella.

"Miss Angel, would you mind if I made a quick stop before taking you home. I can still walk you to the front door." She wore a pair of those roll-up, flexible film sunglasses optometrists' offices provide for patients with dilated pupils. The glasses sat askew on her nose. He worried that the edged of the film might cut into her wafer-thin skin.

"Constanza's cleaning one of Holder's rentals and I agreed to give her a ride back to the bakery. She finished at two."

Miss Angel knew about Panda Bakery; in fact, she had eaten there and had met the family. At one of their book sessions, Magnus and Miss Angel had discussed Holder's attempt to force the family out of the building.

"Have they sorted out the rent business?" she asked. Magnus had told her the full story, including the part about his contacting the immigrant rental assistance people. And about his experience fixing the Holders' computers.

"Apparently," he answered. "Although I didn't know about Constanza. You know, working for them. She's seventeen. They probably pay next to nothing and I doubt they report it."

"Yes. Well, let's rescue the girl from those usurious bastards. Then, after, you can drop me off."

He pulled into the parking area. It was large enough for a half-dozen vehicles. Lee's pickup occupied the space designated for the unit at Haven House that Constanza had cleaned. Magnus parked Subi next to a Sprinter van in one of the other spaces. The van hid Subi, so he got out of car and stepped to the side and within sight of the porch. Constanza would see that he had arrived and was waiting for her. Two minutes of rain and chill convinced him to wait at the cottage and under the wrap-around eave. A hand painted sign in Italianate script identified the structure: *Haven House - Unit 1.*

Something bothered Magnus. He didn't know what, but something was off. Curtains covered the windows on either side of the front door. And the windows on the side of the house. That would make sense if Constanza were closing up. Then he realized it wasn't what he had seen, but something he had heard, a muffled sobbing barely audible over the pitter-patter rain. Magnus, senses alert, quietly approached one of the side windows and listened. He stood motionless, and then heard it again, louder this time and followed by harsh, scolding words and the sudden thump-thump-thump of heavy footsteps across the floor. The front door burst open and slammed shut. Lee Holder, just outside the door, stopped to fuss and fiddle with a tripod and bulky camera bag, rearranging the gear so it would be easier to carry. Fuming and frustrated, he set off for his pickup.

Magnus ducked behind a planter and watched Lee toss the gear onto the back seat. The truck, a Ford 250 refitted with an annoying after-market exhaust system, roared to life. Birds in the underbrush scattered. Magnus didn't move. He listened to the spitting gravel and diminishing rumble of the truck making its way to Laneda.

The door to the cottage, the door nearest the window where the whimpering had come from, opened when he tried the doorknob. Magnus found Constanza. She lay curled up in a ball on the king-sized bed, naked and clutching arms and legs around a puffy comforter. Socks, frilly underwear, and a maid's uniform lay scattered about the floor, chair, and nightstand. She sobbed in gasping breaths.

When she saw Magnus, she backed up against the headboard and further withdrew into the folds of the duvet. Menacing eyes glared at him. Constanza seemed to not recognize him. She appeared to be unharmed. At least no obvious bruising or bleeding.

"I'm Magnus. Remember? It's okay. He's gone." Magnus repeated the same words in Spanish.

Constanza didn't move, but the tension in her body lessened. He gathered up the clothes and tossed them on the bed next to her. "I'm getting Miss Angel. She's in the car. I'll be right back."

Magnus exited the front door and nearly knocked Miss Angel over. There she stood, dark roll-up glasses in hand, squinting even in the dim light. She spoke before he got out a word.

"I saw Lee tear out of here. There's no love lost between you two. I was concerned."

"I'm fine. Constanza's—"

"Oh dear!" She brushed past Magnus, dropping the dark lenses to the ground, and rushed into the bedroom to Constanza. Constanza had put on one sock, undies, and the white nurse's blouse.

Miss Angel wrapped one arm around her. With the other arm she tucked and made the duvet into an oversized papoose within which she wrapped Constanza and rocked her.

Constanza buried her face in Miss Angel's shoulder. In one hand she clutched her other sock, in the other she held a black miniskirt. The crying subsided. She sniffled and cleared her throat.

Magnus sat in a chair, trying to figure out what the hell had happened, telling himself to not jump to conclusions and to not do something really stupid.

The Video

Constanza refused to speak English. Miss Angel's academic Spanish was sufficient for her to get the gist of what Constanza was saying, but not the nitty-gritty. Between breaks for breaths and sobs, Constanza explained that a few weeks ago Mr. Holder had asked her if Lee could take a few photos of her for the Holder Real Estate website, supposedly for an ad regarding the company's cleaning services. He had clarified that reducing the rent hike at her parents' business was contingent upon her complying with his request.

The following week Lee had taken a few photos and nothing untoward had transpired. Lee subsequently requested a second photo session. This time he asked Constanza to model a maid's uniform, a uniform with a very short skirt. Constanza had been uncomfortable with the request, but again had complied. The week after that, Lee arrived with video equipment. He staged the furniture in the bedroom and Constanza donned her uniform."

The shoot soon went off script, at least off any script that Constanza had expected. Lee had reminded her that she had to do what he asked or her family would lose their business. She was terrified, but went along. Through angry tears, she described Lee as *un monstruo*. She had been afraid that he would hurt her.

Miss Angel asked Constanza to repeat what she had reported, this time in English. Magnus replied, in fluent Spanish, that he would translate later for Miss Angel. Hearing him, Constanza ignored Miss Angel and took Magnus's hands. "I only tell you, Magnus. No one else. Okay?"

"Okay."

Constanza, Magnus assumed, was in shock. She would reconsider after she had had time to think. It was understandable that she was embarrassed and afraid, and that she took refuge in speaking Spanish.

She was a minor and not someone Magnus knew well or had any right to make decisions for. Still, she had trusted him. He didn't take that trust lightly. She had to speak to the authorities. That was the right thing. The challenge for Magnus was to avoid involvement that might reveal his actual identity.

Miss Angel interrupted his thoughts and, as if reading them, addressed Constanza. "My dear, sweet child. We need to call your parents and the sheriff. But first a physician."

"No!" Constanza grabbed Miss Angel's forearm with both hands, imploring her. "You can't. No! You don't understand."

Magnus's focus was on Constanza as he addressed Miss Angel. He wanted Constanza to give him some indication if what he was about to say would be acceptable to her.

"Miss Angel, Constanza needs time to figure out what to do. Her situation is complicated."

Constanza gestured for Magnus to continue.

"Complicated? Young lady, is that what you think?" Miss Angel was obviously upset with Magnus for siding with Constanza. "Magnus, do you trust this poor girl to think clearly about her future? And under these circumstances?"

Constanza's gaze caught him, confirming what he told to Miss Angel. Taking her time, speaking with care so that Miss Angel would understand, Constanza made her argument.

Magnus translated and paraphrased as she spoke. "She is afraid to speak to her parents because her father is a violent man. . . . He would punish her for getting into so much trouble. . . . And she is even more afraid of what he would do to Lee." This following had been difficult for her to say. "Her father had been in jail in Chihuahua. For a long time. . . . Constanza does not want to lose him again."

None of this explanation pleased Miss Angel. Her head fell back; she closed her eyes. "Christ. We're going to at least get medical help."

Magnus waited for her, and in the silence noted the backdrop of waves pounding the beach. He had not heard them before, drowned by the steady rain. Miss Angel's next statement surprised him. Not the words per se, but the vehemence with which she uttered them. "Frankly, I'm afraid of what I might do to that man!"

"I suspect," Magnus added, "the Holders are cozy with the police and the sheriff's offices. There's a risk the story gets twisted around and Constanza becomes the perp and Lee the victim. Constanza's family will face deportation or worse."

"Magnus, how can you say such a thing?" Miss Angel admonished him. "You don't know the police or the sheriff. The sheriff has a new deputy. They're intelligent, decent people."

Magnus couldn't tell Miss Angel about his own difficulties with the law, but he gave her something else. "I hacked Holders' computers. There's some kind of shady business crap going on with a guy in the county office—a part-timer, not a local. And money transfers. The sheriff's clean."

Miss Angel's lips parted, searching for the right word and not finding it. Her thoughts seemed to have coalesced at the same time.

Her restatement of what he had confessed could have been an attorney's cross-examination. "You hacked a computer that Shortley Holder had trusted you to fix?"

Her expression was a combination of being extremely disappointed with Magnus's behavior while curious about what he had discovered.

"Not exactly. I ran across this stuff by accident. It wasn't intentional."

"Better Magnus. Marginally better."

Constanza eased out of her papoose enclosure. Magnus turned away to give her privacy. She reverted to a mix of Spanish and English.

"Entiendo lo que pasó. I want to wash my mouth. And go home." The broody, self-confident teenager had re-emerged. She was resilient, bouncing back, or she had been more in control than she had been letting on.

"Constanza can clean up at my place. Then, I'll run her home. Miss Angel can you—"

"Yes," she anticipated the ask. "I'll come with you."

Miss Angel was not prepared to let things slide. However, she didn't seem well, as if the excitement had been too much for her. Constanza noticed Miss Angel's discomfort. She feigned broken English. "Are you okay? Please Misses, thank you. I am fine. I want to go home and explain to my parents. It is better for me and for them."

"Young lady, I want to speak with your father or mother. I'll wait until after you talk to them." Miss Angel turned to Magnus, "Can you make sure she understands the importance—"

He didn't let Miss Angel finish, but, continuing the charade, repeated words in Spanish that he knew Constanza had understood perfectly well in English. Constanza bowed her head. She hugged Miss Angel and kissed her multiple times, on both cheeks, on the eyes. "You are a kindest person, thank you."

Magnus broke in. "I'll call Hero and see if she can reach her father."

Miss Angel raised a hand in the air, as if asking permission. "Are you not afraid of the attention, Magnus?"

"No." A few seconds later, he'd reconsidered. It was unclear if he was speaking to Miss Angel or himself. "Yes. I am."

Magnus called Hero. She—like Miss Angel—had become someone he could go to when the universe threw him a curveball. "You gotta get over here right now."

"You're such a drama queen, Magnus." Dishes clattered in the background. She was at work. "Wait, you're not going for a swim or anything? Where's here?"

"No, no, no. Home. I'm fine." Satisfied that he had quelled the panic in her voice, he took a breath to calm his own. "Do you remember Constanza, from the bakery? She's just had this for shit experience and needs to see a doc but won't go to the clinic. Can your dad look at her? Here, privately?"

"Yeah, of course I remember her. Where's here?"

"My place. The incident happened at a rental she cleans—one of Holders' rentals. This is serious." His tone of voice conveyed the gravity of his concern. "She's in a world of trouble, can't talk to anybody, including her family. Can you call your dad? Now. I mean, well, maybe he can come by later if he's at work. But Constanza—"

Hero interrupted, her words short: "Drugs or rape?"

"No, not drugs. Maybe the other. I don't know."

"What do you mean? You don't know!? Shit. Okay. Dad's home. My shift's as good as done. I'll be right there."

"Your dad—"

"Yes, right away—" She hung up.

After Hero's exclamation, Magnus pointedly queried Constanza. Although awkward for both her and Magnus, she had insisted that Lee had not raped her. He wasn't sure he believed her. Nor was he in the least clear about what technically constituted rape.

Two minutes later, Hero called back. She skipped the niceties. "A nurse trained in sexual assault exams is on the way to your place. Dad said Constanza shouldn't clean up or do anything until the nurse gets there."

Hero continued. "Rape or no, there are STDs and other injuries. I don't know what they do in the exam, or how much the nurse can do there." Hero paused, thinking as she was speaking. "Is there anything I can bring for Constanza? Does she need a place to stay? And Magnus, exactly why is she at your place?"

"Hero, just come over. I'll explain. Miss Angel is here too."

He heard her relief. "Good. She's smart. I'm on the way."

"Yes, she is. Very wise, that is."

Miss Angel heard the compliment and stiffened her posture. She *was* smart and wise. She damned well walked the walk.

Constanza lifted her hand. "Water."

"I don't know. The nurse will be here—."

Constanza repeated the request. "Water, please."

Miss Angel pulled her closer. "In a minute, dearie. Let's see if the doctor says it's okay."

He and Miss Angel were both ignorant about the appropriate protocol. Magnus assumed an exam would be both forensic and medical. When in doubt, try the internet. In seconds, he had found a site that described the responsibilities of a Sexual Assault Trained Examiner.

He read aloud: "No water. They'll want to swab her throat. And keep the clothes separated."

This prompted him to text Hero to ask if she had spare clothes at work and could she bring them.

Would Manzanita follow the same procedure as big-city Detroit, where the presumption would be that the assault had been a crime? There, the examiners would gather, seal, and store evidence for potential identification and prosecution of the offender. The more Magnus read, the more serious the ramifications for the offender and for Constanza seemed. The incident could draw the family into an impossible imbroglio. Constanza was young, but far from stupid. He showed her the site on his phone. She carefully read the entire article.

"Dearie, you don't have to read that." Miss Angel was upset about his sharing the information with Constanza. "In fact, I don't think you should—"

Constanza cut her off, demonstrating a better command of English than Miss Angel had expected. "I want to read. I want to know what happens to me and to my family. And to the men who do this."

Magnus picked up on the "men," but didn't want to grill her about the plural. Anyway, the nurse would ask.

Constanza fidgeted, wiggling and adjusting the ill-fitting socks, skirt, and blouse. The maid uniform was just plain weird. She asked for her pack she'd brought with her from when they had left Haven House. In the pack, neatly folded, were her actual clothes.

It was so obvious. Lee, and maybe someone else, had been making a porn video. Why? The obvious answer: They would market the video. Another possibility was that the video had been for personal use. But the Holders were all about the money. Or it could be both. No wonder, Magnus reflected, that the Holders had been touchy about the dark web logins and their TOR and Freeway accounts. They had a side gig, a dirty one.

A car and a scooter pulled into the parking lot at the same time. There were two voices, one being Hero's, and then footsteps clomping on the porch below.

Miss Angel, her hands shaking, announced that she was not feeling well and had to leave. She preferred to walk the few blocks to her own place. "To get some air."

"Will you be alright?" Miss Angel asked Constanza.

Constanza seemed to have regained her composure and confidence. "Fine. I am fine. You are very kind. Thank you. Magnus will take care of me."

"Yes, Magnus will take care of you." Miss Angel was unconvinced. "Young man—"

"Yes, Ma'am." He wanted to ask her why she was leaving, if she was unwell, and how she would manage with the dark glasses.

"I have," she apologized, "an appointment at home that I can't ignore."

"Shall I walk you?" he asked. "Or Hero can."

"I'll be fine, thank you. I can see better. And I need the air," she smiled, "wet or no."

On the stairway, Miss Angel briefly spoke with Hero and then had a slightly longer conversation with the nurse. The nurse was younger than Miss Angel, maybe mid-forties. They knew each other. Magnus reminded himself that everybody knew everybody in Manzanita. Constanza would be in good hands. Hero helped Miss Angel with the porch steps and walked her to the street.

* * *

* * * *

A quarter-hour after the nurse's arrival, Constanza emerged from Magnus's bedroom, cleaned up and wearing her own clothes. The nurse—her name was Riley—delivered a brusque summary of the exam and follow-up. Constanza was physically fine. Riley had given her a referral to a cost-free trauma specialist who would honor Constanza's right to privacy. Riley announced further that she would respect Constanza's desire to not report the incident, although, given her age, she recommended otherwise. The medical data, a plastic bag with her maid clothing, and a full report of the event would be on record at the clinic. If Constanza failed to follow through with the trauma therapy, Riley would be required to report the incident to the sheriff's office.

"C'mon!" Hero spat out the words. She clearly believed this should not have been Constanza's decision.

Riley ignored Hero's comment. She continued, speaking as if Constanza were not standing beside her. "People, Constanza made very poor choices. She told this guy, the photographer—she won't give up his name—that she wanted to make a sex video for her boyfriend. She claims the photographer had not forced her to do any acts she performed. In the middle of the filming, she reconsidered, and had a breakdown. She's eighteen, or so she says, old enough to know better. She claims to have no official birth record, which I find hard to believe.

"If you ask me," Riley went on, "that's all baloney. But I can't force her to do or say anything she doesn't want to do or say. Fortunately, she is physically one hundred percent okay—assuming the tests we run come up clean. She said her parents would be deported if the incident was reported. I'm going along with what this very bright-in-some-ways and not-so-bright-in-other-ways young woman wants. But I think her story stinks."

Riley wasn't finished. "And who the hell are *you* people? Estelle vouched for you, but I'm not forgetting."

Hero turned combative, "You did *not* talk to Miss Angel when we arrived."

"No, smarty pants," Riley huffed. "I spoke to her a few minutes ago by phone. You're both in my notes."

Riley gathered her things. "I'm going, but I'm going to keep an eye on Constanza." She took Constanza's hand. "You remember what I said?" Constanza acknowledged her. Riley, in a slightly warmer tone, told her to "Take care. Check in tomorrow."

Constanza read the card Riley had given her.

Riley repeated the warning she had given to us and Constanza in passable Spanish. She didn't wait for us to walk her out or say goodbye.

The three of us sat in silence until we heard Riley's car back out of the drive and turn down First Street.

"Eighteen?" His doubt was obvious.

"There's no proof I'm not eighteen. Maybe I am? It's better this way."

"I don't know, Constanza."

Hero broke the somber mood. "Pizza?"

Even Constanza laughed at the suggestion.

"Helado. I want ice cream."

Hero suggested Marzano's for pizza and the Little Apple for ice cream.

"How's about mint chocolate chip?"

All hands went up. Chocolate chip diplomacy was going to be more effective at restoring Constanza's mental well-being than Riley's advice.

Constanza eased carefully onto the Beast, testing the deep cushion before committing her weight. She pointed, suggesting that Magnus should sit next to her. He hesitated, thinking that she wouldn't be big on cozying up to another man, any man. She patted the cushion again and Magnus sat. He reached for the remote and put on the game—any game. It was women's soccer. They watched in silence.

Magnus thought about what had transpired and what, if anything, he could do to make things better for Constanza and her family, and what, if anything again, he could do to make life hell for the Holders. One question among many nagged at him: Was Holder senior as involved as Holder junior?

He had an unrelated idea, or partial idea. Sometimes one says something before thinking it through. "Constanza, would you talk to my mom?"

"Why?" Constanza asked.

"Well, Mom is Cuban. She's street smart."

"Street smart?" Constanza was unsure of the term.

"Astuta," Magnus translated. "I love her and trust her, and she always gives good advice. I was going to call her. You can talk to her about anything. She's not going to judge you and she's not going to talk to anybody about you."

That may or may not have been enough to convince Constanza, but since she didn't object, Magnus made the call, placing it to a burner phone he had left with Mari.

Pizza

Magnus caught Mari at a bad time, but when he told her it was important, she asked for a minute to cancel something and then called right back. He explained to Mari that he was going to pass the phone to Constanza and that Constanza would explain what had happened and could she, his mother, be her normal, wonderful self and talk? He also reminded her of the importance of retaining his cover as Magnus Krum. Constanza took the phone and went back to the bedroom. She closed the door, a door that was about as soundproofed as the thin walls of the apartment. Within a couple minutes, Constanza was laughing, crying, and engaged in, at times, somber conversation that included details that Constanza had not shared with Magnus.

Reclining in the Beast, he threw his arms back behind his head and thought about what to do next. Hero stood behind the sofa and leaned over him, comfortable letting her breasts press against his arms and wiggling her head so the braided strands of hair brushed against his ear.

"That tickles!"

"Sorree." She flicked her head to the side, tossing back the hair and braids.

"And you're breathing down the back of my neck!"

She scooted around the sofa and plopped down beside Magnus. "Aren't we touchy! Fine."

His mind was jumping from one thing to the next. "Why do you work?"

"What do you mean?"

"Your mom is sick. Shouldn't you be with her?"

"We'd drive each other crazy, me doting on her night and day."

"Still, working in a diner?"

"You're showing a lot of attitude about a girl working in a diner, fella."

"Nothing derogatory meant and you know it."

"I know." Hero tossed her head back. "I had to keep busy or I'd go nuts. And it's just for now. When Mom needs me more, I'll quit. The owners are super nice and understand."

He repositioned himself, laptop on knees and legs on the table in front of the sofa. The thing that had been nagging at the back of his mind jumped to the foreground. "There's something I gotta do asap. Fuck, I should have figured this out sooner."

"Whatcha gotta do asap'?"

"Erase the video, the one Lee made."

"And how, Mister Krum" a skeptical Hero asked, "are you going to do that?"

Magnus generally downplayed his IT skills. He had jokingly implied that he had winged his way through a few easy, local consulting gigs. This reticence was one side of a tacit agreement between Hero and Magnus about limiting details about their respective histories. The reflection prompted Magnus to think about his relationships with women, its contractual nature and immaturity. He decided that although he didn't trust Constanza's story, he accepted enough of it to move forward with the hack.

"You can watch, but no interruptions. Not a peep. Okay?"

Hero saluted.

"I'm gonna order pizza. Any prefs?" She shoved her phone in front of his face. It displayed Marzano's menu.

"For fuck's sake, Hero!"

"Sorry, sorry—"

"I need to do this quickly."

"Why?"

"Hero! Shit, okay. Because if the Holders change the passwords on their logins, I won't be able to access the file with Constanza's video. Assuming I can find the damned thing. Please, let me do this."

He logged in to Holder's network and Lee's computer, hoping that no one would notice the remote login icon on the taskbar. He waited. "Do not touch."

"What happens if I do? Or if you do?"

Magnus pointed. "That's Lee's desktop; I'm using it real time. I booted him out of the program he was on and he's going to have to log in again. He'll probably do what he normally does and that *might* show me where he's uploaded and stored the video."

"But it could be tomorrow or the next day. Why do you think he'll upload it now?"

"What he's doing is illegal. So if I were Lee, I'd want to get the video off my camera and uploaded someplace private as soon as possible."

Hero ordered pizza, her choice of toppings. Magnus waited, nervous and doubting himself.

Ten minutes later, the screen on his laptop came to life. He had set his computer to record the screen. Within twenty minutes, he knew where Lee had stored the file and how to access the specific folder. Hopefully, the passwords, though displayed as asterisks, still correlated with the website and folder password list he had photographed at Holders' office.

Hero watched him work and, without asking, brought a beer from the refrigerator and a bag of Smart popcorn. He took the beer and ignored the popcorn.

Hero tore open the bag. "I'm starved."

"C'mon asshole," he swore at the screen.

After Lee logged out, Magnus broke off the remote connection.

"Cross your fingers" to Hero.

Hero literally crossed her fingers. "Why?"

"Because the old passwords may or may not give me access to the site and folder where the video is stored."

He held his breath. And then the magic happened.

"Bingo! We're in!" He quickly found the right folder and the video. Amateurish identifiers tagged the file's place and date.

"Can we watch it?" Hero asked.

"We could, but we're not going to. I don't think Constanza wants us or anybody to see it."

"Can you download the video? I mean, what if she wants us to give it to the sheriff's office? Maybe not now, but maybe later."

"Right. I'll make a copy and delete the one on Holder's site."

As the file downloaded, Hero put her hand on his arm. "Magnus, I appreciate that you respect her privacy."

"I'm no hero, Hero."

Her phone buzzed with a text. Hero rose and headed for the door. "Ice cream, I'm gonna pick up ice cream at Little Apple. And the pizza. Be right back."

"Is it still raining?" he asked.

"Clear sailing."

So it was, Magnus reflected. Clear sailing, at least for now.

* * * *

Hero arrived with Marzano's pizza and pricey Lopez Island mint chocolate chip ice cream. Magnus opened the bedroom door and pantomimed eating. Constanza held up a finger. She was finishing the call. The conversation with Mari must have been full of questions and answers that required a lot of sharing. Constanza should have been emotionally exhausted. Instead, she was almost chipper. Whatever she and Mari had discussed, Constanza was in a decidedly positive mood, even seemed to have an appetite.

"How'd it go?" Magnus asked as he and Hero separated to make room in the middle for Constanza. When she took her place, the sofa sagged and pizza crumbs rained on the carpet. He waved a hand.

Constanza took a slice. Hero handed her a coke, appropriately a Mexican. "Gracias." She dove in on the pizza as the soccer game played out in front of them, a Portland Thorns game.

"You know," Magnus spoke over the soccer announcer's voice, "when I first rented this unit, Holders' office manager assured me that the place was clean. My first night here, this room smelled real funky. I sniffed around."

He imitated a dog sniffing around and got a laugh from Constanza.

"I was on hands and knees, crawling all over. I found the source of the odor when I peeled up a corner of the rug, and under the rug and this gross fibrous underlayment, there was a cache of old food, candy, little animal figures and plastic soldiers, and an old, *used* Band-Aid. And mouse shit, a lot of mouse shit. It was disgusting. The previous renters had kids, and the kids hid whatever under the rug. I cleaned it and trashed the underlayment. This fucking couch is the heaviest fucking couch in the universe—"

"Magnus! Language, please. And we're eating!"

"That's when I named the sofa the 'Beast.' The first discovery made me paranoid about other garbage, so I dug between the cushions and, sure enough, found another cache as gross as the first."

"This slipcover is new, I hope?"

"Yeah. But underneath, deep in the Beast, I think the cooties still live there. When it's quiet, I hear them, this rodential chewing and off-gassing—"

Hero wiggled in her seat. "Gross, stop it!"

"The what? Rodential?" Constanza asked through a mouthful of pizza.

"Mousy-like," Magnus answered.

"Cooties?"

"Cooties are . . . I don't know. Magnus would know better than me!" Hero crinkled her nose and looked to Magnus to explain."

"Thanks, Hero." He pressed on, unoffended. "Germs. And creepy crawly stuff: lice, bacteria, maggots, old scabs and fungus. Stuff you really don't want to touch, smell, or be anywhere near. Cooties are the essence of gross. It's what little girls say about little boys—ewy, he's got cooties!" Magnus poked Hero. She made a face back at him and stuck out her tongue, a very gross tongue with bits of food on it.

Constanza loved it. "Lee Holder is a cooties," she tested the meaning.

"Kind of," Hero agreed. "A big bad cootie, but you've got the right idea. A better word is *scumbag*."

"Scum. Bag." Constanza enunciated each syllable.

"Better yet," Hero added, "a total prick."

"Culero, entiendo prick," Constanza laughed openly.

The laugh, tangible and real, touched and lifted spirits. Maybe the trauma she had experienced had not been as bad as he had thought. Or maybe he didn't know shit about sexual trauma and how people deal with it.

Magnus asked again about how things went with his mom. Constanza's expression darkened, not a defeatist darkening, but a defiant, brave darkening. "I love your mother. She said you would fix things; you always do. Then she said to tell you to not get into trouble! You were in enough trouble, but she wouldn't tell me about enough trouble. I asked!"

"More than being a hacker?" Hero added.

"Magnus is a hacker?"

"He said so, yes." Hero faced Magnus, a pizza crumb on her lip. "That right Magnus?"

Constanza brightened. "Cool!"

"I'mmmm gonna get some paper towels." He picked the crumb off her lip as he got up. "And feed the cooties."

A half-hour passed before Constanza's mother, Carmen, arrived. José waited in the car. Hero had left; Carmen and Magnus exchanged not a word. She had already been given a complete account. Still, her unease and distrust were obvious. Magnus was too burned out to care.

The family had not taken his advice. You can't fix everything, Magnus told himself, even if your mother thinks you can.

The New Normal

Two vacant and uneventful weeks drifted by. The Fourth of July came and went with a poof. In past Fourths, the city had allowed pyromaniacs with rocket-propelled grenades in the backs of pickups to transform the beach into a war zone. Wisely, the City of Manzanita eventually banned the freewheeling fireworks.

The main event, a parade up and down the length of the city on Laneda and Manzanita, showcased floats and classic automobiles and groups from supportive businesses and community organizations like the Little Apple, NCRD, the Hoffman Center, Heart of CARTM, the Emergency Volunteer Corps, local lumber and hardware stores, and more. Fire engines tapped sirens, and kids lined the streets and scrambled for candy tossed to them by virtually every float. Representatives of the right (e.g. NRA) and left (e.g. Women's Choice) waved flags and behaved themselves and set a good example of adult behavior—Congress take note.

In the aftermath of the incident at Haven House, Magnus had visited Panda Bakery but learned little more. Carmen and José avoided talking about what had transpired. A brief conversation with Constanza had confirmed that the Holders had reneged on the rent deal and once again threatened the family with eviction. The flip-flop confirmed that yielding on the rent had been in exchange for Constanza being a porn asset. The big news—per Constanza—was that soon, a Reyes family friend whom they referred to as Tio Félix, would visit from Chihuahua.

Constanza had explained that he wasn't really her uncle, but that's what she called him. The Uncle and José were going to talk about bakery finances and alternative locations. Félix, Constanza explained, was a contractor.

Magnus learned from José that Félix wanted to meet with him to talk about work. What kind of work was unclear. Magnus assumed IT.

The same uneventful status applied to Miss Angel. In polite silence, Magnus drove her to the Coop in Astoria and to a follow-up visit to the ophthalmologist. Miss Angel explained to Magnus that she needed to "idle" for a spell and had asked for a few weeks' reprieve from tea and reading. She had made one brief inquiry about how Constanza was doing. Magnus reported "fine" and that was the end of it.

Hero kept in touch and nagged Magnus about crabbing. He had given it two seconds' thought and a hard no. Crabbing grossed him out. He wanted to fit in as a local, but only to a point.

Folks in Manzanita were nuts about crabbing. Some families shelled out fifty grand for a boat and another fifty on a pickup to tow the boat, all of which gave them the opportunity to spend four or five boring hours monitoring a handful of crab traps while puttering around Nehalem Bay in the icy drizzle.

Hero's unrepentant response: "Get a life!"

Even Riley, the social worker, dropped off the radar.

Within this foggy calm, Magnus drifted. He had a recurring dream about reaching out to touch people—literally to touch them, say put a hand on someone's shoulder—but the moment he got close he turned into a two-dimensional, cardboard cutout with geek glasses.

The home front proffered the same no-news, but not necessarily good news. Mari and Ari decided to caravan with Vinnie and Alejandra for a road trip to a period inn in Amish Country, choosing it as the only option they could agree upon among any number of better vacation ideas.

The Twins reported they had leaked Zaidu's generous donation to the press. He reveled in the upgraded social status. But thugs don't forgive and forget.

Mom mentioned that the local police seemed to have found better things to do than hunt for a kid who printed Green Cards for immigrants. Dad, being in a credible position to opine on the matter, confirmed that my case smoldered on the back burner.

Uneventful day after uneventful day added to the disembodied quasi-normality of it all. The new normal depressed the shit out of him.

* * * *

* * *

That had been before Lee showed up at the front door. Magnus had been at the stove and had just done a masterful job of releasing a twisted fistful of pasta in a pot of boiling water. The strands fanned out in a perfect circle. He used a wooden spoon to coax the stiff ends down as the ends in the water grew pliable. A soccer match narrated in Spanish played on the tele and masked the footsteps on the porch. Magnus heard the door open and someone walk up the stairs. Hero, he thought.

"You motherfucker. I know it was you, you shithead. Did you make a copy?"

Magnus tried to not appear surprised and guilty. He glanced at Lee Holder and returned to the stirring the pasta.

"Lee, my man, how you doing? Want some pasta? No clue what you're talking about."

"Ain't no one else coulda done it, fucker!"

Magnus shook his head, playing dumb. "Sorry, no clue."

Spoon in hand, he walked over to the front window and saw no sign of Lee's pickup.

Lee intercepted Magnus as he walked back to the stove. He shoved him, knocking Magnus into the Beast. He put one hand on Magnus's throat and the other on his shoulder, banged him on the table, and rolled him onto the floor. Magnus tried to get up, spoon in hand. Lee walloped him across the face and sent his glasses flying. This surprised Magnus, who had irrationally thought that glasses protected him and that a thoughtful assailant would at least wait for, or ask him to remove his glasses. Under a second blow, Magnus went down hard on his knees and landed next to the broken, lens-less frame. He rolled to his side too late to avoid a boot connecting with his ribs and underbelly. His body had practically lifted off the floor. He rolled onto his back, clutching his rib cage, spoon still in hand, and stared up into the barrel of an old-fashioned six-cylinder revolver hovering about six inches from his face. Lee rested the pointed toe of his boot over Magnus's crotch, leaned over close enough for Magnus to smell cologne and breath mints, and rammed the barrel of the revolver into Magnus's cheek. The cold metal of the front sight cut the flesh.

Magnus threatened Lee with the spoon, fully aware of what a useless gesture it was.

"Where is it?" Lee shouted. The "where" had two syllables: long, a "wah" elided into the "air".

The pain in his ribs made breathing impossible. Words came out in a raspy, staccato gasps. "Not . . . here . . . tomorrow. Tomorrow."

Lee realized that his anger had gotten the best of him. Probably not for the first time. Instead of patiently extracting what he had wanted from Magnus, he had lit into him and practically killed him.

"Listen up!"

A tendon in Lee's neck spasmed. Magnus couldn't stop staring at it.

"You got 'til tomorrow night, you understand. And if you ain't got that video or if you spread it around—I been lookin' for it—you're a dead man. You got that?!" The barrel of the revolver came down across the side of Magnus's head. Blood trickled from the head wound and seeped between the splayed fingers of his hand.

The wooden spoon dropped to the floor. Scalding hot, foamed water overflowed and hissed angrily when it spilled onto the burner flame.

Hugging his ribs and unable to speak, Magnus nodded. He had understood, and he also knew that there was only so much Lee could do. It was nine p.m.; neighbors were home from work. Too much racket and someone would call the cops. And Lee wouldn't kill him, not if he wanted the video. Where was Hero? He feared she might walk in the door.

The painful throbbing in his head refused to go away. He lay there in the fetal position, hoping he wouldn't shit his pants or pee. Lee walked to the deck window to see if anyone might have seen or heard him. With a parting, threatening glance at Magnus, he descended the stairs and quietly let himself out.

The hiss from the stove had grown to a roar. Magnus crawled to the stove, reached up and turned off the burner. He tried to sit upright by leaning against the kitchen island across from the stove. Boiling water had burned his hand. He tasted blood in his mouth and spit it out, wondering if he had lost a tooth. On the tele a player scored a goal. Magnus, inspired by sports commentator's long-voiced *Goooooooal!*, crawled to the table in front of the Beast and found his phone on the floor under it. He dialed 911, staying conscious only long enough to give his address and smell the lingering odor of Lee's cologne.

Seaside Clinic

"Good morning, Magnus. Welcome back. Do you know where you are?"

Memories assaulted Magnus: The first responders' arrival; being strapped to the stretcher; a Black man, thirtyish, with a lumberjack beard, beat-up Pirates hat with brim to the back and Doc Marten boots good for stomping on the head of a dude wearing the wrong color; a Latina woman as short as her partner was tall, skin wan to his black, and stocky, five-hundred-squats stocky. Tats owned real estate on the woman. A multi-headed snake spread like disease up her neck and slithered into hair. Black baseball cap, bill forward this time, and black hoody. Three gold chains for Lumberjack. Goth Girl wore a silver skull necklace—plus the nose, lip, nostril, and waterfall ear piercings. She sported black driving gloves with holes at the knuckles, fishnet tights, and mid-shin lace-up boots. Magnus recalled feeling relieved when they arrived, reassured, because these were his kind of peeps.

The pair wore matching khaki shorts and crisp, white collared short-sleeve shirts. Radios in leather cocoons swung from their belts. Plump beetle mics clung to shirt collars. A patch on the sleeve displayed the company logo. Without the uniform and logo, a lot of folks—he had had this thought and felt smug about not having reacted this way—wouldn't have let these guys in the front door.

A vivid magical-realist experience found a permanent place in memory: being rolled out the door headfirst on the gurney and his body rising in the air and floating into the back of the ambulance van. A rush as he left the earth's surface.

He would make it a point to forget the other memories: Lee's fury and blows; childhood fights he had lost; fear of confrontation and vulnerability. He searched for Hero, for her ice-grey eyes, amid a collage of determined faces searching for him.

And then he was home, dancing to Bachata Rosa, an old Juan Luis Guerra number, his mother back leading.

* * * *

Overlarge eyes behind 60s wire-rimmed glasses filled his field of vision. It took a minute to recognize Hero's father.

"Dr. Wheelwright?"

"Yes. You were dreaming. And talking a mile a minute—"

Magnus remembered dreaming, feeling pressure but surprisingly little pain. Bandages wrapped his torso and head.

"I was?"

"In Spanish and English. You asked for Hero." Wheelwright poked at Magnus like the EMTs had done. A light in one eye, then the other. That thing physicians do to see if pupils dilate and contract and if you still have a brain.

"How do you feel?"

"I feel like I had the shit kicked out of me."

"I'd say that was an accurate medical assessment. Cracked rib, multiple contusions, concussion, possibly internal bleeding. We were concerned about splenic bleeding and the concussion. We need to keep you for the night."

Magnus bounced from health worries to legal worries to Lee worries. He had met Dr. Wheelwright, Hero's dad, once at the Farmers' Market and then once at an emergency preparedness event.

Folks in Manzanita take emergency preparedness seriously. October 14, 2016, a tornado ripped through town. A month later, there was a tsunami scare. Local authorities had sent a reminder to every household suggesting that residents prepare an emergency go-bag with radios, water, food, a space-blanket, flashlight, and other supplies.

Magnus had helped Miss Angel assemble items to update her old go-bag. When he had finished, the go-bag was so heavy that she couldn't lift it off the ground, much less carry it to a higher ground location. She insisted, unreasonably, that it didn't matter. Disregarding the fatalistic old-folks' talk, Magnus repurposed a canvas boat bag at her house to hold a handful of truly essential items, not forgetting her little yellow radio so she could listen and call neighbors even if the phones were down. If there really were an emergency, well, he would try to help her make it to higher ground.

"Magnus, are you with me?"

"Sorry, the brain's on walkabout. I was thinking about emergency preparedness."

Wheelwright, using words instead of an AED, shocked Magnus back to the here and now. "Hero told me she was worried about you, a lot worried, but nothing specific."

He continued, back in doctor mode. "Are you taking any medications? Any medical preconditions we should know about?"

Magnus shook his head no.

"Any substances? Tobacco, recreational drugs, alcohol?"

"Nada. A beer once in a while. I'm a runner."

"Good. I've prescribed several medications for you. My PA will go over them with you."

A young male assistant showed up beside the bed with a clipboard and a form asking for patient and insurance information. Magnus didn't know if this was the PA Wheelwright had referred to or someone else. "When you have a moment," he said.

The PA stepped away, stopped, and turned to face Magnus. "De dónde vienes?"

"I sorry, I don't understand. Can we do this later?"

He was Latino and couldn't be bullshitted. The "no te creo" expression said as much.

"Blame Duolingo," Magnus tried, but the words sounded lame.

If that's how you want to play, the assistant's expression said. He turned and headed back to wherever he had come from.

Dr. Wheelwright glanced at the readings from the pulse/ox monitor. "The police may want to talk to you."

His pulse surely skyrocketed. He looked, and it hadn't. Probably the meds. "Can you talk to them?"

"Me? And tell them what?"

"Tell them it was a friendly fight that got out of hand. No desire and no need to press charges. The cat next door, you know."

"The cat next door?"

Dr. Wheelwright didn't read Peanuts.

"Kidding," Magnus coughed the word. "I'm begging you, Dr. Wheelwright. No police, please. I'm seriously begging you."

"I'll see what I can do. Get some rest, Magnus. I'll stop by tonight."

With his IV-free hand, he tugged Dr. Wheelwright's sleeve, worried about annoying him with a second request.

"I don't have insurance. But I have money. Can I pay something now, maybe the rest later?"

Dr. Wheelwright scowled the way a parent might, implying the wagging finger but not actually doing it.

"No insurance, you say?"

Magnus answered by not answering.

"Very well. There is an assistance program. The beneficiaries are often migrants. The staff is Latino. My aide will give you a pamphlet about the program when you're discharged."

"Thank you."

"Is there anyone we should contact for you? Your parents perhaps?"

"No. Thanks, though. Thanks for everything."

"There must be someone."

Magnus agreed. It would attract unwanted attention if he were to ask for no one.

"Wait. Could you call Miss Angel. She can contact my family. Do you know her?"

Magnus gave him Miss Angel's number. "You can text her directly, or ask Hero to call her."

A few minutes later his cell phone vibrated. It was in a plastic bag of personal effects on the table next to the bed. He glanced at the message without retrieving the phone, struggling to turn toward the tray and read the message sideways. His glasses were next to the phone. Adhesive tape replaced one hinge and attached a cracked lens to the frame. He had a vague memory of Lumberjack in the back of the van doing something with his hands as they careened down the road to the hospital. The EMTs must have seen the phone and boxed it up with the glasses. *Thank you, you lovely, amazingly competent people!*

<<HW: Dad said you're ok and I can give you shit.>>

He searched for a snarky comeback but came up empty.

* * * *

That feeling of being watched. Everybody knew it existed, but science couldn't explain it. He scrunched his face a few times to get the sleep from his eyes and saw Miss Angel in a chair beside the bed, focused on her reading, the metronomic rise and fall of her chest, the careful way she turned a page. She closed the book—a massive volume—when she noticed him stirring. The book's title and author's name sprawled across the cover: *Infinite Jest,* by *David Foster Wallace.* He'd not read or heard of the book. A dozens neon green Post-it flags marked passages. The worn spine was more binding fabric than paper.

"It's evening, Magnus." She rose. "How are you?"

Her chair, oversized and comfortable, had not been in his room before. She noticed him looking at it. "Yes, I asked them to bring a chair from the waiting room. These old bones, you know." Miss Angel put her hand on his shoulder.

"Thank you for coming. I didn't know what to tell Dr. Wheelwright. About my family."

"I presume you told him exactly what you had told me."

This confused Magnus, as did her announcing that it was evening. If anything, he was foggier and more drugged than before. She closed the book before she spoke.

"Exactly nothing."

"Did you talk to him?"

"Do you mean, have I spoken with Dr. Wheelwright? . . . Yes."

"What did you tell him?"

"I told him that you were the nephew of a friend in Germany, whose sister, a comedic actress of some renown, had abandoned you and moved to a survivalist commune in Costa Rica where she was in recovery from heroin addiction. Oh, yes, and that she sketched exotic plants in the manner of Ellsworth Kelly. Have you seen his plant drawings. Magnus? They're lovely."

"Good grief. Miss Angel, who would believe that?"

"Everybody, dear. Everybody. People believe anything I write! I wrote it down, to make it real. It's in a margin here . . ." She reopened the book and flipped through a few pages, unable to find what she had written. Or maybe she was pulling his leg. "Ah well, seems your history is lost. Hah!" She winked, pleased with herself, very much liking the story she had fabricated and whatever her allusions had alluded to, and then lost.

The gay mood gave way to a serious expression. "This was Lee's doing, I presume."

Magnus didn't respond.

"Argumentum ad nauseam?"

"What?"

"If you assert that this was not Lee's doing enough times, then it is not his doing. Must I ask again?"

He relented. "We compromised. Well, I might have compromised a little more than he did." A chuckle turned into a grimace. "It hurts when I laugh."

 She nodded and changed the subject. "The nurse, a very handsome gentleman of Spanish descent, questioned me."

"..."

"He said, and I poorly quote: 'I theenk heez accent is Cuban!' " She did an embarrassingly poor job of imitating the man's accent.

Magnus played it straight. "And what did you say?"

"Oh, I said, so true. Yes, Cuba, certainly not Costa Rica. Oh wait, perhaps it was Columbia. I told the dear man I didn't remember things the way I used too."

She had hidden behind her age. Miss Angel wasn't addled and she forgot nothing.

"I want to ask you a question, Magnus."

"Fire away."

"Where in the hell *are* you from?"

He couldn't lie to her. Not after she had had his back. "Between us . . ."

"Fine. Between us. I shall leave the boundary of ethical behavior for the indefensible hellhole of tribal loyalties. This is one of those shunts that characters in my books inevitably regret."

"Detroit. Mom's from La Habana. Contenta? Happy?"

Miss Angel raised a finger at my attitude. "Don't push your luck, young man!"

His phone buzzed. He heard it, but the phone was no longer on the tray.

"I borrowed a charger," she explained as she reached down to the floor beside her chair. She unplugged the charger and rose to hand him the phone, charger, and, from his side table, his glasses. She briefly examined the patched-up frames.

He took the glasses and put them on as if using them to read the phone. A message on WhatsApp got his attention. It was from Harry, one of the Twins, but using a different name:

<<KZ: Someone trying to find MK>>

Another message followed, this one from the other Twin, Charlie, also using a false identity:

<<PK: Seeker hid Manzanita IP. set up redirect.>>

Magnus didn't text back.

Lee had been hunting Magnus online, causing Charlie and Harry to sprinkle a few crumbs out there to throw Lee off. They probably led him up a dark alley on the dark web, likely a path that exposed him to truly malevolent players. No wonder Lee was pissed. Magnus couldn't repress the grin.

"Magnus," Miss Angel asked, "are you going to tell me what's going on?"

Whether it was drugs or just hearing from the Twins, his mood brightened. The cracked lenses distorted the image of Miss Angel, creating a seismic split down the middle of her face. Stupidly, Magnus found this funny and tried to suppress the Cheshire smile. "Nope!"

Clam-Lips

Attired in hospital gown and slippers and unable to sleep, the revenant Magnus traveled the hallway in an elliptical orbit with the bathroom and nursing station as foci. He shuffled down the hall; he shuffled back. He shuffled down the hall; he shuffled back. He tried, with eyes half-closed, to navigate the journey by nose, noting the odor of disinfectant cleaners in the hallways, pleasant human odors at the nurses station, and not so pleasant human odors—vomit, urine, feces —as he passed various rooms. At one room in particular, he detected, or perhaps imagined he detected, the saprogenic odor of decomposing flesh. From the door leading to the kitchen came the universal aroma of tasteless, saltless, fatless food, and je ne sais quoi of stale coffee. Another tour, he navigated by sound. He half-hummed and half-whistled a salsa number that he could never remember the words to. After the fourth or fifth lap, an orderly—or maybe it was a nurse—ordered him back to his room.

"You can't parade around here singin' and all, Magnus. People got to sleep. Shoo yourself back to that room or I'll shoo you back myself!"

She laughed, being one of those people who seemed to laugh after everything they said. The laugh wrapped you in warm, confidence inspiring parens. A good (nurse) laugh is, as they say, the best medicine!

The meds made him batty, no question there. No pain though, he felt no pain. Head low, acting the scolded child, he returned to his room and, still unable to sleep, stood with his hands braced on the footboard of the bed and practiced salsa shines, coordinating the footwork and voicing the clave, "bop . bop . . . bop . . bop . . bop . . ."

Uncountable hours later, the artificial illumination outside the window deferred to the pre-dawn glow. Sounds from the hospital and the world outside merged: a siren, the lonely groan of a semi tapping air brakes, a slam of a delivery van door, the low-frequency whir of an electric vehicle, paging pings, beeping IV pumps, heart monitors, huffing mechanical ventilators, muted staff conversations, a rolling cart with a squeaky wheel, a floor cleaner whirring and thrumping into objects, a high-pitched snore from a neighboring patient. On the other side of 101, out of sight but not out of hearing range, waves collided with the beach in a drunken cadence influenced by the new moon and clocking winds. By mid-morning, man-made road noise dominated the soundscape: lumber trucks ground gears, impatient pickups convened at job sites, delivery trucks labeled Amazon, FedEx, and UPS jockeyed for road time. The hospital didn't officially discharge Magnus until well past ten a.m.

Loopy from meds and antsy as hell to leave, he was dialing *WeDrive!* when someone knocked at the door. A beaded braid swung into view and gave her away before she ducked back behind the door.

"You decent?" Hero asked.

She had seen him and made the comment for the benefit of someone else. And for Hero, a rather uncharacteristic deference to modesty.

"No! Not decent. Not in the least!"

The odors of cleaning products and urine clung to the room and embarrassed Magnus. That, and he hadn't showered since forever.

Hero told whoever she was with that they could go in. She held the wrist of the mystery companion, but let go when they entered.

"You look bad!"

Ah, that was the Hero he knew.

"I mean. Fuck."

Her fingers traced his face, from hairline to cheek to jaw, and with her other hand mirrored the path on her own features, comparing their respective contours. The unknown guest waited at attention.

She recovered from the tracing distraction and spoke, "Magnus, this is Henry."

" . . . "

"Henry, Magnus. He's new here."

Magnus was confused. Which was the new guy?

"Not a patient," Henry joked and anticipated Magnus's next question. "We met at Vassar. I was a full-time student. Hero was there for a summer abroad—but backwards abroad. *Her* home was Rome."

"And" Hero added, "Henry is Uncle Theo's wife's son from a prior marriage."

"Isn't Vassar a women's college?" Magnus stuck with a topic he might understand. Tackling who was what relative of whom was beyond him, as was how Vassar and Uncle Theo fit together. Maybe it was random.

The new arrival put a hand on his hip and shifted his weight to one leg. He tossed his head to the side. A poor taste stereotype of womanhood. "You can't tell?" The falsetto grated.

Her last visit Miss Angel had described a male character in *Infinite Jest* who, for professional reasons, had given up his sexual identity. There had been a sadness in the loss, some satisfaction from the authentic sacrifice, and painfully little understanding of what it meant to be a woman. This, Miss Angel, had commented, was an unfortunate oversight. He was drifting again.

"Vassar has been coed since '69."

"..."

"Henry, don't act stupid."

Magnus resented Henry's grinning map, his handsome physique, the clam-lips that framed a mouthful of overlarge teeth and underscored the rugby player's pugilistic nose. He had lacrosse player hands and forearms. Magnus had dancer hands and intersex features.

"Henry works at an investment bank in San Francisco."

"Really. How interesting." Bully for you, Magnus thought. Then he questioned himself. Who was he, to be so rude? Had his remark been sardonic or sarcastic? How about dumb? He'd ask Miss Angel, grammarian and civility expert.

"Really," Henry good-naturedly qualified her introduction, "Vassar was the only place a fat, Jewish kid like me could find a date. And I'm little more than a glorified intern at the bank."

"Right," Hero said. "You're so fat!" She poked his tummy, and Magnus imagined the rugby abs tense under the shirt. Did he even play rugby?

Hero turned toward Magnus and soberly announced the purpose of their visit: "We're here to give you a ride home."

Was Henry a Jewish name? He'd known a Jew in Detroit named Henry. The name reminded him of Prince Hal. Now there was a pair— Hero and the hero of Shrewsbury. Nice of Henry in the flesh to have made fun of himself. The other Henry ditched Falstaff and took himself way too fucking seriously. Miss Angel and Magnus had reread Henry IV Part II and wrote off the reformed Hal as a jerk because he wouldn't laugh at a fart joke.

"Cool." Magnus couldn't think of anything more intelligent to say. His brain was back on St. Crispin's day, 1415, or whenever it was.

Maybe Henry the Clam *was* okay. And it was he, Magnus, who should question his own soundness of mind. Did Hamlet? Just how jealous was he?

"Aren't you supposed to be at the Wave?"

She gave him the dodo look. "It's Suundaay. I'm off." This warranted a little dance.

"Right." Magnus mechanically conceded and came up with an excuse for the oversight. "Bedpan coffee, you know. You sure it's Sunday?" A behind-the-eyes headache pounded the inside of his skull. Caffeine withdrawal.

Henry spoke up: "Brew 22?"

Magnus wanted to kiss the clam lips. Brew 22, a drive-thru coffee shack, was his Seaside coffee go-to. Lively baristas chatted up clientele; the playlist rocked 90s grunge.

Hero punched Henry in the shoulder. "He's not supposed to have caffeine."

Magnus disapproved of the punching. He was about to say something but forgot what it was. He didn't want to talk. It hurt to move his jaw, to breathe. It hurt to fart.

"Yes," he said aloud. "I, Magnus, can drink coffee."

A nurse interrupted the party. She handed Magnus his discharge papers and a plastic bag with his bloodied clothes. The thought of having to wear them again dismayed him and reminded him of the shame that went along with his having had the crap beaten out of him.

Hero took the bag from Magnus and reached into the daypack on the floor and leaning against her leg. Magnus had not noticed it. He had been obsessed, he realized, with how her beaded braids flopped around and if there might be a way to characterize their dynamics. Lagrangian?

"Clean duds."

"Where did you get my clothes?"

"They're mine. Baggy stuff. We'll be twins."

"We already are twins, I don't know . . ."

Hero placed the clothes on the bed. "Henry and I will wait for you at the front desk."

* * * *

* * *

Falstaff mode Magnus bumbled through the discharge process. The nurse in command said something predictably not funny, "hope we don't see you soon," and handed him a fistful of paperwork. Magnus repeated the words back to her, equally unfunny.

"Magnus," Hero chided. "Be nice."

"No more Sir John," he said, confusing everybody. He zippered his mouth with his finger and traipsed after Hero and Henry. The group came to a stop in front of a blue-black Porsche 911. Hero squeezed into the back seat, sitting sideways. Magnus painfully eased into the passenger seat.

"What kind of mileage does this thing get?" Magnus's tried bro-talk. He wasn't into high-end cars, but he was a car whisperer. The Porche broke a hundred grand, meaning it was keen to be talked about.

Hero's bare foot rested on the shoulder of the seat. Magnus believed Henry was going to use her big toe as a microphone. When she wiggled her toe it added to his confusion.

"Twenty on the highway, eighteen in the city."

"Like mine," Magnus bro-like responded.

"You have a Porsche?"

"Subaru. Used." The Zio Vinnie imp on his shoulder spoke up: "A lot used."

"Magnus." Hero twisted to face him as the Porsche came to life and made a lovely rumble. "Did they give you a toothbrush and toothpaste?"

"I don't know."

"Your breath is yucky."

"Open the window." His hands kept a gentle pressure on the rib cage. It helped with the pain.

Hero reached over him to put down the window. Her breasts and arm pit leaned into his shoulder. The scent and warmth of her body were intoxicating. His broken glasses tilted to the side. He closed his eyes when she placed her hand on his thigh for support. He wanted her.

"No," he said aloud. The referent was lost on everyone.

A strand of Hero's hair snagged the hinge of Magnus's glasses. Despite his altered state and cracked rib, he quickly and deftly took hold of her wrist between his fingers, as if he were partner dancing, clear about his intent but gentle in execution.

"Easy. We're tangled—"

"Shit, sorry."

Hero relaxed and nestled into him as he separated the trapped hair fibers. She, upon release, lightly held his fingers. A tactile conversation ensued. Magnus implied that he was sorry for being so out of it. She gave his fingers a playful squeeze, telling him to not be jealous of Henry and his Porche, and more.

Clam-lips, no slouch in the ways of the world, laughed. "You two are cute."

At Brew 22 the baristas recognized Magnus and praised his girly pajama-wear. Five minutes and a half-latte later the drilling behind the eyes ceased.

Henry, despite having the fastest car on 101, settled into a slot in a crawling queue of campers and trucks. His driving style made clear the journey of his life. He would become one of those super-smart financial advisors who, in a low Vassar voice, tells the client to stay the course, ride out the corrections, and invest in index funds.

Before that moment when she had let him hold her wrist, Magnus had imagined Henry and Hero as a happy-ever-after story, and that their progeny would be rich enough to avoid the struggle to survive on an Earth ravaged by climate change, greed, and political violence. Note to Dante Alighieri: *Add tenth circle for assholes destroying the planet. As for me, I'll see you on the eighth floor.* Here, he visualized the escalator arriving at a floor filled with mannequins of con men and fraudsters. The escalators perplexed Magnus. His escalator ascended. It should be descending.

Ten miles later—halfway home—Hero woke Magnus. She put her lips to his ear to be heard over the road noise but not shout.

"Can we talk about what's going on. Or maybe a thank you."

He was carsick and depressed and confused. The meds were wearing off and the pain worsening. Clam-lips, sensing Magnus's confusion, acted like the nice guy that he was. Someone had put Magnus's coffee in the cup holder.

Clam-lips' front top teeth grew bigger, awning the lower lip. When he spoke, the awning flapped. "No need Magnus. Rest up."

"Didn't want to breathe on you." He was unable to finish the thanks because he couldn't remember if the *th* in thanks was a voiced or voiceless fricative. He remembered it being backwards in that the voiceless *th* was the sound that was accompanied by a puff of air.

"I'm sorry, Hero. It's the goddamned drugs. I'll shuddup. Thanks. I mean it. You too, Henry. I don't want to be an ungrateful ass. Thank you."

She scrunched her nosed and blew him a kiss to acknowledge that she was good and that Magnus had done his best.

Henry repeated what he had said earlier: "You guys are cute."

Chicken Soup

"It seems our roles are reversed, Magnus."

Miss Angel, a veteran caregiver, carefully handed him a mug of hot chicken soup. She had dropped by to see how he was doing. The care basket beside her had contained a thermos of soup, two still-warm three-cheese sourdough biscuits, and six chocolate chip cookies. Magnus was about to try the soup.

"Thank you, Miss Angel."

"Don't burn your tongue!"

His lenses fogged when he whistled air across the hot liquid. He would have hopped up to get an ice cube from the fridge, but that wouldn't have been consistent with his convalescent state, plus he didn't want Miss Angel to feel unneeded. And it really might hurt.

"Could you please get an ice cube for me?"

Miss Angel rose and retrieved a few ice cubes from the icemaker. Magnus held out the cup and Miss Angel, without ceremony, put two small pieces of ice in the broth. She tossed the extras in the sink.

"New glasses?"

"Backups."

"Good."

"Shouldn't you be in bed?" she asked.

"No bed. In fact, Dr. Wheelwright said the opposite. Moving is good. Not overdoing it, no running for a couple weeks. Mostly, de-stress. Watch the blood pressure. Usual drill for a sixty-year-old."

"Heaven forbid! Sixty, we can't have that."

"Sorry. No offense."

She laughed. "No offense taken. Hah! My blood pressure is one-twenty over sixty-eight, my dear."

"I've been worried about you," Magnus declared his concern. "We haven't been reading. I've hardly seen you, even around town. And you seemed down when you visited at the hospital."

Miss Angel objected. "Ah! That was because you were quite *up*. Those not on opioids or whatever you had taken might have *seemed* down to you."

"Yeah, well, sorry. It was a double whammy, worrying about Lee and the meds messing with me."

"Your assessment of my condition is not entirely off the mark. My funk is intellectual, not physical. It's a damned book I'm reading."

"The one you were reading at the hospital?"

"Yes."

"So let it go."

"I can't. I finished it. Once. But I now must re-read the work . . . chronologically."

"For self-punishment? Subject?"

A hand wave dismissed the question, though she answered anyway: "Addiction, entertainment, Hamlet, tennis . . ."

"Hamlet and tennis?"

"Yes. Tennis was quite popular in Shakespeare's day. *Henry V*, there's mention of a gift of tennis 'B.A.L.L.E.S.'—if I recall correctly."

"Miss Angel," Magnus thought the snarkiness endearing, "if you don't want to talk about it, that's cool."

For the next few minutes they sat in silence, Miss Angel thinking and Magnus eating.

"Magnus, dear Magnus—"

He let his spoon rest in the bowl.

"A brilliant, labyrinthine work." She was still answering his earlier question. "Two notions resonate, or are what I would describe as apt, well-suited to our conditions. One—I'm thinking of you here—is the author's deep dive into what it means to lead an authentic life."

"An athletic life?"

He had misheard. She corrected him. "An *authentic* life. But yes, the author does a fair description of what I imagine an *athletic* life to be. That is, for a professional or near professional athlete. This, perhaps, is apropos to you as well."

"Because I'm a dumb jock?"

"No. It's because of how you use your athleticism. A living metaphor: seeking excellence; running from things.

"Yeah, like running from Lee."

"Hogwash! Don't play the child. I . . . Well, people can run from themselves, from something authentic they're afraid to acknowledge."

Magnus returned to the soup, had a sip or two.

Miss Angel backpedaled. "Authenticity, too, can be a sort of posturing. Perhaps the life less examined is not so bad. What do I know!"

"The other notion?" he asked.

Miss Angel didn't hesitate. "Ah, there's *my* burden: flow."

His brain wasn't ready for this. Magnus wanted to move on to chocolate chip cookies. "Do I ask?"

"That one—" The notion amused her, as if a quiet, inner, comedic conversation were happening. "That one, my dear. Oh, I own it!"

"Would it help if I read the book? We could talk about it."

"No. Not now. Not yet."

Magnus considered asking why she thought he should put off reading *Infinite Jest*, but he had lost interest—maybe that was exactly why she had suggested deferring the read. Their conversation overwhelmed and tested his attention. Yet one realization followed: their book-reading sessions filled gaps not only in his literary knowledge, but in his life.

He kept it light. "Sounds depressing, not fun."

"Both, yes. I can't shake it. The work—which, ironically, is both incredibly funny and shockingly gruesome—has cast a pall over my own efforts. My work, by comparison, is so common, trivial, banal . . ."

Miss Angel lowered her head and tossed her arms up in the air, a gesture of futility. "Enough! Here I am, talking about myself. It is your silent power, Mr. Krum, to deflect and distract and with a wave of the wand—or soup spoon—to exact the truth from those around you. Are you even aware of this?"

"Got a whole fistful of truth from Lee, alright."

Magnus ate quietly. He gave the impression that he had been thinking about Miss Angel's words, but really he couldn't think about anything. That health issues had not been the source of Miss Angel's worries was a relief. Writers, he generalized, were an awfully moody, self-involved lot. And people, he generalized again, honestly didn't think that much about other people.

They sat on the Beast, not speaking for a few minutes. Miss Angel had something more though, he could feel it.

When the clock had run out for Magnus to speak, she began. "I told Dr. Wheelwright not to worry about the bill."

"What bill?"

"*The bill*, Magnus. If you don't want to apply for support, I assume you have a good reason for not doing so. I know you have some money, but medical expenses are no joke. I shall pay the sum you owe. The hospital has my billing information."

Without sounding overbearing, Magnus declared. "You can't do that."

"I can and I did. Consider it a gift, young man. I never loan money. If you gift something back to me someday, fine. If not, that's fine, too. It changes nothing in our relationship. I'm uncomfortable with what *loans*, what money, does to relationships."

She was right about the giving versus loaning. He had never thought about it, but he liked the idea and vowed to adopt the policy. Another plus, the obvious one, was that the financial obligation would not raise identity issues at the hospital. He would pay her back, in kind if not in cash.

"Thank you. I *will* pay you back."

"More important, Magnus, what are you going to do about Lee Holder?"

Magnus had been thinking about little else since leaving the hospital. "There's the rub, Miss Angel. There's the rub."

Stair Fall

The next day, feeling better, Magnus drove to the Nehalem Bay Health Center in Wheeler to fill a prescription ordered by Dr. Wheelwright. Being in a small-town, care at the Health Center was personal. It was his first visit. But the next time he walked through the door, the staff would recognize him. This meant that he would have to remember his story—a tumble down a slope while hiking up Neahkahnie—and again, since this was a small town, eventually everyone would learn about Lee. Eventually, he would need an alternative story to explain why he hadn't told the truth in the first place: he hurt too much, Lee had been going through a troubled time, the truth embarrassed.. It would be a story that was easy to believe, that people could identify with and therefore would want to believe.

In the reception area, arriving patients and clinicians inquired about each other's families and caught up on topics of interest to the community before addressing whatever medical issue that had been the reason for their convening. Magnus enjoyed this custom. It gave him a glimmer of hope, a bit of faith that everyday people were okay. Who knows? Maybe the world would meet the challenge of climate change and people would become less divisive and stop senselessly slaughtering each other. Clearly, his mood had improved.

On the return, back in Manzanita and driving down the hill on Laneda, he slowed for a crowd that had gathered in front of Shortley Holder's home, a cedar-sided two-story affair with the main entrance at street level on Laneda. An in-bloom, eight-foot-tall escallonia hedge wrapped the entire backyard and separated the house from the empty lot next door. A lilac encrusted arbor marked the entry to the backyard. Stairs from the enclosed garden led to a private deck and separate entrance on the second floor. Potted roses, as ambitious as the escallonia, sprawled across the railing of the rear deck.

Besides the pedestrian onlookers, several vehicles—including an ambulance, a car from the Manzanita police and one from the Tillamook sheriff's department—blocked one lane of Laneda. Police were stringing the front of the house with yellow tape. The Holders were nowhere to be seen. The sheriff put his arm around someone's shoulders, consoling them. Neighbors gawked and gabbed.

When he saw Miss Angel in the crowd, Magnus stopped and lowered Subi's window.

"Miss Angel!" He hollered to get her attention. She turned, startled.

"What's going on?" he asked.

She wore a coat too warm for the weather and Magnus wondered if underneath she was wearing only a nightgown or pajamas and had quickly put on the coat when she had heard the commotion.

"Lee will be devastated. Though I feel little sympathy for the man. His father—you know his father, Shortley? Well, of course, you do."

Magnus nodded yes. They had talked plenty about the Holders. Something had rattled Miss Angel. She seemed distraught."

A less circumspect neighbor standing beside Miss Angel spoke for her. "Shortley took a tumble. Broke his neck and that 'lectric wheelchair o' his broke up all over him."

Behind Miss Angel and the neighbor, I glimpsed the EMTs rolling a gurney with a draped body into the back of the ambulance. With his outsized temper stilled and the body detached from its weighty electric wheelchair, the form appeared frail and shrunken.

"Bet somebody shoved Shortley," another gawker volunteered. She must have known Miss Angel as she directed the comment to her.

"Yes, I suppose that could have happened," Miss Angel replied, then leaned over to speak to Magnus. "Terrible things like that don't happen in Manzanita."

The gawker, eavesdropping, added, "Not since Jeffrey fell outta that tree he was trimming. He made it but his brain didn't."

The commenter, uninvited, joined Miss Angel in bending down to speak to Magnus. Magnus leaned out the window to listen and then wished he hadn't.

"I think it was foul play, real foul. That's what I think. These days, you gotta look out for number one. You got a gun, dontcha?"

He ignored her, although she tried to stare a response out of him.

"Can I give you a lift home, Miss Angel? Would you like me to stay at the house with you?"

Miss Angel brightened briefly. "Ah ha, *Les Assassins en Fauteuils Rollents* lose one of their own."

The private joke flew by Magnus. His knee-jerk reaction to the French and pseudo-French was the universal Spanish response: "Mande?"

"Sorry, yes. Both would be nice. But I'm only down a street. And the people next door are home. I mean, at their place, next-door."

Nothing Miss Angel had said made sense to Magnus. He, in the role of caregiver, the dance partner, insisted: "A ride, anyway. C'mon."

Her coat fell open; the nighty fluttered. She was shivering and needed to get out of the cold and damp. "Please. Get in."

"A gun, Magnus. Can you imagine?"

He thought about O'Conner's short story about the Misfit, about how the peaceful setting for the story lured the reader into complacency. Magnus wasn't an escaped convict, but he was a wanted man. Had he brought bad luck to the townspeople? Prior to his arrival, nobody in Manzanita had fallen down a flight of stairs and been crushed by their own wheelchair. He remembered maneuvering Holder through the gravel at Panda Bakery. The damned thing probably weighed a hundred pounds.

"No guns, thanks. I'm thinking more nuclear weapons. Wave the flag, go big or go home." Magnus's poor attempt at humor conjured up the image of Lee's revolver. The image homesteaded in some part of his brain. When he looked in the mirror, the purple bruise on his cheek refreshed the memory.

Miss Angel walked around the front of Subi. Magnus popped open the passenger door. They drove to her place and arrived as usual, greeted by the address sign swinging by a single nail. Once inside, Miss Angel excused herself to change into warmer clothes. Magnus put water in the electric kettle for tea.

A half-dozen yellow, letter-sized notepads cluttered the top of her cherry wood desk and shared the space with mounds of colored index cards stacked in a manner that revealed a readable corner at the top right of each card. Obviously, she was working on something. He hadn't opened the book she had given him, unsure why. Was he afraid that his impression of Miss Angel would change? What if her work turned out to be sophomoric dribble? He didn't want to be disappointed. On the other hand, would it matter?

Behind the desk a paned glass window framed a twenty-year-old rose bush about to explode into blossoms. Midsummer, with the window cracked open, the aroma from the roses would fill the room.

The hot pot whistled for attention. He would ask her to tell him about the book she had lent him. And then he would share his fear of starting it, knowing that the discussion would distract her and make her laugh. One treated the elderly with the same parenting tools one used for the very young.

Over tea, Miss Angel avoided talk about the accident, talk about Lee and his threats, and talk about how Lee would deal with the loss of his father. Some other matter preoccupied her. Whatever it was, it was sufficiently grave to overshadow the last few days' drama, and it was sufficiently personal that she would not share it with Magnus. He assumed it was the *flow* business she had alluded to at the hospital. She was onto his waiting game and not about to be tricked into talking.

When Magnus brought up the book she had given him, Miss Angel switched the topic to bees, and reminded herself that she would have to put up screens when the Oregon Grape bloomed. The mature shrub shared the window frame with the Nootka rose, another bee-attracting shrub. Miss Angel swatted and waved her hands overhead, telling and demonstrating how bees swarmed the plants when they bloomed.

"That's the only time I need screens," she repeated. Her mind was elsewhere, batting away things she didn't want to talk about.

Magnus listened, then reminded her about her book. The question was not a deflection. "The book?"

"Yes. Be patient, Magnus. It is about . . . bees! Read it. You'll understand." She seemed annoyed that he hadn't been listening or that he hadn't started the book.

They parted some minutes later. Magnus left, feeling unfulfilled. Something, there was something going on with her. She had followed him out and stopped at the doorway. She had raised a finger as if she were testing the breeze or about to call him back.

Félix

Five days passed without a word from Lee Holder. In the interim Magnus had collected everything he could about the Holders' porn operation and stashed it on a server only he and the Twins had access to, leaving instructions with the Twins to give the file to the appropriate authorities should anything untoward happen to him. Magnus had recast Constanza's threat and given it teeth.

A chance encounter with Holder's receptionist, Meredith, failed to explain Lee's absence.

"He'd said something about urgent business in Portland. I'm guessing it's about his father. Or some estate thing. So sad, isn't it. Anywho, I was off visiting my sister in Missoula and Lee hasn't called. But you try me tomorrow. Better yet, come by!"

When Magnus failed to respond, she cheerfully added, "Can I give him a message?"

Not a lot of remorse there, Magnus noted. If anything, she seemed pleased that Holder senior's grumpy presence would no longer grace the premises. Could she be in a relationship with Lee?

Magnus couldn't separate Lee the man, from the memory of staring down the barrel of his revolver. He resolved to put an end to the bullying; he would turn the tables. "Tell him thanks for *all* the videos. Be sure to say *all* of them. He'll understand."

Tomorrow—assuming Lee was back—he would confront him. Any threats would lead to a sweeping disclosure of Holders' dark web business. Magnus bet that Lee's decision would come down to money. Was harming Magnus or revealing his identity worth the risk of Magnus destroying the family's shady enterprise? Lee well knew Magnus had the chops to do just that.

With Holder matters in abeyance, Magnus turned to the next item on the agenda. At the request of Constanza's father, Magnus had agreed to meet with a trusted Reyes family friend who was visiting from Mexico, the man Constanza had referred to as Tío Félix, although he was not a blood relation. José had not explained why he had suggested the meeting, beyond that it was work related and connected to what had happened to Constanza. Regarding Constanza, José further requested that Magnus give Félix a thumb drive containing a copy of the video Lee Holder had made, and that Magnus delete any other record of the video.

Shortly after their conversation, Félix called from José's number and set the lunch location and time for Trio Loco at noon. When Magnus told Félix he had other commitments—the other commitment being an errand for Hero—Félix, in few words, told him that he, Magnus, did *not* have any other engagements. A time constraint, Félix apologized. Magnus figured he could catch up with Hero later, so he accommodated the change in plans.

The go-to dive for Latino workers and tourists who wanted a reasonably priced place to eat and no epic wait was El Trio Loco, a Mexican restaurant not unlike innumerable family friendly and family run Mexican eateries cloned and thriving in anywhere, USA. The unremarkable, predictable food made Magnus homesick every time he ate there. He usually sat near the kitchen and eavesdropped on the cooks' palaver. Menu item labels were an English-Spanish composite; one might argue the same for the food—the exception being a few seafood dishes. The service was friendly and fast.

He arrived to find Félix at a booth in the small room next to the primary dining area. Félix surprised.

The first surprise was that he spoke excellent English. The confusion in Magnus's expectations had been because Constanza had described him as a contractor and said nothing about his speaking English. What's more, José had mentioned that Félix had driven, not flown, from Chihuahua. The distance suggested that Félix was someone with more time than money. The next surprise—this one, perhaps only an extension of the first—was the disconnect between the worn Carhartt work attire and the polished manners; between the thick, muscled hands, and the manicured nails. Félix moved with physical and social ease, and had greeted Magnus in a purposeful, professional manner that implied that he was all business, as in a man of affairs with little time to waste, a man comfortable managing people, a man without an ounce of self-doubt. He was mid-forties and a solid two-hundred-plus pounds, balding and with a thick block for a head that seemed smaller than it was only because of the massive stump of a neck the head sat on.

The black Chevy Suburban he had parked in front of Trio Loco had tinted windows and Texas plates. Someone had inscribed "wash me" and a big heart in the dust on the rear door. Caked mud and dirt lined the vehicle's wheel wells and underbody. Magnus casually scanned for and failed to find a rental sticker on the car. This prompted him to memorize the plate number and make a mental note to track down the registration. A few things about Félix, as with Magnus, didn't add up.

Magnus ordered tortilla soup; Félix went for steak fajitas. When Magnus added a Modelo Negra and tried to order a beer for Félix, he declined politely and asked for an horchata. He didn't drink, not while he was working. Therefore, Magnus concluded, this was a working lunch.

"Thank you for making time to meet with me today. I'm imposing my schedule on you, and I am sure you are a very busy man. You see, I have to leave day after tomorrow."

"José mentioned you had driven here from Chihuahua! That's a hell of a drive."

"You are not mistaken! Without stopping, not counting the border crossing, the trip takes thirty-one hours. For me, it was several days longer!" He laughed to himself and continued. "I went here," he gestured, "I went there," another gesture. "Too much in one trip. Too much driving! I rarely visit the North. This trip was my opportunity to see dear friends along the way, sort out one or two unimportant business matters, and to convince myself that I was a tourist on vacation."

"Did you succeed? What was your favorite part of the drive?"

"Ah!" Félix's grin—a suspension bridge across the wide, square face —expanded. He was reliving moments from the drive; his expression changed with the panorama in his mind. "Somewhat, yes. A success. It is a challenge, when you work, work, work, to—as they say—stop to smell the roses. Ah, but the waterfalls in the Columbia Gorge, Multnomah Falls. Magnificent! They reminded me of Basaseachi. You know this fact perhaps, that Cascada de Basaseachi is the second tallest waterfall in Mexico."

"I did not know, but now it's on my radar—"

The waiter interrupted. He placed their drinks on the table.

"The falls are located in the State of Chihuahua, to the west." Félix took a long drink of water, emptying the glass and following up with an approving sip of his horchata. "But to business. Carmen and José called. Carmen was very, very worried. The Reyes are family to me, you understand?"

"Yes, so they've said." Magnus gave the expected response, drawn into the stilted politeness of the conversation. He wanted to bring it down to Earth. "José said you were a contractor or something. Are you going to help with the bakery?"

"Yes, of course. I will help, but more in the capacity of, let's say, a developer."

After he had answered, he veered in a different direction. "It was terrible, what these unscrupulous men did. You know the men I'm referring to?" He waited for a nod of agreement before continuing. Magnus delivered the nod. "It was terrible how they took advantage of little Constanza. Would this be extortion?" Magnus added nothing and let him go on. "I would call it extortion. I suppose," he added, "human nature being what it is, bad things can happen anywhere. Even in this a shy, little town, this pearl by the sea."

Magnus squeezed the lime into the top of his beer, leaving it in the bottle and not bothering with the chilled glass. He tasted the beer, needing to clear his throat.

Félix, quietly, but still in a voice loud enough to make Magnus uncomfortable, sang: " ' Jalisco, Jalisco, Jalisco . . . la perla más rara.' Do you know this song, Magnus?"

He did, and added the line after the opener, saying, not singing the words: 'Tú tienes tu novia . . .' "

"There, you don't know your geography. But you are a romantic, a man who remembers lyrics to a Mexican folk song. Constanza said you were a man with corazón!" He bowed his gigantic, square head. This, apparently, was worthy of honoring.

Magnus noted beads of sweat dotting the top of his head except for a discolored swath of scar tissue, evidence of a burn, perhaps a childhood mishap. He looked at the scalded red patch on his own hand.

Félix behaved as though the remembrance of the incident with Constanza caused personal pain and sadness. The dark expression in his eyes remained as he lifted his head. His eyes telegraphed an unfamiliar emotion, one that Magnus didn't understand and that made him feel sufficiently uncomfortable to look around and see if other people in El Trio Loco had noticed. In a flash, it came to him: Cruelty.

"Such things," Félix was back on what had happened to Constanza, "such things traumatize a woman of any age. She is very young, you know."

Magnus nodded back. His neck was sore from all the nodding. His lunchmate continued. "The family, their little business. Threatened. You ask if I, Félix, am upset?" He answered the unprompted, rhetorical question: "Yes, Félix is upset."

The food arrived. Magnus thanked the waiter. Félix stared straight ahead, transfixed.

The dark direction of the conversation was uncomfortable. Magnus asked, "Your English is native?"

Félix returned from the dark place as deftly as he had entered it. He opened his hands on the table, turning them palms up, acting the supplicant.

"Yes. So is yours, and for a similar reason. Constanza said your mother is from Cuba. Mine was a Chihuahua native. Fue profesora de Inglés." The corners of his mouth turned down. "Very serious, and very strict!"

"Was, you said was?"

"She died last year. On her deathbed she asked me what I would say at her memorial? I told I would say that *I was always treated kindly*! Hah!" He feigned anger and waved his massive finger at the air. "Remember, she is on her deathbed. She sits up and scolds me! 'Mi amor! Don't use the passive voice!' Those were nearly her last words. She quickly realized I had made a joke to make her smile. The tears, oh my God. They flowed like Basaseachi!" He laughed and tapped the thick finger to his blackboard sized forehead. "In here, I hear her voice!" He opened and closed his hands, again displaying them palms up. "I feel her tears. Even through these callouses, I feel them."

The image of his strict but caring mother hung over their conversation. She might as well have been sitting at the table. Magnus said he was sorry for Félix's loss. He was. Someday he would experience a similar loss, a loss that would never leave. Félix had made it feel real.

"Your father?" Magnus kept the conversation going, pausing to eat.

In a small, private voice, Félix recited grace. He bowed his head. Magnus noticed the cross hanging from a silver chain nearly lost in the folds of skin around his neck and shoulders. He started in on his food, finishing each bite and putting aside his fork to speak.

"A geology consultant, originally from the Midwest, from Chicago.

The West side, if you know it. He worked for mining companies all over Mexico and fell in love with the country and, of course, he fell in love with my beautiful mother. They met at a grocery store when he offered to carry her bags. She instantly knew he would be her hombre. He carried her groceries for fifty years!"

Small talk filled the next three-quarters of an hour. Magnus's answers to Félix's innocuous inquiries sounded increasingly false. Félix must have picked up on it, but consciously chose not to challenge Magnus. He had taken sides. Félix claimed he was a consultant for a Chihauhua-based project development company that sold its services to foreign companies setting up shop in Mexico. He implied that the company was a spinoff of McKinsey, a company that once had, and perhaps still had, a large presence in Mexico.

For the moment, his story sounded credible. Magnus and Félix had agreed to accept each other's bullshit, whatever it was. The plates were half-empty, and the stomachs too full. Such was the serving size at Trio Loco and one of the many reasons the restaurant was popular with the work crowd.

Félix put his hand over Magnus's. The pleasantries, a social necessity between Latinos, were over. It was time for the ask.

"So, my friend, do you have the memory stick?"

José had told Magnus that Félix was going to question him about what had happened to Constanza. The other request, to which Magnus had agreed, was to give Félix a thumb drive with a copy of the video. Separately, Magnus had checked with Constanza to confirm that she was okay with her father's request. Maybe it was wrong to trust a minor—if she was a minor. Even so, it was her call. Constanza had replied yes.

Magnus reached into his pocket and held out the drive. Félix wiped his hands with a napkin and took it.

"The only copy, yes?"

Magnus considered lying, but didn't. "No. I have a backup in the dark web. No one else can access it."

"This is what you do, computer work?"

"IT, yes."

"Have you watched the video—"

"No." Magnus answered the rest of the question before Félix asked. "I knew if I watched the video, I would think about it every time I saw Constanza. I don't want to think about her like that. There's one copy online, in case you don't do what you promised Carmen and José."

"You think you know about things you don't know about." He waited a moment, then laughed. "You are young."

Was that arrogance? No, he was stating a fact. Félix twirled the drive around in his fingers.

"If I tell you to destroy the copy, will you do that?"

"Sure. If Constanza's family is okay with it, I'll destroy it. If they want another copy, or a partial copy, for the authorities or something, I'll give it to them. They know I won't do anything stupid with the video."

"You didn't answer my question, so let me give you the correct answer." As if by design, the eyes in the oversized head intimidated. Magnus defanged the threat by imagining Félix's head as a big russet potato with little plastic eyes, a Mr. Potato Head. "If I, Félix, tell you to destroy the video, then you say 'yes Félix, I will destroy the video.'"

Magnus refused to be intimidated, not by a potato head. "Félix, what's your game?"

"Not a game. I can insist, Magnus. And I am a very persuasive man." Still twirling the drive, but faster. Was *he* nervous?

A scramble for a middle ground ensued. "How about a compromise?" Magnus suggested. "I erase the copy in a week. That gives the family a window to think it over, and time to confirm it's okay to delete the online copy. That's not a big ask."

Félix leaned back. The backboard of the booth creaked. He focused on Magnus, then slurped up the last of his horchata like he was sucking the life out of Magnus. For whatever reason, his gaze jumped back and forth between the Suburban and the waiter at the Trio Loco's reception desk. The empty glass alit silently on the table and that Golden Gate grin returned. "I see why Constanza likes you. You should take her dancing. Le encanta bailar." He held the thumb drive up to my face. "It would take her mind off of *this*."

"I know. And I will."

"Prométeme."

"Si, lo prometo."

The few words in Spanish reminded Magnus of promises he had made to his mother, to Carolina, to Zio Vinnie, even to IBM and the NSA. Magnus closed his eyes and let his head fall back, re-logging the litany of promises and pseudo-promises he carried in his heart.

"I've got to stop making promises." He uttered the words aloud, not at all meaning to. The thought, so sincere, so deep, had escaped on its own. He tilted forward and opened his eyes and faced off with Félix's square mug and junk-yard grab-jaw hands. He visualized the hydraulic forearms overhead, a hand palming his head and ripping it off. *Maybe*, he thought, *I should start now.*

Félix laughed. He seemed to have not heard Magnus or had simply ignored him. "What is important in life?" Félix asked.

Magnus did his usual. He waited, again assuming the question to have been rhetorical.

"Only two things, Magnus. Survival and Love. People need and use each other for both."

Magnus thought the comment half-baked, philosophically speaking. He humored his interlocutor. "Am I using you right now?"

Félix leaned back in the chair, the amused teacher waiting for his slow student to catch up. "You are. I'm not sure if you know you are."

"And the Swiftie bracelets?" Magnus didn't know what made him bring that up.

Félix beamed. "She showed you! That was love, Magnus. *Love!*"

He checked his watch, a vintage Timex—a touch of Vinnie—and pronounced lunch over. Then put a hundred-dollar bill on the table and shook Magnus's hand. With a tip of his head but not a departing word, he was out the door, leaving Magnus to settle the bill and a host of unanswered questions. His last word stayed with Magnus. "Love."

Magnus checked his phone. He had silenced notifications but had received several texts, including several from Hero.

<<HW: Can't meet later. Have to drive Mom to Portland for tests. And I gotta see my shrink.>>

<<MK: Everybody ok?>>

<<HW: Mom's great. Considering. The shrink, not so sure.>>

<<MK: hmmmm>>

<<HW: explain later. Back tomorrow or day after. Important we talk in person.>>

<<MK: Call now?>>

The suggestion got a thumbs down. Whatever Hero wanted to tell him would have to wait.

A Perfect Day

After the depressing events of yesterday, Magnus was determined to make the best of the new day. The day, for its part, cooperated and oozed perfection. A few morning clouds and a temperate breeze followed him down to the jetty and then, as if on cue, the breeze changed direction and was at his back for the return run. The wet sand was firm but not too firm, ideal for running. But Magnus had walked. The ribs hurt when he ran.

He had encountered a group of snowy plovers working the wrack line, feeding and finding nest material and then zig-zagging up the sand toward a nest site. Although he couldn't see the nest, Magnus wanted to record the location so Hero could put it in her log. She would want the time and weather, plus data about predators, disturbances, and tracks. He photographed the plover tracks—they were the distinctive pigeon-toed track a plover makes—and he pinned the location on Google Maps, adding notes. No corvids in sight; a Cooper's hawk, some distance inland. For good measure, he marked the location with three sticks of driftwood which he placed just above the tide line and in the shape of an H. The sighting had been at the midpoint of the shore restoration zone, another data point that would make Hero happy. The Oregon Parks and Recreation Department project was a leveled section of the dunes where invasive species of European and American Eastern beachgrass had been eradicated and replaced with Western beachgrass to re-create a sustainable habitat for plovers and other shore life.

The ocean tides temporarily washed away thoughts about Mr. Shortley Holder's sheeted, crumpled corpse. Near the end of his walk, an ornery gull aped the scratchy voice of Miss Angel's neighbor: "Somebody shoved Shortley!" Like a needle stuck in the groove of an old LP, it played and replayed in his head.

Relieved to be home, he stood for ten minutes under a stinging hot shower. Routine chores followed: check mail at the Post and hit the Manzanita News for coffee. He chastised himself for driving, especially the two-block segment between the Post and News, but the recovering body had had enough physical for the day.

No mail was the norm, but Magnus enjoyed the ritual of going to the Post Office and chatting with the Postmaster. Occasionally, he did receive mail: a catalog from REI, newsletters from the Tillamook PUD, and resident directed advertisements.

The atmosphere at the Manzanita News was anything but normal. The unpleasant aftermath of recent events revealed itself in a nervous edge in people's voices, a quirky self-consciousness in how customers moved. Even the inanimate objects—knick-knacks, magazines, espresso machine, puzzle-boxes—seemed outsized and overly bright. The eyes of sparrows, usually harmless in intent, instead appeared as predatory, furtive, and threatening.

Because the Manzanita police station was across the street, the News was the watering hole for officers and staff. As Magnus entered, Jock, a handsome new guy on the force, wrapped up a breezy tête-à-tête with the barista. The racket from the coffee grinder and milk steamer overlaid the conversation.

"For real?" Morgan, Magnus's favorite and very talented barista—a straight-A student—sounded shocked. This was not ordinary coffee-house banter, whatever they were discussing. Black lashes fluttered at certain words. Her jet black nail-polished fingers dispatched with mundane tasks—charging a card, taking an order, toasting and cream-cheesing a bagel—to free up moments to catch what Jock had been discoursing about.

"For real," Jock, the cop, matched her tone, though at a lower pitch. This was not a discussion about frothing oat versus almond milk.

"You're not shittin' me or making this up?"

"I am not. It'll be all over town by midday. Hell, it'll be national headlines."

"Holy Mary Mother of Jesus!" Aileron-like lashes lowered, and Morgan threw her head and hair back as if to pray. The tips of ten black fingernails—two giant five-legged black widow spiders—crouched atop the countertop, ready to pounce.

Other customers tuned in.

"Where'd they find it?" An older woman with hair tied into a tight, white, bagel-shaped bun had been close enough to have overheard. She asked those around her: "Should I call it *it* or *him*?"

"What are you talkin' 'bout, woman?" her silver-haired husband asked.

Bagel-bun lady muttered, more to herself than to him, "I suppose it could be a *her*. Where was it?"

Jock exhaled; he breathed easier now that Act I was under his belt; the cat was out of the bag. He knew that eventually he would have to go public and add details. But so far, the reception had been satisfactory.

"North end of the beach, about where the rocks start. Right there. Bobbing around in the surf and rocks, like one of those foam beach balls."

"Who found what?" Another question from another customer.

Morgan answered on behalf of the police officer. "Jock said it was the nice old man who lives in that place with the big glass windows."

"Harrison, Willy Harrison," someone else added, "the artist. I know him. Lived there forever."

Jock tried to pay, but Morgan waved him off. He thanked her and announced to her and the assembly that he had to get back to work. Several people wished him well and good luck and keep us posted.

"Old Willy Harrison was on his deck, getting ready to paint." Morgan had the attention of the crowd. The steaming and grinding paused. "He paints before it gets windy," she informed. "Artists like morning light and all that."

Bagel-bun lady, her voice sympathetic: "Is the poor soul okay? He's got to be eighty."

"I assume. I mean, Jock didn't say."

"What'd it look like?"

"Jock said," Morgan took center stage, "at first Mr. Harrison thought it was one of those Japanese glass floats covered with seaweed—"

"I like those floats. I found one in Lincoln City, that event they do—" someone interrupted.

"That's not the same," another customer commented.

Morgan waited a moment, then continued. "Mr. Harrison thought nothing of it. Then his wife came out. She's a birder, y'know. She had her binoculars and focused the binoculars on it and screamed bloody hell."

A woman in the know and with an appropriately shrill voice agreed. "Christ! I'd scream bloody hell!"

Being next in line after Jock, Magnus stepped up to the counter and ordered a twelve-ounce triple shot latte with oat milk. Morgan knew his regular. Before he had asked, she had written it on the cup and passed the cup to her co-worker.

"You heard about it, right?" Morgan asked Magnus, who was at a loss and trying to not think about anything.

He asked anyway. "About the beach ball thing?"

"A head. They found a *human* head on the beach."

He thought he had mis-heard Morgan's words. He leaned over the counter. The bean grinding that had restarted, then stopped. Same with the steamer. Both baristas, as if co-conspirators, wanted to see his reaction.

"A *human* head," Morgan repeated. "They found a human fucking head. A *fresh* one."

"*Fresh*, you say?" Magnus asked. "Not stale?" He regretted the dumb-ass comment before he'd finished saying it. Christ, she wasn't joking.

"Not funny, Magnus. A fucking head, a real *human* head, was up in the rocks up there by James Road. You know where that is?"

"I do." He tried to sound apologetic.

"Jock said nobody knows, like, who it belongs to. Not yet."

"Belongs to?" Magnus couldn't wrap his brain around the head talk and all of Morgan's "Jock saids." How the hell would party A have lost party B's head? They were not talking about the head of a bear in Central Park. That had a reasonable explanation—sort of. Right. Wrong. Clearly, he was confused and needed coffee. "I assume it was a boating accident."

Morgan shrugged her shoulders, tilted her head, and raised her hands in the air beside her ears. She could have been posing for a scary Halloween photo or preparing to leap to the ceiling and hang there by her fingernails.

Magnus struggled to not overreact. Because, what if wasn't a boating accident? Of course, not reacting was equally compromising. "Well, they'll figure it out. But holy crap."

"Holy crap is right," Morgan continued. "Jock said it was really fresh."

That word, fresh, refused to go away. "I'd guess that would make it easier to ID. Do they know who it is?"

"They do, but Jock won't say. I don't think he would, 'cause he's a cop."

The man behind Magnus had been quiet until now. "Yeah, could mean it's someone local. That would be sad, really sad for everybody."

"Yeah, local. Not good." Morgan had a habit of repeating what people said. In her defense, she had to do that with drink orders, to make sure she'd heard the order correctly. Her co-worker placed his latte on the pickup counter. He tested the drink. Perfect temp, perfect foam, perfect ratio of espresso to oat milk, but not perfect enough to get the *head* out of his head.

When, for example, had the head, being fresh, had its last coffee? What was it going to do now? Go on ice? Pose for a weird mug shot? Lucky some kids hadn't found the damned thing and spiked it on top a driftwood pole à la *Lord of the Flies*. What would be the first thing a medical examiner would do with a head without a body? Magnus was afraid to read the news, even the puzzle. What if the *Wordle* word was *fresh*? He'd lose his fucking mind. The day, the perfect day during which he had planned to not think about Holder's death, Miss Angel's writer's angst, Hero's struggles with her past and her mom having cancer, the dread of the next confrontation with Lee, and his own self-imposed miseries—the perfect day—had gone to shit.

Some part of his brain put the pieces together before Magnus consciously did the same. With the latte still warming Subi's cupholder, he drove a few blocks east to the Highlands, a recent housing development on one of the few remaining large parcels of buildable land in Manzanita. Residents occupied a dozen homes; another six were under construction, some with footings poured and the bones of wood-framed walls in place.

At one of sites a framing crew orchestrated the placement of pre-built roof trusses that a mobile crane was lifting off a nearby flatbed truck. The man standing beside the truck and directing the workers fit the profile: a tank sized Latino about the same height as Félix and dressed in well-worn Carhartt attire. Magnus parked Subi and waved to him. Plans in hand, the supervisor removed his hardhat and walked over, turning his head once or twice to check on a worker spinning a large truss and lining it up with three other trusses that were already in place.

"Sorry to bother you."

"Can I help you?"

"I live here and I'm thinking about buying a lot nearby and being my own general contractor. I'll need a framing crew and wanted to see if you'd be interested."

"We are very busy." He made a sweeping gesture with the hand holding the plans. "Are you a GC? Do you have a license?"

"No, but I'll be the homeowner and I'm an engineer. And I'm not in a hurry. Could we, you know, talk about your schedule and terms."

"Do you have plans?"

"Yes, a small place, two-thousand square feet place. I've found a lot that's flat, easy to build on. No permit work done yet."

The man shook his head. "Permit here takes a while." The supervisor checked on his crew again and donned the hardhat. "I should go back." He waved to one of the crew, signaled some directions and said something Magnus hadn't understood.

"How about this," Magnus continued, "you're probably gonna have lunch. Can we meet at El Trio Loco? I buy lunch and show you the plans. And you give me ballpark costs and dates, or maybe a referral. No commitment, except to enjoy lunch!"

The sup grinned knowingly and waved the plans toward Subi. "What's your budget?"

Magnus had expected the question; two minutes of research on his phone had given him the answer. "Three-fifty to three-seventy-five a square foot."

"Yeah, that's good. Any less and you're kidding yourself. Okay, sure, why not? Eleven forty-five. I got a half-hour. You're buying!"

"Deal." They shook hands.

Magnus drove straight home, hopped online, and for two-hundred dollars downloaded a set of plans for a very basic two-thousand square foot beach house. He printed two pages of the overall layout and then, out of habit, erased all records of the search and download.

After the lunch with the first contractor, he later, the same day, found a second Latino contractor at another project site and arranged lunch for the following day, again at Trio Loco. He wanted the Trio Loco lunches to blur together for anyone who had seen him, and for the word to get out that he was building a place and talking to contractors—some of whom were Latino.

Félix was gone. The construction project provided cover for their meeting—a routine search for a contractor. It didn't take a rocket scientist to connect the dots: Félix's visit, the relationship to Constanza's family, the video, and Holder's death. Magnus didn't want to be one of those dots. He had no evidence for it, but Magnus believed the odds were even that the fresh head rolling around in the surf had once belonged to Lee Holder and that the man who had separated it from its body had been a square-faced Latino from Chihuahua.

To deepen his cover, shallow though it was, Magnus sent a note to Hero, announcing that he had been thinking about building a place in Manzanita, and then a second email to Constanza's father, José, thanking him for the introduction to Félix and in the note referring to Félix as a contractor/developer. He assumed José would support his version of the story. He was also certain that, if questioned, José would say nothing about his daughter's experience with the Holders. José might have to explain Félix's cameo in Manzanita, but he could easily make up a credible story, claiming that Félix was a family friend, a contractor needing work, or simply that he was one of a thousand other tourists seeing the sites along the coast. Hopefully, Magnus's name would never come up in any conversation about Félix.

A Shorter Shortley Jr.

The following day the Oregonian ran an article on the front page that asserted that the authorities had designated the beheading as a major crime and not an accidental dismemberment. The status upgrade meant that the case required engagement from a slew of agencies from the city, county, and state. Soon, the state would announce which agency would lead the investigation. The article surmised that because the severed head had turned up on a public beach, the burden of the investigation and medical examination would be the responsibility of the Oregon State Police and the State Medical Examiner.

The Manzanita police, Jock to be specific, had been the first to suggest that the head had been Lee Holder's. After Shortley Holder senior's fatal accident—which had not been treated as a crime—Jock and friends and relatives of Holder the elder had tried to contact the son. Junior, aka Lee, had not been home, hadn't shown up for work, and wasn't answering or responding to calls or texts. Lee was missing. Jock made it official and provided the State Police with a comprehensive report, including a time-stamped list of calls and interviews and a promotion-worthy summary and analysis of his investigative effort.

Overnight, Jock became an ah-shucks-just-doing-my-job celebrity. The ever-reliable baristas at the News reported that Jock hated being interrogated by the State Police because he hated tattling on neighbors and friends in Manzanita. He expounded at length to the media how "most of all" he abhorred the media.

As in any small town, word spread quickly. Supposedly, the cause of death had been the prop of a crabbing boat. Then the cause of death became the foil or fin of an errant kite-boarder. Next up was a machete wielded by a crazed antifa-fisherman, or whatever flavor maniac suited one's politics. Liberals put their money on QAnon conspiracy nuts. Whoever the perp was, most folks got onboard the "machete" bandwagon.

Fortunately, Jock the cop, whose last name was Esposito, had had firsthand experience with machete assassinations carried out by rival cartels in his childhood hometown in Quintana Roo, Mexico. He had been the first to recognize that Lee's death had been no accident, and the first to suggest a machete as the murder weapon. He had wisely advised County and State to double back and review Mr. Shortley Holder's accident. Jock, not wanting to speculate officially, nevertheless officially speculated that the two deaths in the same family in the space of a day or two were likely committed by the same person or persons.

As if it were common knowledge, everybody agreed that the head had to have been in the water for at least a couple of days for the decomposition gases to cause the tissues to bloat enough for the head to float. Everybody in town was an instant forensic expert. It was further rumored that regarding his public statements, Jock had conferred with barrista Morgan about the use of the subjunctive.

* * * *

Dr. Wheelwright had invited Magnus to stop by the house for a quick checkup, thus saving Magnus the trouble of driving to the clinic in Seaside. The two spent the first few minutes comparing notes about the double murder. An exam done in the kitchen took another ten. The update on Peggy Wheelwright's cancer was in line with Hero's report. The update on Hero's well-being was not in line with Hero's self-report.

Wheelwright showed nervousness about betraying his daughter's trust, yet seemed to feel that he owed an explanation to Magnus. "You are, of course, aware of the event at Alder Creek?"

Magnus stated the obvious, holding onto his mistrust, feeling protective of Hero. "I was there, you know."

"Yes, I know. Hero explained how you helped her. Peggy and I are grateful for your help."

"I didn't do much."

"She trusts you. She's been through some difficulties that make it hard for her to trust people."

"I understand."

Dr. Wheelwright struggled with whatever he was about to say. Magnus grew impatient: "So, what else did you want to—"

"I suspect—well, more than suspect—that she had another episode a few days ago. Holder's death triggered something."

"Is she okay? Was she violent?"

"God no, not violent. She heard the news—in town somewhere, not from me. When she came home she was terribly withdrawn. I don't know if she's told you, but she has struggled with depression. She takes medications. I mention this only because I want the best for her. I think you do as well. Other times when she's had these kinds of sinkings—that's her non-clinical term for them, 'sinkings'—she talked about what precipitated her reaction and how she felt. She openly shared with us. This time was different. Peggy and I got the brick wall treatment. So—"

Wheelwright shifted his weight from one leg to the other and lost his train of thought.

"You should sit down. I'm the one who should be standing. You know, from a rehab perspective."

Wheelwright took a seat across from Magnus. This seemed to make it easier for him to talk.

"I wanted to ask. Has she said anything to you about what, if anything, might have happened?"

Magnus questioned the appropriateness of Hero's father talking with him about her with Hero not in the room.

"I don't know Hero all that well. And, I don't mean to be disrespectful, Dr. Wheelwright, but I'm really uncomfortable with this conversation."

"Yes, of course. You are not being disrespectful. Quite the opposite in fact."

"Thank you." Magnus remained polite though wary.

Wheelwright continued in the same vein, undeterred by Magnus's avowed reluctance. "Whatever it was. Whatever set Hero off, she was unwilling to share with Peggy. I think this is because she didn't want to burden Peggy. And Peggy, you don't know, but she doesn't let things go. My dear wife is action incarnate, and I think that's the reason Hero didn't say anything. Peggy and I both feel Hero needs someone to talk to."

Magnus hoped Wheelwright wouldn't get into his daughter seeing a therapist. If he started, Magnus decided he would walk out the door.

"So you asked Hero to tell you what was bothering her?"

"I tried," Wheelwright answered.

"I guess you need to be patient," Magnus advised.

"Maybe she'll open up to you, Magnus, when she gets back. I'm not asking you to do anything, except to be aware that she might be . . . struggling. That's all."

"Back when?"

"I think tomorrow night. Another round of tests in Portland. Peggy's tests are part of her treatment plan. She and Hero have a few other things to do, big city errands."

After an awkward silence, Dr. Wheelwright declared Magnus as sound as could be expected. He recommended Magnus continue with moderate exercise. The kitchen "office" visit ended.

They made their goodbyes, and Magnus drove up the hill to 101 and back to his place in Manzanita. He had stopped at the market to pick up fixings for a homemade dinner: parsley, oregano, thyme, spaghetti, beef and pork sausage, tomatoes, onion, garlic, breadcrumbs, and eggs. He would make meatballs and spaghetti tomorrow—an easy, comfort food dinner, and he would text Hero to join him.

I have no past

A mix of sounds announced the Vespa's arrival. A tire chirped on the pavement; then the *vrrupp* petered out. The chassis squeaked and tipped forward as the handbrake brought the macchina to a halt and the spring-action kickstand *bronged*, mashing driveway stones under its lily pad-shaped base. Ribs complained, but Magnus descended the stairs two at a time. Six p.m., an hour late. He didn't care.

"Hey. How was Portland?" They performed a perfunctory hug. Hero held a helmet in one hand and a paper bag with a bottle of wine in the other. Magnus's ribs were not big on hugging, not yet anyway, despite protests from other parts of the anatomy. The ground fog had thickened. Smoke from wildfires to the south of Manzanita added to the malaise.

"Mom's tests went okay," The empty words had none of Hero's usual spunk. "Not worse."

"Meaning."

"Same ETD—Estimated Time of Death."

Mrs. Wheelwright had less than six months. Hero had to live with that. The family had to live with it. And Magnus too. A person's imminent death factored into every interaction with that person and the people with whom they were close.

"I'm sorry. How are you holding up?"

She avoided the question. "Smells good. Magnus. Thank you for the invite. I need me-time out of the house. Mom and Dad are extra special annoying. I love them, but—"

"Totally get it. Well," he tried to cheer her up, "this is a no-annoying zone. Chill out and experience the wonder of a spic making whop food."

A smile snuck out. "I'm excited!"

"You've never had Italian the way I make it."

"I'm afraid that that might be true," she half-closed one eye and cocked her head to the side. The expression asked: Had he forgotten Hero had spent much of her life in Italy?

With some flare, Magnus released a fistful of spaghetti into the boiling water, trying to get the pasta to fan out in a circle across the top of the pot. The night Lee had been his uninvited guest, he had executed the move perfectly. This time strands bunched up to one side. He separated the pasta by hand. He had to move gingerly to avoid the hot water and steam.

"What do they call that thing, the bundle of sticks Roman emperors held?"

"Fasces," Hero answered. "Sounds like two words: 'Fass and kays.' "

Hero helped and nudged pasta into the water with the concave side of a wooden spoon.

"Bravissimo, amore mio!"

"You know what I do with spaghetti?" Hero offered.

"What do you do?"

"I break it in half before I drop it in the water. Easier to cook and easier to eat."

Magnus feigned offense. "Sacrilege!" He inspected the meatballs in the oven and started a burner to rewarm his homemade red sauce.

He dipped a finger in the pot and tasted the sauce. He dipped the finger a second time and offered a taste to Hero. She took his hand and sucked the sauce off his finger.

"It's good."

"What? No *amore mio*?" Magnus exclaimed.

She leaned into him and pressed his arm. "Don't get your hopes up!"

His hopes were up. Not because he hoped to get lucky, but because she seemed happier than when she walked in the door.

Hero rummaged around the flatware drawer and found a corkscrew. She removed the wine, a Left Coast Cellars Oregon Pinot Noir, and prepared to uncork it before noticing that the bottle had a screw top.

"Can I help. This, I can do."

A *Frank Morgan* set played softly in the background; the light from the propane fireplace offset the gloom outside. Over the next hour, Hero and Magnus enjoyed dinner and talked about nothing. Magnus patted himself on the back for executing the delicious, Zia Alejandra meatballs recipe. Hero ate enough for two, explaining that she had eaten little the last couple of days. After dinner, they moved to the Beast and watched the always-different-always-the-same flicker of the fire and glow of steel logs that never crashed or spit embers across the floor.

Magnus recounted the conversation he had had with Dr. Wheelwright.

"Yeah, well I'm out of sorts and Mom and Dad are worried. Good news is they're less keen about the shrink now that he's out of the picture."

"Now that what?" Magnus asked.

"Now that he ran off with a twenty-something yoga instructor."

"You're kidding, right?"

"Nope. The dude had Ivy League cred. Dad did a residency with him years back. Not the yoga teacher."

"Fuck. Hero, I'm sorry about that. We don't have to talk about it."

"I kind of want to. Unless you don't want to hear."

Magnus smiled warmly, and Hero continued. "He's handsome, a hip dresser for his age. Not a frumpy dad type. Curly, wet-black hair. His wife is a Harvard MD, and they have a kid. Ted—the shrink's name is Ted—fancied himself an artist. He had this piece in the waiting room of his office—a five-by-five tableau of clear plastic and splattered all-over à la Jackson Pollock but with neon acrylics in drippy, galactic swirls. The first time I saw it I told him it was the ugliest painting I'd ever seen. I didn't know he had painted it. For a guy with twenty years of psychology under his belt, Ted didn't take it well. I should've walked then."

"When did he and prana girl—"

"Night before my appointment. He got drunk, dropped oxy, sent a gushy, incomprehensible email to a bijillion people, Mom included. Mom said he should have slashed his wrists while he was at it."

"Your mom can be so compassionate—"

"She was pissed. Called him a whiny motherfucker and called Visa and demanded a refund for a recent payment. He's not, though. He was always professional with me. And smart." Hero paused her story for a bite of pasta she had wound around her fork. "The good news— well, maybe it's good—is no more shrinks for Hero. Right after we got the news, Mom took me to a bar and we drank Bloody Marys."

"Corrupting you and killing herself," he quipped. "I'm sure she's not supposed to drink."

"Do tell." Hero sipped her wine and continued. "Magnus, she doesn't give a fuck. Remember, she refused chemo. Says she wants her 'tits, wits, and martinis.' That's her mantra."

The *Frank Morgan* set ended. Magnus switched to *Coltrane*. They listened, chatted little, watched the fire, and enjoyed their food.

"I didn't ask, but your dad implied there was something else bothering you. And that you didn't want to talk about it. He's worried, Hero."

"Funny he talks to you about my personal stuff. I should be upset, but I'm not." She snuggled closer. "And I don't."

"Don't what?"

"I don't want to talk about it."

Hero drew close to Magnus, their faces inches apart. She carefully removed his glasses—the spare pair. He thought she was about to kiss him.

"Magnus. I have no past."

He let the statement marinate before responding. "I get it. I truly do."

Having to be so careful about his own past, he understood what she had meant.

She was quiet for a while, then changed the subject, moving on to *the* subject of the day. "Did you hear about *the head*?"

"The whole fucking world has heard about *the head*. I've been trying to get *the head* out of my head."

"Me too. I didn't want to mention it while we were eating."

Magnus relayed the "fresh" conversation he had had at the News, describing how he had retreated to his apartment, intending to hole up for the day and crack open the book Miss Angel had given him.

"She's a writer? I didn't know."

"Nobody knows. It's her little secret and if you tell anyone, she'll hate me. Please don't."

Hero winked okay.

Magnus showed her the book and read the title aloud, *Sappho's Tears*. He opined that the pen name, Angela Steel, connoted feminine strength and sophistication, mystery and a sort of international appeal, and, of course, romance. She took the book from him and flipped through a few pages.

"The author's name," Hero observed, "is a mash-up of her real name. And the title is a *whoa* title. Deep stuff. " She shifted her attention toward the kitchen island. "Do I smell popcorn?"

Magnus reported that he had made a gigantic pot of popcorn for lunch.

The winter eyes thawed. "That's what I smelled when I walked in. At first, I thought it was old socks. Did some piggy eat it all?" She tickled his tummy.

Without answering, he rose from the Beast and returned with the bowl covered with a checkered dishtowel and still half-full.

She removed the dishtowel and announced, "I'm in heaven." Magnus retrieved the salt filled ramekin from the kitchen island and pinched a hefty volume of coarse sea salt and sprinkled it on. She caught his hand and licked the salt off his fingers. He let her manipulate them.

Hero turned her attention back to *Sappho's Tears* and opened the book to a random page. Her eyes lit up; the smile lit up the room.

"Holy shit. Miss Angel, I am shocked!"

"What?" Magnus was super curious.

"*Whoa* was the right word! Listen up!" Hero read the passage:

"Within the oven-dark duvet their bodies warmed where flesh met flesh. A bead of his sweat crossed his ribs, leapt to her body and, traversing the parabola of her breast, stopped at the nipple. She awaited its release."

Magnus plopped down on the beast. "Yup. Holy shit, Miss Angel!"

"Yeah, but I want the back story. I mean whose body's where? Steamy stuff, Magnus!"

"Tantric yoga? How else—"

"Next time you see Miss Angel—"

"Yeah, for sure. I'll ask."

"So you haven't read it?"

"Not yet. Now I feel like I need parental permission! Fuck. You want popcorn?" He asked as innocently as he could, as if the question hadn't been a distraction. His face reddened.

Hero turned the book in her hand to examine the jacket. "She probably wrote this when she was really young."

"Publication date?" he asked.

Hero read the publishing information on the inside cover. She tried to say it with a straight face: "Oh . . . last year."

"No way!" Magnus raised his arm and made a shaka fist, thumb and pinky extended.

"Uh-huh. So, what goes on in those 'reading sessions' with Miss

Angel. You're pretty cute, y'know. Young and cute."

Hero rose, put her wineglass on the island and helped herself to an Izzy from the fridge. Out of nowhere, she asked Magnus if he could look at some mechanical problem she was having with the Vespa.

"Sure." He rose and stepped to the sliding door that opened to the front deck. He could see the Vespa from there. The fog had lifted. "Right now?"

"No, no. Just sometime."

"Check out the sunset?" he asked and then qualified the question. "If we can see it."

He clicked off the fireplace. They made their way to the four-by-eight-foot deck, the one facing the street and the ocean. One could hear the waves a few blocks away and see the horizon but not see the actual beach. A bank of spruce and cedar trees and houses blocked the view. The fog had dissipated. Smoke in the air transformed the sun into a dirty yellow bruise.

They kicked back in the deck chairs, feet up and resting on the sagging cable strung between cedar posts. The rusted turnbuckles no longer turned; the cable squeaked when weighted. Magnus held the bowl of popcorn in his lap. Hero reached over to help herself, sometimes jiggling the bowl for the salt at the bottom and stirring up more than popcorn.

"Did you run this morning?" she asked.

"Nah. Hurt too much to run. And then it got smoky. Gordon's weather report called it. The wildfire smoke. Are you cold?"

They watched the sun drop behind a foreboding offshore fog.

"Lovely colors." She scanned the horizon. "Sort of Willem de Kooning yellow and grey."

"De Kooning?"

Hero got out her phone. It took a minute, but she found a few examples of his work. She pressed closer to show him.

"Great colorist," she added.

"How can someone hack off someone else's head. We're not talking about chickens. These are real people."

"Even a chicken is gross."

"What about compassion and empathy," Magnus stated. "Am I nuts to think people should be nice to each other?"

"There's a choice—" The words arrived between bites of popcorn. "—I don't think you can prove that human nature is innately good or bad. You choose. It's a belief, not something you can know. But you *can* rationally argue for or against certain practices."

"I suppose we can make an argument that it's not a good thing to take away somebody's rice bowl. Unless you're starving or trying to save the life of your child."

Occasionally they reached into the bowl at the same time, or his hand stayed and Hero gathered a bite from around his fingers. They did this deftly, the mingling of salty fingers.

Hero had found her voice and confidence. Maybe the topic was something she'd hashed through in college. "Even then, Magnus, we base the decision on our beliefs. We choose to take or not to take that bowl of rice. We choose good will over avarice and greed and other self-serving ends. You gotta start somewhere."

"Yeah. Well, I'm a little tired of pushing the good-will rock up the hill. It's exhausting to explain away bad behavior. The counterexamples are emotionally overwhelming."

"That is why," Hero continued her argument, "you've got to give up trying. Accept that regular people are okay and live with the consequences. Stop pushing. The pushing implies that you don't really believe it, you're trying to force it."

"Close your eyes and say people are good? That's denial."

She handed the Izzy to him. He took a sip.

"Denial? No. Denial is a defense mechanism where you refuse to believe something real. Choosing to believe—you can't simply automatically believe something—is about engaging in practices that align with the chosen belief. That's all I'm saying. Then all that exertion can go a different, better direction. Do something kind and justify the belief by making good choices. Then tell yourself, if I can be a good person, maybe so can my neighbor."

"Is that your parents' line?"

Hero laughed. "No way. Mom thinks people are total shit. She describes herself as possibly more shitty than most. And Dad, he doesn't think about things. He acts; he cares for the sick. And that works. He's living proof of Aristotle's argument that repeating good deeds makes a person virtuous."

"I get that," Magnus agreed, not inclined to get too technical.

The philosophy talk had dulled the sexual edge. Why, Magnus asked himself, was he afraid of intimacy? Hero's words showed an intellectual confidence that Magnus had never had. He was plenty confident leading someone on the dance floor or turning a wrench or writing code. The moral ledger in his mind was simplistic. Good actions in one column and bad in another. His accounting was inadequate; it was childish.

"Well, Félix scares the shit out of me."

"He doesn't sound very—who's that guy, the painter, the teddy bear guy with the afro and the soft voice?"

"Bob Ross," Magnus answered and continued with his report. "Félix and I bromanced over lunch. I made a deal with him. I gave him a thumb drive with the video Lee made. And I agreed to destroy the online copy in a week or when Constanza's family lets me know if they want it."

"Why would they need two?" Hero answered her own question. "Because you don't trust Félix to give it to them. Understandable."

"If Félix said the sun was going to rise tomorrow, I'd have second thoughts. That's how much I trust Félix."

Magnus babied the ribs as he got out of the chair. Hero followed and took his arm. Inside, she kept his arm as she closed the sliding door and locked it.

"Tea? Water?" He asked. The sky had darkened. He reached toward a lamp. None of the lights were on.

"Can we leave it off? I want to sit here, next to you, and just be quiet."

He left the lamp on the side table untouched and let her ease him onto the Beast.

"Hero, I know so little about you. Usually, people unload their life stories on me. It's weird. You're like me."

Not wearing the therapy hat, but being a caring friend, Magnus asked. "Want to talk about Alder Creek?"

He had expected a negative reaction. Instead, Hero snuggled closer. She kicked off her sandals and tucked her feet up onto the Beast. She leaned heavily against Magnus's side. It hurt, but he didn't complain.

"Anger got the best of me. Different than *your* stunt."

"*My* stunt?"

"Or maybe it was not so different. But mine was directed at someone who had hurt me. Yours was directed at yourself. Both were destructive."

He understood what she had meant. Not, however, agreeing.

"That was a rip tide. I didn't know about rip tides."

"Magnus," she tried to not sound condescending. "If it hadn't been that rip tide it would have been another. A fucking excuse, my friend." Her back stiffened. "We are friends. Or getting to be friends, right? I don't have room for confusion."

He struggled to be as honest as someone living a lie could be. "We are friends, Hero. No confusion here."

She had understood something he had had difficulty admitting to himself. She had accepted him. Magnus decided, then and there, to reciprocate. He would accept Hero unconditionally. He gently put his arm around her.

They sat a while before Hero spoke. "I'm so weary, friend."

"Me too, friend."

They closed their eyes and rested in the quiet warmth of each other's arms. The fog rolled back in and brought with it a chill eager to penetrate the poorly insulated apartment. Magnus found the remote and clicked on the fireplace. He freed the cotton throw on the back of the Beast and pulled it over Hero's shoulders.

Eso Es Todo

The new day brought with it renewed purpose. That purpose, to Magnus, was not to solve the mystery of Holders' deaths, but to continue his effort to distance himself from the investigation into the murders. At the top of the list was a visit to the Panda Bakery for a conversation with Constanza.

Hero, who had joined him, sounded concerned: "You know all that money you're swimming in? Have you considered a first-class ticket to Rio?"

"And leave you to deal with the fallout. Ain't gonna happen."

"Thank you, Magnus. But I'm serious. I can't leave, because of Mom."

Her tone implied resignation, but not capitulation. She was as cooly determined as he to deflect any attention that might link them to the Holders and Félix.

Seven days. That's how long it had been since Shortley Junior's head had washed ashore. With little to show for it, eager, macabre-minded beachcombers had scavenged local beaches for other "fresh" body parts. Conspiracy theorists and wannabe criminologists predicted the next discovery would be a sneaker containing human remains. Such claims usually accompanied discussions about how long it would take for the rest of the body to decompose.

From the scuttlebutt, Magnus had learned that sneakers were both buoyant and remarkably good at preserving their human contents long after the rest of the cadaver had decomposed. Per the *Victoria Times Colonist*, since August 2007, at least twenty detached human feet had surfaced on the coasts of the Salish Sea in British Columbia, an area located a mere hundred miles north of Manzanita, less by sea. Lee had probably worn cowboy boots. Were cowboy boots buoyant?

"We're here," Hero announced.

Lost in buoyancy thoughts, Magnus had missed the turnoff for the Panda Bakery and had to double back. A fog stuck to the coastal lowlands, a result of warm inland air rising and creating a low-pressure area that sucked in the high pressure, moist cold air off the surface of the ocean. There was parking between a couple of pickups. Mist-softened light from inside the bakery gave the place an eerie but cozy glow. The view depended upon one's predisposition. A waft of air from inside carried the smell of freshly baked pastries and swung Magnus to cozy.

José stood at his station at the stove. This normality was a relief. He had not contacted Magnus about the backup video, but he had not skipped town either. Carmen was probably out back. Constanza cleared dishes from a window table and carried them to the kitchen sink. She welcomed Magnus and Hero with hugs and led them to a table in a small alcove off the main dining area. They didn't mess around with small talk.

"You read the papers?" Hero asked.

"Yes," Constanza replied, "and online. I read everything I can find. It is horrible."

Hero, they had decided, would ask the questions. She took and held Constanza's hand. "Are you okay?"

"I'm good, yes. And you. You are good?"

Constanza knew what was coming. She seemed prepared and answered their first question before Hero asked. "Riley, the lady your father sent, did not call. No one called."

"Nothing from Riley," Hero repeated. "Any word from your uncle?"

"My uncle?" She hesitated and then understood. "Yes, you mean Félix? He is my mother's cousin."

"I see. It's similar in Italy—maybe not so much in the U.S.—calling him 'uncle.' "

"Yes, I think."

Constanza released Hero's hand. Neatly stacked paper napkins and a bin each for forks and knives sat on the checkered tablecloth. She, or someone earlier, had been prepping for diners and rolling up a knife and fork in each napkin. She fiddled with a knife before continuing, drawing faint lines across a folded napkin, making a cross sign. Magnus wondered if this was a conscious act, and then reflected on how difficult it must have been for Constanza to defend herself.

Something *was* off. She carried herself differently. Constanza, named for "constantia," meaning constancy or steadfastness, exhibited a change in demeanor. She had withdrawn, but was still in control. The observation led Magnus to speculate about Hero's past, the past she didn't want to acknowledge. She was so different from Carolina. Then again, his perspective relative to each of these strong women had been that of a clueless male.

They said nothing for a minute. Then Constanza spoke. "Tio Fe is gone. He went back to Chihuahua. Something important; he didn't say."

"Does anybody else, anyone in Manzanita or Wheeler or Nehalem, know that he was here?" Hero asked.

"I don't know. He was here a lot, with us."

"Where was Félix the day of the accident, when they found Mr. Shortley Holder?" Although Hero had focused on Constanza, the question had come across as performative.

"I know nothing about Mr. Holder's accident. I mean, about Tio Fe. But he stayed with us all the time, except he and Magnus had lunch at Trio Loco. He might have gone out sometimes. I think once to the market, once to the Costco in Warrenton. We needed things for the bakery. He went for long walks on a beach."

"Beach where?" Hero asked.

Constanza shrugged her shoulders, then perked up. "Short something beach, the surfing one. He watched the people surf."

"Short Sand Beach?"

"Yes, that's the one. He was a surfer, when he was a niñito.

Hero leaned to one side and peeked out the window. "He slept in your family's trailer?"

The Reyes trailer was a small camper unit mounted on cinder blocks and in the middle of a lot next to and behind the bakery. Even for two, the trailer was cramped.

"He slept in his car. Sometimes the storage room here, if it was cold. He has a bed and camping stove in his car. We use the bathrooms here, in the bakery."

"So, he rarely went out," Hero restated what she had been told, "except the market and beach walks." She paused, then moved on to a couple of questions that she and Magnus had been curious about. "Did he go to a bank in Manzanita? An ATM to get money? Or shop at Fresh Foods, the big market in Manzanita, or the Manzanita News coffee shop across from the Police Station?"

"I don't know. I don't think so. Why?"

"Constanza," Hero continued, "there are cameras at or near those places. There's not a car in town that matches the one he was driving. The cameras could place the car or Félix near Shortley Holder's home and office. Someone might have seen the car and described it to the police. Being an out-of-towner and being present when all this stuff with Holder happened . . . it would be natural for the police to want to question him."

"He was in town," Constanza faced Magnus, "at Trio Loco."

"Well, maybe," Hero surmised, "that's all there was."

Without prompting, Constanza provided information that some might have considered damning. "There was a long black box in his truck. You could sit on it and it was locked with a big lock. You need a key for the lock."

"A padlock?"

"Uh-huh."

Hero and Magnus exchanged glances. They were dancing around the obvious question. Do they straight-up ask Constanza and her parents if Félix murdered the Holders? Hero was tapping her fingers on the table. The unease had no place to go.

Carmen surfaced. She and José stepped up to the table. They had been listening and had nodded hello but hadn't interrupted. She stood behind her daughter and put her hands on Constanza's shoulders and gently stroked them.

Magnus studied José. He was less opaque than his daughter. "José, did you get the thumb drive?"

"El me lo mostró. Dijo due no había nada. Se rió y dijo que no me preocupara."

"Do you think Félix murdered Shortley Holder? And Lee, his son?"

Constanza's eyes froze. Her parents shook their heads. The pencil moustache twitched. Carmen, genuine sadness and disappointment in her voice, asked: "How could you think such a thing?"

After the head shaking had settled down, Carmen posed an equally direct question. "What would you do, if you thought our Félix did this terrible, terrible thing. Would you call the police?"

What indeed, Magnus asked himself, should one do? And how, he reflected, how had his life become so complicated?

"Carmen," he softened his voice so he wouldn't come across as accusatory, "can you tell me more about Félix."

"Are you sure you want to know?" She turned toward Constanza: "Hija, estos jóvenes les gustaría comer algo."

Constanza left the table and went to the kitchen, ostensibly to prepare something to eat for Hero and Magnus.

"In Mexico, maybe he is a dangerous man, yes. But we know nothing. He was here to help us. He gave us money for the bakery. I spoke with him after Mr. Holder tried to make us move out the second time. It was not fair to us, to make Constanza work. I told all of this to Félix. He said don't worry, he would talk to him. That is why he was here. To give us money. We were so embarrassed, ashamed to ask, pero tienes que entender, he adores Constanza. Eso es todo."

Magnus saw Constanza leaning against the doorway, listening closely and out of sight of her parents, being not at all the cowering child. Hero had picked up the knife Constanza had been drawing with and was retracing the cross patterns on the napkin.

Carmen put a hand over Hero's. "Eso es todo."

Jock

The last thing Magnus expected was to be asked to help the police. After Jock had learned that the Holders had hired Magnus only days before the murders, he grilled Magnus about their office setup. He wanted to know if the Holders had been agitated or troubled, if Magnus had noticed anything unusual. Magnus assumed the State Police had already scoured the company's computers and discovered the porn operation. Doing so would have given the authorities a small army of suspects.

Jock had presumed that Magnus must have known something shady had been going on at Holder Real Estate. He did not appear to think of Magnus as a suspect, given that the interrogation venue he had selected was an outdoor table at the News and not a room at the police station across the street. Not disclosing a neighbor's difficulties or oddities would be the norm in Manzanita. Magnus's having not mentioned the Holders' pornographic interests would not be something that Jock would hold against him.

The warm air and the wind-free sunny day had put the townspeople, Jock and Magnus included, in a cheery mood. A butterfly hovering over a huckleberry blossom prompted Magnus to think of Count Rostov's comical assertion in *A Gentleman in Moscow*: "Fate is determined by meteorology!" The logical Magnus, inclined to seek counterexamples for any broad claim, then jumped to that serene and fateful day at the conclusion of *All Quiet on the Western Front*, the butterfly's appearance and the sniper's bullet. He scanned the perimeter of the News. No snipers, only butterflies.

"So, did you catch'em yet?" he teased Jock.

That morning, Magnus had logged his first jog since the beating. He sat in a metal chair and rested his tender-from-disuse feet on a nearby

175

stump. A bacon and egg breakfast bagel, still in its wrapper, warmed his hands. Sandals hung loosely, the breeze wound round his toes. In the background, the sculpted-concrete fountain chortled. The usual feathered suspects were there, drinking and bathing and flitting back and forth between the bird feeder and huckleberry and salal.

"No, I wish." Jock exhaled, the disappointment obvious. "Thanks for meeting with me," he continued. "I wanted to ask you something."

"Fire away."

"The State Police didn't seem interested when I suggested this. They're hot on the tail of some internet bad guy. I don't understand that stuff."

"I'm listening."

"Shortley's appointment calendar had a big 'X' blocking out a few hours and your name was next to it. And Meredith said that was shortly before the Shortleys were murdered."

"Was that intentional?" Magnus laughed; Jock didn't.

"Were they both there, at the office? You did what they asked, I figured, because Meredith cut a check for you."

"I did. And they screwed me out of an hour they owed me. That was after we'd had a conversation about exactly that issue. I'd refused to do the job for what they had originally offered. I'm sorry they died, but they were cheap."

"Between us, Magnus, you're not the first. They have—had—a reputation for it. Smart people here always got something in writing. You learn after a while. Kick me once . . . Whatever."

Magnus smiled and agreed. "I'm obviously not one of the smart ones. But I wasn't pissed enough to, you know, off them for a hundred bucks."

Jock relaxed. "Well, you got off light." He leaned forward and rested his elbows on his knees and folded his hands together. He did not want others to overhear what he was about to say. Other than their avian companions, Magnus and Jock were alone in the patio area. The precaution seemed silly.

"You sure, now, they didn't act strange? Nothing fishy?"

"Well, yeah! They're weird people."

"How so?"

Magnus sipped his drink, an iced oat milk chai, and had a bite of the bagel sandwich. Jock waited for him to finish chewing and wash the food down.

"For one," he wiped his mouth with a napkin, "after the brief episode about how much an hour I get paid and how long the job would take, I asked them for a description of the hardware and programs they were using. The hardware was obvious. I was more interested in anti-virus info, email services, cloud accounts, browsers. The usual stuff."

"And?" Jock asked.

"I noticed that they had a couple of messaging and email services that are typically used for dark web activities."

"Would that be unusual for their business?"

"For a real estate and rental services company, yes. There was no actual need for that level of security. At first, I thought maybe they had foreign clients. I asked if I should wipe this stuff off the server and they panicked. Not panicked literally, but they clearly didn't want me to touch it. So, I didn't. Other than I made sure that all the programs, including the questionable ones, had been updated."

"Was that it?"

"Pretty much." Magnus sipped his drink. "Except, there's a little thing. I mean maybe this is more. They gave me a list of passwords to access the accounts. After checking their browser history, I saw several sites that they had accessed but that I didn't have passwords for. I asked if the password list they had given me was complete. They said that it was."

Magnus took a sip of his chai and bit into his bagel. Jock's eyebrows lifted. He tilted his head a funny way, somewhat forward and sideways.

"When I was working on my own—over lunch when no one else was in the office—I ran across a program and site they used a lot. I didn't see the password for it, so I opened the desk drawer and rummaged around. Every small office hides the password list someplace handy. I assumed that the first list had been incomplete. Sure enough, I found another page and another set of sites and passwords. I snapped a photo to add to the photo I had taken of the first list—"

"Why" Jock interrupted, "do you photograph your client's passwords?"

"Because when they call in the middle of the damned night, when there's a system crash, I can log in remotely and fix whatever has to be fixed and not repeat the hunt-for-passwords fire drill. Each client's password list is in its own secure cloud folder. The client can see and update the folder. I hadn't done that yet for the Holders."

"I see. That makes sense."

Magnus had expected that the State Police would learn that he had accessed the Holders' accounts, and that Police might want to reconstruct his interactions with them. He had scrubbed the drives but left the photos of the password lists. His strategy was the same as it had been with Vinnie's records. Leave a few details for the authorities. They'll feel satisfied that they had done their jobs, but their discoveries will not have been enough to warrant further investigation.

"Did you go to any of these sites?"

"Yeah, I was curious. Took a quick peep. It was your basic porn stuff. People are attached to their porn. I'm not judging."

Jock was interested. "What kind of porn? What did you see?"

"Some tits and ass. Not my thing. I didn't linger. And I was on the clock."

"You didn't know what kind of porn it was?"

"No clue. I'm not into that stuff. The first sign of anything gross, I'm outta there."

The answer satisfied Jock and must have accorded with his expectations. He repeated an earlier question. "Anything more about their behavior? Did they seem worried about anything? Say anything peculiar?"

"Nothing really." Magnus didn't want to embellish, especially about things that he might mess up if cross-interrogated by a different agency. "They were jerks about the money."

"Jerks. I'm with you. Wealthy family," Jock offered, "but jerks all the same. Thank you, Magnus."

Jock shook my hand and rose. He turned toward the station. Beside the parking lot there was a basketball pole and rim with a weathered, torn net. "Play basketball?"

"Not much. Love the game, though."

"Thursday nights. It's staying light now. C'mon by. You can bring that tall honey of yours, if she plays." He winked.

Magnus offered a sure-why-not, grateful-for-the-offer shake of the head. "Cool. That would be fun. I'll ask her. Thanks."

Off the hook, at least for now, Magnus checked his calendar. He had made an appointment for Subi at a local garage. The mechanics, after a conversation about Subi's needs, recommended selling the car, but in the end agreed to let Magnus work on Subi in the garage in exchange for a few hours of free IT work. The post-Holder murder publicity had generated more IT business than Magnus had time for. Later that day, and since Subi would be up on the blocks, Hero would pick him up for dinner at her parents. This upping the ante in their relationship had made him uneasy, the kind of uneasy one got when crawling under a car and using only a tire jack for support. One tremor and you're toast.

Dinner

Hero whispered. "Do you think it's true, what José said about Félix?"

"Hero, not now. Not exactly a conversation to have around your folks."

"They're deaf and dumb."

Magnus didn't laugh. "We're in their kitchen, their house, benefiting from their kindness and generosity. You're acting like a child."

Hero had been all for his meeting her parents. But after Shortley Holder's death, her enthusiasm had waned.

"Sorry. Dad really got to me today. A lecture about *moving on* in life and *grief therapy*. I mean, there's nothing to grieve yet. He can be so pedantic. And now going out on the town after we eat—on a double date with my parents! I don't need this, Magnus."

"It's great grief therapy, the best! Why shouldn't they do something fun? Suck it up, girl."

They continued bickering as they prepped vegetables for a salad, their—and in Magnus's opinion, paltry—contribution to the family dinner. Dr. Wheelwright had tossed a couple of game hens in the oven. A sauce made from herbs and giblets warmed on the stovetop and smelled delicious. He and Peggy enjoyed cocktails on the deck and watched low clouds from the north roll toward the western horizon.

The view from Neah-Kah-Nie Meadows captured the entire seven-mile-long beach. Above, a tired sun longed to call it a day. Below, a sleepy lace-hemmed ocean agreed. The ogre-y shadow of Neahkahnie Mountain rose behind the housing development's fastidiously tended grounds. Barbered bushes dotted acre-plus lots of uniformly architected homes that cost a million-and-a-half a pop.

Hero once summarized her opinion of the development by sticking her finger in her mouth. Magnus disagreed, and Hero quickly qualified the gesture, stating that what she had objected to was not the architecture per se or the stunning location, but the inflexibility of the HOA and the requirement that all homes conform to a particular style. She followed up with a lecture about Manzanita's history and how developers, politicians, artists, settlers and Native Americans had responded to the remote location and coastal environment and capitalized on local resources like timber and stone.

She repeated the legendary story of Governor Oswald West, who, in 1913, had the bright idea—one of his few, he humbly claimed—to declare the entire coast a highway, thus thwarting private ownership and making the coast forever available for public access. And she described how the depression of 1929 had resulted in land developers indebted to the county having to forfeit properties for back-taxes. These properties eventually became Nehalem Bay State Park and Oswald West State Park and, within the park, Short Sand Beach.

Magnus followed the coastline as far as he could see, imagining it as a highway—as West must have done—and then returned to the present. In two hours, the uppermost edge of the sun would dip below the horizon and, for an instant, the atmosphere would refract and magnify its last rays. The patient and attentive would see a green flash.

Dr. Wheelwright's agenda included: Dinner, the green flash, and a short drive to a bar in a neighboring town where a local celebrity and her band were performing music from the forties. As awkward as Magnus expected the dinner to be, he was excited about getting out of Dodge and listening to live music, any live music, even if it wasn't Latin.

"Your mom's behavior is not what I'd expected. She doesn't seem —"

"—like she's dying. That's her generation. She's tough as nails. Seriously, Magnus. She could kill you in seconds."

"I believe you." He smiled and thought about what had inspired Hero to describe her mother in those terms. He returned to his original question. "What kind of cancer? Am I crossing a line here?"

A voice from behind answered. "The kind that fucking kills you, Magnus. A goddamned brain tumor. I don't recommend them, especially one as feisty as this little bugger."

His knife paused over the carrots. "Sorry. I didn't mean to pry—"

"Of course you did. And it's a fair question." Mrs. Wheelwright did not act like someone at death's door. "And *your* parents," she asked, "are they well?"

"So far, yes." The knuckles of the hand holding the knife tapped the butcher block. "Both are well. Healthy as horses."

"What do they do, their jobs?"

"Dad's an attorney and Mom's a teacher."

"Dad should change careers. But Mom, a teacher! Wonderful. What subject? What level?"

"Not a proper teacher. She teaches ESL part-time. And she teaches Latin dance."

"Please! Respect to your mama! ESL is important. And hell, a dance teacher *is* a proper teacher. Where did she train for dance?"

"The Malecón, Habana." Mari was a street dancer. Her first exposure to dance had not been in a studio.

"Ah, Avenida de Maceo. What part?" She asked.

Mrs. Wheelwright's familiarity with the city and her Spanish surprised Magnus. "Old Habana. She studied voice in school. Her parents sailed to Florida. Mom didn't want to go. She was nineteen and was afraid they would all drown."

"Horseshit government but the best damned education in the western hemisphere. Especially music. Yes, and theoretical physics and medicine. What the Cubans lack in material goods they make up for with intelligence, training, and hard work. They're good people."

"So you've been to Cuba?" Magnus set the knife down. He had so many questions.

"So I have. Love it."

"Hero said you weren't well, Mrs. Wheelwright. But you seem so healthy? Before, that's why I asked."

"Please. It's Peggy. I'm a humble Peggy. And I am far from well, señor. About six months from maximally not well. Hope to die before the goddamn rain starts. You haven't been here in the winter. Don't stick around. Gale force winds, rain, rain, and more fucking rain. Maybe I'll go to Cuba. Die there. Far from vermin relatives hoping for handout." Her expression implied that she was seriously considering the Cuba option. "Inexpensive. Though the food's only marginally better than what I'd get in the hospital."

"Mom," Hero jumped in, "don't be morbid." Hero turned toward Magnus. "She's really not like this. Usually, Mom is—"

Hero searched for the word; Peggy supplied it: "—circumspect, sweetie. But, you know, me and diplomacy have gone our separate ways."

Peggy had more. "Thing is, I'm intrigued with this Magnus guy. I don't have time to waste. I want to know him better."

"Mom—"

Magnus headed off whatever it was Hero was going to say, trying to avoid an argument. The undisguised attention flustered him. "Well, thank you. I'm a pretty regular guy, Mrs. Wheelwright. Joe Average, not much to know."

"Yeah, so I heard. Ace mechanic, computer savvy. My daughter adores you." She stepped closer to Magnus, brushing against him and speaking conspiratorially. "And a successful thief."

"Hero said I was a thief?!"

"Why not? And, she said you feared confrontation and had cold feet about a new relationship. Something about an old flame, or afraid of getting caught and folks finding out who you really were? I forget. Sooner or later, the ugly truth wiggles out! Am I missing anything?"

A hearty, alto laugh devolved into an unpleasant coughing fit. Peggy cleared her throat, coughed up phlegm, and spit into the sink. Magnus imagined Peggy biting off the end of a fat Habana cigar and spitting it onto the street and hanging out with the Santeras and calling on Orishas. Mari had studied orisha chants and songs. Most were sung in Yoruba, the sacred language in Santoria. A little like Latin to the Catholic Church.

"Though maybe not," Peggy continued. "I've had plenty— identities, that is. After a while, it's like slipping on a pair of shoes. No, that trivializes the experience." She paced the kitchen floor, as if it were a stage. "It's more an opportunity to perform, to be on an evolving set with a very demanding audience. If they don't buy your act, they kill you."

Peggy opened the oven to check the hens. She froze in the middle of the act. She was thinking and staring at Magnus. With the oven door open, heat poured into the room. Her hands shook and her shoulders trembled. Something—an emotion, a nervous spasm, adrenaline, a shot of pain—something merciless, something out of her control coursed through her body. She breathed with difficulty.

"Make my day," she half-coughed, half-spoke. "Marry my daughter before I *fucking* die."

"Mom!" Hero practically screamed. "Close the oven!"

Magnus leapt to Peggy's side and put his arm on her waist to steady her. He gently supported her as he closed the oven door. Hero and Magnus stared at each other, searching for what to say.

Peggy's voice was resolute. "You heard me right." The seizure had passed, her breathing evened out. Suddenly, things were as they were pre-seizure, as if nothing had happened. "Back to work, you two. Hens come out in five."

She stopped at the doorway as she was exiting the kitchen. "I did my homework, Magnus. You and your two made-in-China pals, what are their names?"

He responded before thinking. "Harry and Charlie. They're not Chinese."

"I know, I know. I tell you; I love those two. Yes, Harry and Charlie —Charlie, née Charlotte. You did good work at IBM and university. You keep bright company." As she stepped out, she winked at Hero, "He's a keeper!"

"What the fuck was that about? Her homework? These are the friends you had mentioned? I never said a word to her. I swear. I'm so embarrassed, Magnus. She's not well."

If Peggy had intended to rattle Magnus and Hero, she had succeeded.

"So, how the hell does she know? Your dad, too? What *did* you tell them? Shit, I don't remember us ever talking about Harry and Charlie. Maybe in the hospital, when I was doped up."

"Nothing. God, no. I would never—and I mean never share personal things you didn't want me to share. I'm sure Dad's in the dark. He and Mom have this long-standing agreement. Dad has been trained to not ask questions. Mom rarely talks about work. But sometimes—I don't know why—she does. I'm as surprised as you."

Peggy had certainly been snooping around. There was something raw and personal in her disclosures. "Do you think she talked to Clam-lips?"

"Who?"

"Henry. Your boyfriend. Was I blabbering nonsense when he gave us a ride?"

"Don't be an idiot, Magnus. Boyfriend? Of course she talks to Henry. He's Theo's wife's kid. His wife had two kids when she and Theo married. You know, my uncle owns the Neah-Kah-Nie house."

"Wait, I thought it was Vassar where you met?"

"It was. Theo was on an academic sabbatical and met Henry's mom there."

Hero was ready to give up explaining anything. "You're as bad as Mom. You're both weirding me out."

"What the heck was she in Cuba for? And she knew about the work that Harry, Charlie, and I do in Ann Arbor? She's got to be a seriously high-level spook. The shit we do is fucking more than top secret."

Hero had calmed down. "You said 'do.' "

"They do. I'm . . . on a break. I think. My friends made up a story for our boss."

"Mom is a not so nice spy. She was—and still is, head-to-toe—a flag-waving, big cheese in the CIA's Operations Directorate. She's right out of a thriller and was about to be promoted to the top."

"And then the cancer," Magnus added.

"And then the cancer," Hero confirmed.

Hero focused on her hands, as if she were mad at them, angry that there was nothing they could do to help. Like Magnus, her emotions often had a physical aspect

"Glioblastoma means she has a nasty, fast-growing brain tumor. She has few symptoms now, except for random seizures. She collapses. I was afraid she was going to fall into the oven! Everything in her body —her legs, balance—gives out. Her mind goes blank; she remembers nothing about what happened. A minute or two later, she wakes up and wonders why she's on the floor and her head hurts." Hero teared up. Magnus took her hand and waited for her to continue. "She has hurt herself . . . when she's fallen. . . . We try to be with her or have somebody keep an eye on her."

"Bet she loves that."

"She's impossible. Fucking hates being cared for. Absolutely *hates* being dependent upon anybody."

Dishtowel in hand, his arms wrapped around Hero.

Peggy peeked in from the doorway, smiling as if the oven incident had never happened. "Where the hell's the salad? Did you forget the hens!"

"Crap," Magnus yelled and dove for the oven. The game hens were fine. He moved them from oven to stovetop.

* * * *

The scene in the dining room was Normal Rockwell normal. No one talked about the cancer, the CIA, or troubles in Detroit. Dr. Wheelwright, who had since asked Magnus to address him as Leonard, made some innocuous inquiries about his past. Magnus answered relatively honestly, admitting to having attended the University of Michigan and having studied mathematics and literature. When asked about why Manzanita, Magnus told Leonard he was working on a book about modern politics in small town America. In a way, he was. He was certainly making mental notes about how to survive in Manzanita and environs. People here, he had stated, were not so different from people in Detroit. The banal observation embarrassed Magnus.

Leonard, perhaps feeling an obligation to give Magnus better material, described his role at the local hospital, the pros and cons of a small-town practice, and how locals recast national policy during the Covid epidemic, an action that had led to heated disagreements about hospital policy and patient treatment.

The table talk had been interesting. The take-aways were that Dr. Wheelwright was engaged in his work, happy that his daughter was living at home, and deeply committed to making the best possible life for this mysterious woman he had married and clearly worshipped. He was a quiet man who listened and gave others the opportunity to express themselves, a refreshing humility that Magnus would not have associated with a physician with Wheelwright's experience and credentials.

Hero spoke only when spoken to. She cringed when her mother briefly mentioned "difficulties" in Italy and "uncertainties" regarding extradition. Magnus was full of questions. When he started in on one, Hero kicked him under the table. Clear evidence of their becoming an item.

The huge surprise of the evening, after they had finished dinner and a rich marionberry sorbet from Buttercup, a Nehalem maker of all manner of foodie delights, was that Leonard and Peggy, though the hour was late, still wanted to go out.

"Dancing? You can do that?" The surprise showed on Magnus's face, along with a bit of cringeworthy embarrassment about his acknowledgement of the obvious fact that Peggy was sick, that she was going to die.

"Magnus," Peggy addressed him directly and spoke softly, understanding that he was young and well-intentioned. "This ain't the movies. I'm not a drama queen. No Wagnerian angst, thank you."

"Mom's not big on Wagner," Hero rejoined. "Me neither."

Magnus didn't know Wagner from watermelon. He understood Hero was exhausted and dreading the double date. But he was excited. None of the Wheelwrights had any idea about the depth of Magnus's dance experience or suspected that he was wiggling in his seat.

Elks Lodge

The Elks Lodge in Seaside was nearly identical to the Lithuanian Hall in Detroit where Mari regularly sang and taught: the same stained wooden bar with a limited selection of drinks; similar food options—in Seaside it was barbeque pork sandwiches that were delicious and inexpensive; a dance-seasoned wooden floor; round, fold-up community tables that sat eight; floor space for twenty couples; a raised stage for the band. The featured singer was an incredibly talented woman who could have gone pro in New York or LA. Someone mentioned that she cleaned houses for a living. That this was case was not unusual. Small coastal communities are a magnet for people with interesting stories to tell. Magnus wondered if someday he would be among them—assuming the ending to his story wasn't a jail cell or worse. On the other hand, a little time in the slammer might add color.

The designated drivers, Hero and Magnus, nursed beers. Leonard and Peggy worked their martinis. Leonard did not need drink to brave the dance floor. He politely asked his wife to dance, took her arm, and walked her to a clear spot on the floor. He then led her through a textbook, challenging foxtrot routine. During those years at medical school, the guy had paid his ballroom dues.

When dancing, Magnus often imagined himself as the follow. This was to understand what the follow experienced and how the lead could make the dance experience pleasant and memorable and, most of all, fun. Would this be, he wondered, Peggy's last dance? Ever. She moved gracefully, swaying and twisting her head back, her ribs glued to Leonard's. They were one being with four legs and four arms. It was stunning. Would Hero understand? It was something he couldn't explain.

"What's wrong, Magnus?"

"Nothing's wrong." His feelings were on display. "I'm blown away by your parents' dancing. They're beautiful!"

"Do you know how to dance?"

"Not foxtrot, but yeah, I can dance."

The beer lost its chill. They listened to the band and watched Hero's parents strut their stuff. When Peggy and Leonard returned to the table, Leonard was tired and Peggy beamed. Leonard wiped his brow and face with a handkerchief and plopped down in a chair. He downed a full glass of water before returning to the martini. The next number was starting up, a sultry number from well before Magnus's time. Peggy, still standing, extended an arm.

"I'm not gonna wait all night."

His heart rate went stratospheric. He was being asked to dance and in a place where people actually danced. Magnus remembered the endless hours of salsa with his mom, and being ten and Mari reaching out to take his hand. Yes, he was a dancer, a good one, and he would step up the plate even if he didn't know the specific patterns for a specific dance. That's what a brave salsero did!

"Heck yeah, let's do this."

Peggy beamed. Magnus sensed she trusted him.

"Ever dance West Coast?"

"I've seen it. Very sexy, very cool. I'm a salsa dancer though . . ."

Her eyes lit up. "If you can dance salsa, you can do this. I'll walk you through the basics. Don't be shy. This is a very casual place. We'll stay on the side over here. Out of the line of dance."

Hearing the familiar term, "line of dance," relaxed him. Peggy had one hundred percent of his attention. As for shy, we'll see about that. Magnus was happy, genuinely happy.

They walked to a quiet section of the floor, away from other dancers and other tables, and stood there, wondering who was going to flinch first.

Magnus stepped forward, took her hand and put an arm around her, resting one hand on her shoulder blade—basic closed position. Again, that spark in Peggy's eyes. He swayed with the beat, unrushed. Magnus was familiar enough with West Coast to appreciate the mix of brief, explosive or showy moves, and then pauses when the tension built and the lead offered subtle hints to the follow about what was next. He knew the give and take of the dance.

Peggy back-lead him through a few moves, the sugar push, sugar tuck, left and right-side passes, a simple whip—a move that was on an eight-count instead of a six-count. One time through a move and Magnus owned it. He took the basic vocabulary she had given him and mixed in leadable salsa moves that fit the context and rhythm of the melody and/or the beat. He missed the conga, always his rhythm reference point.

Their dance was glorious fun. At the end of the song, an elated Peggy thanked him and suggested they do the next dance together. She led Magnus to a nearby empty table.

"Sit tight. I'm going to get my drink and your water bottle, and we, Mister Krum, are going to have a little chat."

He did as requested. The gruff order implied that their chat would not be "sugar" anything.

Peggy had a brief conversation with Dr. Wheelwright and Hero. They nodded. Leonard took Hero's hand for the next number.

Peggy—he had stopped thinking of her as Mrs. Wheelwright—returned.

"So, Omar Adil Papadopoulos aka Magnus Krum, let's talk about my daughter, and then the Holders and señor Félix. We don't have long, so I want to get to it."

"You know? Yes, obviously, you know."

Her eyes were as inscrutable as Hero's. The metaphor about the eyes being the "window to the mind" was bullshit re these two.

"I've told no one. The agency made a few calls. Officially, this sort of request is neither allowed nor encouraged—reason being you're in-country and not part of any ongoing operation. Think of it as a glorified credit check. Though, in your case, I asked for the works."

"Comforting. This was because I was hanging out with Hero?"

"Exactly. I wanted to know if you were in any way connected to what had happened to her in Italy."

"Isn't that fuck-all illegal?" He quickly answered his own question. "Of course, it is. And Hero . . . Hero says she has no past. Can't blame her if she doesn't want to talk about what happened."

"Damned right it's illegal. But what-the-hell can they do? Not like I got much time; and I got chits to cash. Yes, I know your history well, young man, which is why I'm going to level with you. I wasn't joking when I said I liked you. And kiddo, you're a hell of a dancer. I'd love to see the salsa!"

For the first time since he had left Detroit, Magnus was honestly happy, or rather, happily honest. He could hang up the alias in the closet. To be his real self—even for one dance and one conversation—was intoxicating. Truth was intoxicating.

"About that lovely daughter of mine. She's had an average to shitty time with men. She likes you—maybe loves you—and that frightens her."

Magnus thought about saying that Hero sure didn't come across as frightened and that the word 'love' had never entered any conversation between them. That, and that he didn't give a fuck about what Peggy thought. A bit of false bravado which, of course, was only partially true. Magnus did what he often did. He waited.

"Two men in Naples. She got in a spat—"

"So she said." Magnus lied. He didn't know what made him lie until after the fact. Hero had *not* told him anything about any "spat." But he didn't want to hear about Hero's past from Peggy or anyone else. Hero could tell her story whenever and if ever she was ready.

Peggy's surprise was obvious and genuine. "I'll be damned."

They were silent. "You probably heard the redacted version," Peggy added.

"I have no way of knowing. Nor do you."

"It was a deadly incident, a deadly *international* incident. We're fighting the extradition request." Peggy put her elbows on the table, clasped her hands, and cocked her head to one side, chin resting on knuckles. She looked like an older version of Hero. "Magnus, you're really not bothered by this? Hero is wanted for a double murder. There's a fucking mountain of incriminating evidence and witnesses."

Magnus did his best to hide the shock. She was a trained interrogator who would notice if he were tense. He caught himself holding his breath.

"Honestly," he said, "it changes nothing."

Peggy nodded; her head bobbed up and down. "Okay. Honestly."

Shit, Magnus swore to himself. The "Honestly" had been a dead giveaway.

He thought about Peggy and Hero, the Wheelwright family dynamic, and couldn't decide if Peggy was being a shit or a saint. The anger covered his confusion. "You're violating Hero's trust. So's Leonard."

"True. I admire that noble assessment."

Her sarcasm—if that's what it was—fed his protective instincts.

"It's too bad," Peggy added, "that she didn't finish off number two, because now we must deal with this ostensibly respectable, murdering

S.O.B. in court. He's got a lawyer—if you can believe it—and he's arguing that Hero was strung out on meth and tried to kill all three of them. All a load, of course. She only really killed one." Peggy let it rest a minute. Sadness and exhaustion flashed across her face. "I doubted a fair trial would have be possible in Italy, so I whisked her home. I don't know if she told you that part."

"No more, Peggy. Please, I don't want to talk about it."

His tablemate's complexion grew wan. It could have been the light, or the onset of another seizure. "Do you need to rest? Should we go home?"

"Rest, my ass!" A curtain rose, she snapped back. "Regarding the trust matter. Well, yes, a breach of trust. However, mother's intentions are good. I want to jump start Hero's recovery, and I don't have much time. She gets stuck in behavior patterns. You understand what I'm saying?"

"And you know what they say about good intentions. I don't want to be cruel, but you must realize that you are not the only person in Hero's life. Leonard, Clam-lips—"

"Clam-lips? Who the fuck is Clam-lips?"

"Mrs. Wheelwright . . . Peggy—saying Peggy feels awkward," he admitted, and then offered an opinion. "Getting her out of Italy was a good call. Hero's lucky you were there for her."

"My question to you, Magnus, is this: Can you accept what Hero did? Not that I think for a minute that you're a deluded ninny who runs from the dark side of life."

Feeling unsure of how to respond probably put him in the deluded ninny camp. He thought about it: What choices had Hero had? If what Peggy had described was true—which he believed it was—then he would choose to believe that Hero had experienced something horrific and that she had reacted bravely and honorably.

"Mrs. Wheelwright. I.Accept.Hero.As.Is."

"Good. That's good. She needs someone who will stand by her when leaping off a cliff feels like the better option. Living a lie and living with an act your conscience can never let go of, which I've done my entire adult life, does not engender happy relationships. Not me, not at my age, but it makes younger people question their own value. They question if they are worthy of love. It can lead to a relationship where people accommodate each other more than love each other. I don't want Hero and her partner to be sappy accommodators." Peggy practically spit out the "sappy."

"With all due respect, Mrs. Wheelwright. Just stop. You're the best. So's Hero. I don't want to hear another fucking word. Please. Shuddup."

Magnus put his hands over his ears; elbows on the table. The host of revelations screamed in his head. He did not think of himself as a tough guy, not really. He was a romantic and he was an accommodator. Peggy and Hero were from a different universe, one in which they faced gritty matters of life and death. His struggles had been infantile antics, acts committed with little to no forethought about their consequences and directed more by instinct than reason. All the same, his actions had led to a self-destructive emptiness similar in ways to what Peggy had been talking about. Magnus floated above the roiling surface of reality.

Peggy's tough-as-nails persona softened. "Can you handle this? If not, get off the train. Now. But, if you've got the cojones for it, which I think you do, and if you genuinely care about Hero, which I know you do, then be straight with her and demand the same." Peggy drew a bead on him. "All-in, Magnus."

Magnus thought about when he had tumbled off the train—giving her metaphor a literal interpretation. He removed his glasses. No cracks. Then he twirled them around by one of the temples.

"You're an information junkie, Peggy. You gotta know everything. A kid without a parent to stop them from eating too much candy. There's no end and that's self-destructive. We, we being Hero and me, are not addicted. We don't share your appetite, that proclivity that's kept you alive for so many years in so many dark places. It's *your* coping mechanism, not ours. Hero and I know little about each other's past. Little about each other period. Her past is painful, and mine comes with its share of shame and fear. So.Fucking.What! It's the past. It's over. Together or separately, we can go on and lead a full, rich, and happy life. Maybe even an extraordinarily happy life together. Or apart. I really believe that. It is not all or nothing."

Brave words from a not so brave Magnus had found his voice, saying something he had been afraid to admit—for a long time—even to himself. He would not do as she asked. He would make no demands upon Hero. They would bumble along.

Peggy wasn't happy. But she wasn't unhappy either. "You done?"

"No." He blurted it out before thinking. "I love Hero."

Peggy took his hand in both of hers. She sat ramrod straight, eyebrows slightly raised, an upward creep at the corners of her mouth.

Her expression was skeptical, surprised, supportive. "I know, you foolish man. I knew the second you walked through the door."

Sweat soaked through his shirt. A familiar condition, but usually associated with dancing all night in a steamy club. This, however, was not the good kind of sweat; this was smelly, nervous sweat.

"The Holders and Félix," he reminded Peggy about part two. He hoped it would go better than part one. Their time alone had grown conspicuously long. Hero and her dad had finished their dance, the easier social foxtrot. Leonard was flagging. Had Leonard and Hero been through a similar soul-searching conversation? "You wanted to discuss the Holders."

Still holding his hand, Peggy scanned the room, noting the exits out of force of habit. "I've changed my mind. We will not talk about the Holders. Bastards had it coming. Although I don't think that Constanza is the angel she makes out to be. Remember that. Did you ever watch the video?"

So, she knew about Constanza. Hero had shared what had happened.

"No," he answered.

"Not the time to be a fucking Boy Scout, kiddo." She swirled the invisible remains of her martini. "Do the police have the video?"

"I don't think so. I ran into Jock, our local cop. He asked about the IT work I did for Holder. Jock said the State Police have their experts and that they're focused on the Holders' porn business. I deleted the video on the Holders' sites and cleaned my tracks. But you never know. The parents have a thumb drive with the video."

"Who is that guy you and Hero think beheaded the son?"

"We don't know if he did or didn't. His name is Félix. No last name. He vanished."

"I'm curious about him. Describe please: Where you met, distinguishing features, his car, license plate. Humor the information junkie."

Boogie Woogie Bugle Boy played in the background as Magnus gave Peggy everything he knew, down to the manicured nails and the wash-me heart drawn on the black Suburban.

Peggy restated what they both knew. "He's gone and he's going to stay gone. Not on the police radar?"

"Correct, as far as I know."

"If the authorities grill the Panda family, will they give him up?"

"Hard to say. The police and ICE could offer a deal to the family to avoid deportation."

"ICE won't play nice. I could change that, maybe. I don't want to rouse that beast. And it is a vicious beast these days. Let's see what happens."

Whatever else Peggy was thinking, she wasn't about to share it. They sat together, each in their own world. Magnus asked himself how it would feel to be counting down the days? Would some things assume vast importance? And others turn to dust? Or maybe there'd be no difference at all.

Hero approached the table. "I asked the singer if she knew a salsa number, or something Latin."

Magnus rose, interlaced his arm with Hero's, and walked to the middle of the dance floor, a million miles from Peggy, a million miles from Félix, a million miles from Detroit, a million miles from everything except Hero and the music. A dreamy bachata number played. Magnus's trained ear detected hints of its Afro-Dominican and bolero roots. This song, closer to sensual bachata or bachata moderna, was usually danced with the partners in a tight, closed hold. The lead came from minute body isolations. He held Hero close, moving as if they had been lovers for a lifetime.

Sensing his body and trusting his direction, she surrendered to the music, the movement, and the moment.

When the number had finished, Hero didn't disengage. Even without music, Magnus's attention wholly focused on Hero, on the music he sensed in her body. He listened closely, silently, to its slightest tremor.

"I want to go home with you." Her lips deposited the words in the hollow above his clavicle. From there, the words spread through every nerve to every cell in his body.

He talked nonsense. "You were planning to hitch-hike?" It didn't matter what he said.

"Silly. I mean *your* home." Each word touched his flesh and left its mark.

Yes, the body answered.

I got this

The two couples rode in silence. Peggy dozed off in the back seat. Magnus was at the wheel. He dropped off Hero's parents. They seemed unbothered by Hero not getting out with them.

Arriving at his apartment, details jumped out at Magnus: the aroma from the lilac next to the drive; a creaking board as he and Hero held hands and crossed the porch. Upstairs, the odor of leftover quesadillas and tomato soup. The neat apartment exuded calm and peace. Books stacked on the coffee table followed Miss Angel's curated syllabus, physical evidence that reading had displaced social media. No Facebook, X, Instagram, Threads; no feeds from the New York Times (except the puzzle, he couldn't wean himself from the puzzle), AP, or BBC. Magnus had turned inward and accepted the paradox of being a tech-savvy nerd without a digital footprint.

He and Hero walked upstairs. The imminent intimacy presented an uncertainty for which he was unprepared. How to handle the emotional baggage? Would sex be an anxious affair full of furtive self-reflection; or, alternatively, a mind-numbing, escapist, pleasure-seeking performance staged by two actors, imposters in their own skins and greedy for physical release? How would past relationships impact their behavior? Magnus hadn't been in a relationship since Carolina; and Hero, well, he didn't know. Probably some guy in Italy.

These insecurities and others skittered in and out of awareness as Magnus unscrewed the cap on a bottle of cheap local pinot and unceremoniously filled two glass tumblers. They settled into the Beast and fired up the gas fireplace.

"Been a long day. To dulling the edge." He raised a glass..

A cross-legged Hero joined in and swilled half the contents of her glass. She wiped her lips with the back of her hand. "Edge dulled."

195

"Popcorn?" The distraction arrived by habit, uninvited. An avoidance move.

"Magnus, you know I fricking love popcorn, but I saw an article that claimed that eating popcorn was the same as having tiny razors in your small intestines. And it makes you fart."

"Are you worried about the razor part or the farting?"

Hero patted her tummy. "The former, duh. I'm not gonna stop eating popcorn! Do you think I fart too much?"

He acted as if he were taking her question seriously, then grabbed the remote and another opportunity for distraction. "You fart just right. Mama bear. Golden Mean. News?"

"Sure."

The screen came to life with pictures of starving people and billowing smoke from bombed-out buildings.

Their gazes went back and forth between each other and the screen.

"I didn't go home with you to watch the news. You can watch that or—" She twisted to face him, still cross-legged. The Beast was plenty wide enough. "—you can watch me."

Hero unbuttoned her blouse and tossed it over the back of the Beast.

"Easy choice." He hit the remote.

She slipped off her camisole and placed it on top of the blouse.

"You. Watch you."

They knew where this was going. But Magnus didn't want to go further until he had cleared up something.

"Hero. Your mom and I kind of had a serious conversation."

"This reeks of buzzkill."

"Yeah, maybe. She wanted talk about what went down in Italy."

"Did she, now?"

"She started but I told her to shuddup."

"You said that to Mom!"

Hero's expression communicated a funny combination of relief and surprise. She seemed proud of him. Another hearty swig of wine emptied the tumbler. She shifted forward on her hands and knees and then sat back on her heels. "So Mom told you. Do you hate me?"

"No, of course not. She said you killed some guy and were fighting extradition. That's when I told her I didn't want to hear more. It's your tale to tell, not hers. And Hero—to be clear—I do not *need* to know."

"Are you afraid that you'll change your mind. About me."

"Popcorn, the same as popcorn," he joked.

Hero pretended to think about that, as if it were more profound than silly. She gave a snorty laugh and leaned close. "I'm probably not as fucked up as you."

Too eagerly, he concurred. "Yeah, so true. My manly angst."

There, they had had the talk. He was ready to move on. "I haven't exactly been a player, you know, since Carolina—"

"You're going out of your way to make this not easy." She frowned and then smiled like she was holding in a laugh. "You were a *player*?"

A red-faced Magnus swiveled toward Hero and stretched out, almost touching her.

"Fuck, I just meant . . . Shit, I don't know what I'm saying."

"Then don't say it."

Hero tossed her head back and forth, flinging demons into space. Her braids whipped left and right and left and right. Her breasts jiggled.

She put her hands on his ankles and pressed her thumbs against the arches, heels, toes. "Are we done talking?"

One at a time, she pulled off his socks. He drank some wine, too much in one sip, coughed, and set his glass next to hers.

"Basta!"

Her hands slipped under the cuffs of his Levis. The backs of her fingernails skimmed the surface of the flesh above the ankles, up his calves.

Magnus's response to her attentiveness was obvious.

"Now, we're not-talking."

Hero examined him head to toe, then bent forward and swung a knee over his legs to straddle him. She removed his glasses and gamely put them on. He saw his own reflection on her face.

He struggled to find an explanation for what he saw. He could visualize it: the understanding of it in his mind like a physical thing, a conflation of physiognomies transmuted by unshared, disparate events but resolved into a deeply resonate connection that made no demands to justify its existence. It was just there.

"What the fuck?!" Hero didn't hide the surprise.

Her gaze skipped about the room, jumping from the window, TV screen, the door, fireplace, her own hand. He could name each object she focused on.

"Are these prescription? Do you need glasses?" Finally, she focused on him, on his face, inspecting it feature by feature. The scrutiny was physical, the hand of a blind person probing shapes and textures.

He, embarrassed, stared into the ice-grey eyes he could see perfectly well. The sheepish expression preceded the words. "Not really. I just wear—."

"They're a prop," she cut him off. "An actor's prop. Huh."

Somewhat carelessly, she tossed the glasses on the table.

Magnus flashed back to the vision of Hero leaning over him at the beach. He remembered his racing heart, and thoughts of death and sexual attraction. She had killed a man. Fuck. *Let it go*, he told himself. As abruptly as the thought had arisen, it vanished.

She leaned forward on her knees and placed one hand on his shoulder. With the other hand she reached into her back pocket and extracted a condom.

"May I?" she whispered in his ear.

Magnus removed his tee, jeans and baggy shorts, and slid his legs forward and between hers. Hero adjusted her position. What should have been awkward wasn't. The sides of his thighs braced against her knees. He lifted a hand to help with the condom.

Hero slipped off pants and undies. She winked, playful and mischievous, tearing open the condom packet between her teeth as she spoke and mumbling the words. "I got this."

Papadopolish

"Golly, Hero."

They lay together as all lovers do, matching swells of breath in a tapestry of calm and passion spent. Hero's muscled frame lay sandwiched between the cushions and Magnus.

"Yeah. Golly, Magnus."

Magnus straightened his arms and stretched upward. Hero rose with him. Her kisses scampered across his chest, stopping for playful nips. His lips found hollows of sinew and bone in her neck and shoulders.

"Tickles!" She fell back and extended her arms overhead. "That was so fucking great. And so great fucking!"

"Yup."

"Overdue, Magnus."

"Yup."

"Are we here for the night?" she asked.

"You want to go home?"

"No, I mean on the Beast?"

" ..."

"My ass is wet."

Magnus grabbed the cotton throw draped over the backrest of the Beast and tucked it under Hero's back and butt.

"Shit. I see what you mean."

Hero pushed Magnus off, rose and wrapped the throw around her torso. She took his hand and started for the bedroom.

"Wait." He put on his glasses and clicked off the fireplace. In the last flicker of light he grabbed his phone and wine glass and, without letting go of Hero's hand, managed with one hand to reach over to the sink, swish out the wine residue, and fill his glass with water.

199

She navigated through the dark and led them to the bedroom. Magnus put the phone and water on the night table as he and Hero slid under the cool sheets and wriggled around to warm them.

"Hero—" Magnus had waited until they had settled in and offset the chill. "Why, *Hero*?"

"That's usually the very first thing anyone asks. It's telling, Magnus, that you never did. You were trying to not care, weren't you?"

Magnus adjusted his glasses, as if needing them to understand her question.

"I suppose you hear better with those."

He swore he *could* hear better with glasses. Maybe the symbolic act of focusing impacted his hearing acuity.

Hero snuggled up close. "I weighed three pounds at birth. I was born in Lebanon, in a war zone and on Liberation Day. The baby me shouldn't have survived, but it did. Mom or Dad, one of them, called me their little Hero. The name stuck and eventually, when we got someplace where I could get a birth certificate, the name became official."

"I figured Hero as in Claudio and Hero."

Hero immediately got the reference to *Much Ado About Nothing*. "Nailed it. Well done, Magnus. Like I was a vapid gossip! " She tickled him under the arms.

Magnus jumped. "That hurts."

"Didn't hurt a few minutes ago."

Right—his expression conceded—nothing hurt a few minutes ago. "Alright, you're more a Beatrice."

" . . . "

"Witty, clever, hard to get. Annoying!" Magnus couldn't resist: "Or so I've noted."

"Oh, you've *noted*, have you!" Hero played the coquette and reached under the covers, toying with Magnus's nethers, gently and seductively. "Is there more *noting* in my future, my Benedict?"

Magnus drank some water. "Thirsty."

"Should I change my name?"

"Is there love in a name?"

" . . . "

"I love you."

"My Benedict is so sappy!" Neither his Hero nor Shakespeare's Beatrice was big on mushy banter. "Is Magnus you're real name?"

He didn't hesitate. "No."

"Any man I fuck has gotta pony up his real name. It's the way I roll, fella."

"You seemed to have rolled just fine!"

The under-the-covers hand re-found his privates and threatened havoc.

Magnus squirmed, unable to resist or keep from laughing. "Alright, alright! Stop! My ribs."

"Spit it out, mister!"

"Hero, it's not a good idea. If you know who I am. You could go to jail for it."

"Your Hero is not asking for anything more than the name of this sexy man I've given my body to."

The glacial eyes thawed. Even in the dark, he could tell.

"My name," Magnus spoke clearly and distinctly, "is Omar Adil Papadopoulos."

A half-laugh half-snort escaped. "I see why you changed it! Jesus, what a mouthful"

"Hey, I like my name."

"Nothing personal, Magnus. But it's so . . . spanakopita. It doesn't exactly go with the Spanish and salsa?"

"Lady, I adore you. But spare me some dignity!"

Hero planted besitos on his ear. "As you deserve, Mister Pompadapolish!"

Magnus groaned and rolled on top of Hero. He took her hands and gently pinned them to the side of her head. He kissed her. After he let go, she shot upright and rolled him to the side. "Oh fuck."

He sat up next to her. There was sufficient light to make out her puzzled expression. "What is it?"

"I was thinking. I know this is crazy. But you know this weird thing that we're so twin-like? Fuck, what if there's a reason for it?"

"Kinda improbable" he laughed. "How?"

"I just now remembered something Mom said. She was in Cuba eight months before I was born. Could your mom have been there, at the same time? She would have been married, but, you know, stuff happens."

"Holy fuck. You're saying maybe somewhere in Habana there's a horny, green- or grey-eyed—."

"Yes, a super skinny horny guy who was maybe an asset of Mom's."

"An ass-set!"

"Like yours my love. So irresistible!"

"Making us cousins?"

"A little gross—" Her eyes sparkled. "—but manageable."

"Whatever that means?"

"That means no children, dummy."

Magnus reached for his phone and did a quick search for DNA testing. "Here we go. American Red Cross in Portland. We're back and forth. Up for that?"

"You could ask Mari. She a sharer."

"The over-sharing is why I'm scarred for life and don't trust women. No thanks. Ask yours."

"No way she'd talk." Hero brightened, "Maybe we're kissin' cousins, Magnus."

"Speaking of kissing . . ."

An Unkindness

Three weeks passed and no new body parts washed ashore. Manzanita residents were no longer holding their collective breath in fear of the next shocker. As interest and gossip about the Holder murders retreated from the forefront, the investigation progressed behind the scenes and produced a lot of whys but no who. Oregon State Police methodically questioned Holders' friends, relatives, business associates, and employees.

Constanza and her father met with both Jock and a detective with the Homicide Investigation Unit—Constanza, because she was a part-time contract employee and she might have been one of the last people to see Shortley Holder alive; José, because Constanza was a minor, or so Jock had thought. The meeting, Constanza had reported, had been cursory, taking all of thirty minutes.

So far, no witnesses surfaced. None for the decapitation; none for Shortley senior's great fall. The latter, given the lack of witnesses or forensic evidence to the contrary, morphed from murder back to bizarre, untimely accident. Jock, by now a case docent, commented that the investigation had shifted to an examination of disputes and threats among and with Holders' questionable online business associates. "Follow the money" had become Jock's new mantra. The list was long and incomplete: purveyors of porn, customers, resellers, service providers—especially those that the Holders had majorly stiffed.

Jock let slip that the headquarters of the Holder pornographic enterprise was a sleazy studio they owned and managed in Southeast Portland. Their studio was near the once-popular—now closed—Le Bistro Montage, and a half-vacant warehouse where city musicians could go loud and no one cared. A clever investigator who was also a devoted porn researcher and underground music aficionado had recognized a band in the background of a Holder video. A raid of the studio found no videos made in Manzanita or environs. Jock was openly pleased to see the focal point of investigation migrate to Portland.

Félix. Well, it was as though he had never existed. Magnus's fear of entanglement via the association with Félix, in retrospect, had been more paranoia than a credible concern. Even so, Magnus extended the cover story of his house planning. He had replaced the original plans he had downloaded with plans that Hero had sketched. She explained that the site informed the architecture. Acting very much the couple planning their future, the two spent some days identifying potential locations for their bungalow by the sea. Magnus got revised costs estimates from a contractor who, though booked out for a year, was someone he could work with.

The days grew shorter and the number of dark hours gathered momentum. Peggy Wheelwright's health neared freefall and made demands on everyone. Hero never begrudged the time, never complained, and would burst into tears over events that might have seemed inconsequential but were, in fact, reminders of times shared with her mother. Hero had had no further episodes on the scale of what had transpired at Alder Creek. Her attention and energy were directed outward, attending to her mother's needs and supporting her father. She never spent another night with Magnus and had quit her job at Big Wave. That she didn't sleep at all some nights, and that Peggy wasn't the sole cause of her insomnia, was not lost on Magnus. He did Hero the favor of not pestering her. There were nights she would call and they would stay on the phone and talk or not for hours.

There was something waiting for its time. Not about an event from the past, but something relatively immediate and unrelated to her mother's illness. He could sense it but couldn't figure out what or why. The tension lingered, noticeable at night and at afternoon trysts, their "sexy time."

* * * *

"Where to, Miss Angel?"

Magnus had quit volunteering at *WeDrive!* soon after he had resumed work as an IT consultant. *WeDrive!* had served its purpose: the job had introduced Magnus to the Manzanita community and the

Manzanita community to Magnus. Miss Angel—although she knew his name was no longer on the carpool driver sheet—continued to call when she needed a ride, especially if the weather threatened, or at night, or when she ventured to Portland for medical needs. She still needed him for sorties to Astoria to pick up items at the Coop that were unavailable in Manzanita.

"CARTM, in Wheeler. Do you know where it is?"

She pronounced the word like "card-em."

"The name, yes. I think they're right on 101." He replied.

"Reuse, Recycle, Reimagine, or something—is the mission," she explained. "A local version of Goodwill, but more. They call it *Heart of CARTM*. They repair things, you know. *The Repair Cafe*. You could help. That is, fix things."

"Aren't they closed?" Magnus checked his watch. "It's after six."

"The store manager is working late. She's waiting."

Miss Angel handed Magnus a bag holding a vintage, portable Singer sewing machine and various attachments. "A fishing boat a mile offshore is fine. That, I can see. But the eye of a needle—impossible! Even with glasses."

Magnus fidgeted with his glasses, aware of and for a moment embarrassed by the falsely implied impairment.

"And my poor fingers, their little motors shake as much as the bloody machine!"

Keeping a palm of his hand on the steering wheel, Magnus opened, and with no evidence of shaking, stretched and closed his fingers.

"I'm going to give this contraption to someone who can use it."

As with Hero, Magnus sensed a certain disquietude in Miss Angel's behavior but could not sort out what it was. Had he unconsciously done or said something off-putting? And whatever it was, how had he offended both women? Or was there something both women had shared, something they were uncomfortable or unwilling to share? He found it especially peculiar that Miss Angel had been so silent about the Holders and Constanza. Not a word. He considered suggesting they stop at Panda, but then the thought escaped, replaced by the search for CARTM's address.

As they approached Wheeler proper, Miss Angel's lips parted, a familiar reaction when she was mentally preoccupied. A hand rose, a precursor to speaking, then fell back upon her lap. It was only after they had finished the business at CARTM, after they exited the door and stepped onto the boardwalk, that she spoke up.

"Magnus, would you care to walk down to the dock?"

"Of course."

The dock was on the other side of Highway 101 and was the perfect location to enjoy an unobstructed view of Nehalem Bay. A single boat piloted by a man in his sixties or seventies put-putted toward shore. Arm-in-arm, Miss Angel and Magnus crossed the highway and walked down the gravel path to a weathered cedar picnic table near the water's edge and on the deck of a gourmet pizzeria that had recently reopened. Magnus sat on the bench seat; Miss Angel stood and gazed seaward. She wore a thin, cotton, goldenrod-yellow jacket that was too light for the uncaring breeze. An ivory, cotton scarf tied in a European Loop, where the scarf folds in half and the loose ends fall through the loop, protected her neck. Her hand touched his shoulder; he shivered.

"I'm sorry," she apologized. "It's too chilly. We should go back."

Again, a wordless journey to the car and the same on the drive back to Manzanita. He turned on Subi's heater to cut the damp. They turned down Laneda and at Third Street Magnus reached for the turn signal stalk. He had assumed Miss Angel had wanted to go home. She reached over to stop him.

"Not yet. Park on Ocean, please."

He did as directed. Miss Angel opened the door, exited Subi, and again gazed seaward. They walked the short, sandy path parting waist-high seagrass and leading to a dull-toned beach abandoned by both walkers and the sun's warmth. The offshore wind, if anything, was harsher than it had been in Wheeler.

"I cannot keep this to myself, Magnus. Not any longer."

Magnus worried that, given her age, Miss Angel stood before a physical reckoning, a deadly prognosis.

She paused—her pose dramatic, but unintentionally so. "An unkindness of dark possibilities awaits you, Magnus Krum."

Her chilling words had been about Magnus, not herself. An "unkindness," he recalled from Plover Patrol with Hero, referred to a fifteenth century term for a collection of ravens. She faced the sea, expressionless. A gust played with a twisp of gray hair. Sand beat unkindly at her thin, bluing cheeks. She blinked. The storm rolling toward shore had obliterated a remnant sunset and threatened the promise of a quiet night. Magnus stepped closer.

She faced the gathering clouds. "I saw her—"

"Who her?"

Waves lapped at the shore; gulls complained.

"You know who." She raised her voice to be heard over the wind. "I saw her leaving Shortley's place. By the back door—"

"When?"

"Don't interrupt!"

"Sorry."

"No. No, it's alright. I apologize for snapping at you."

"You were saying—"

"Earlier. When they found his body. Remember, I was getting the mail and you gave me a ride home. Then we had tea."

"Why didn't you tell me? Why didn't you didn't you tell me *then*?"

"I didn't know if it meant anything. . . . That's not true. I didn't know until now if *you* could manage it."

"I can." His face reddened, and not just from the wind.

"Yes, I know."

"I've changed, Miss Angel. I'm not afraid."

"That's good *and* bad, isn't it?"

"Yes, good and bad," he conceded. "Have you told the police?"

"At my age, Magnus, memories come and go. What was that lovely metaphor for life's transience? Yes, 'shadows on the waves.' "

He recognized the reference to a poem they had once read together, Herder's *Ein Traum*.

Miss Angel turned her back on the wind's abuse. The streetlights on Laneda flickered to life. Magnus turned with her.

"You gonna stick around?" She could talk folksy when she wanted to.

"I'm not planning to leave, if that's what you mean. I don't know what's right to do. Or what's wrong to do"

"Don't be silly." She pulled the collar of her jacket around the scarf and started up the path, speaking in chorus with the retreating wind.

She apparently thought the answer obvious. Maybe from her perspective it was. Not so from his.

Miss Angel continued: "Well, it seems you're not afraid."

"No."

She twisted to face him. Her expression was a mix of relief, concern, and exhaustion. Impossible to read.

"There." The word came out scratchy, a word off a dusty LP. "I've said it. Take me home, please."

Witness

The resolve, so firm yesterday, refused to materialize. The past, both inescapable and malleable, had tacitly become what he and Hero had agreed to make of it. After the Carolina admission and request for his real name, Hero had neither demanded nor offered anything more. On his part, Magnus had not pressed her, not after the machete incident at the farm, not after Peggy's clouded cautions. He simply offered unconditional support. That didn't mean he didn't care or have serious legal and moral concerns about her behavior and what had triggered it, but he deeply respected that acceptance was at the core of their relationship. The conversation today, Magnus feared, might threaten that status. He was dreading it.

They found an outdoor table at the Offshore Grill and ordered coffees and cups of seafood chowder. Although the sun warmed, the stubborn morning chill refused to leave. A clear and windless sky hinted at a pleasant afternoon ahead. The lunch crowd was light. Drinks and food arrived within minutes.

A double-shot cortado—an antidote to the sleepless night—fortified Magnus. He jumped into the line of fire.

"Hero, Miss Angel saw you leave from the back door at Shortley Holder's right before the police found him. She was on her way back from the Post Office and I bumped into her when I got caught up in the crowd that had gathered in front of Holder's."

Hero blew over the top of a spoonful of hot chowder and checked to see if anyone might have overheard what Magnus had said. "Inferring what, Magnus?"

He didn't want to rush her, and he didn't want to impugn something that might be misunderstood.

"Funny," she observed, "how we're so afraid, consciously afraid, to talk about the past."

Hero had ordered a hot chai, not coffee, to go with her chowder. The chai replaced the chowder as the source of warmth. The aromas of cardamom and cinnamon mingled with that of steamed milk. Her sunglasses lay on the table, ignored. She closed her eyes and tilted her face toward the sun, as if she were giving life to the sun instead of the other way around.

She didn't open her eyes when she spoke. "I don't want to talk about it."

"Holder or the past?"

She faced downward, eyes still closed. Magnus hoped the sun wouldn't fall from the sky. When she looked up, a corona of sunlit hair encircled and framed her head. She was an extraordinary, beautiful woman.

"I didn't think anyone had seen me. Had others? Did Miss Angel tell anyone?"

"Doubt it. I don't think so to both questions."

"I didn't kill the old goat."

How, Magnus asked himself, could she be so calm, so removed and emotionless about what had to have been an insanely traumatic experience? He would have been a train wreck.

He was slow to speak. "Not saying you did. But what *did* happen?"

Her eyes scanned their surroundings a second time. She avoided his eyes, a gesture that concerned Magnus. Hero breathed through her nose, and then, with puffed cheeks, blew out all the air in a pranayama-incorrect exhale.

She leaned forward so he could hear her whisper. "Constanza said he tripped when he was trying to adjust his wheelchair on the elevator platform he uses to go up and down the stairs."

Now it was Magnus who whipped his head around, a sweep to see if anyone had overheard. He struggled to hold back his surprise.

"Constanza was there!?"

Hero shuffle-hopped her chair around the table to sit closer to Magnus, taking care because of the uneven ground. "Constanza had called and asked if I could go with her to see Holder about some money he owed her. You know how he is—was—about money."

"I do," Magnus nodded. It was easy to imagine Holder taking advantage of Constanza, advantage of anybody, for that matter.

"Constanza said she was afraid to ask, afraid to go alone. And she needed the money."

"She should have called me. Or gone with her dad."

"She mentioned that. She thought about it but said you had done so much already and she didn't want to bother you."

They sat quietly. A couple with two children walked by and entered the restaurant. The children stopped to pet a tail-wagging, wire-haired terrier leashed to a wrought iron bench next to the front door.

"Half-assed reasonable. From her perspective. Was the money for house cleaning, or filming?"

"It was unclear."

"So, what happened?"

"We went up the stairs in the back, the side away from the street. The back door was locked, but Constanza had a key. I guess she had cleaned the place before. Holder was in the bathroom. The bath is just off the landing and close to the stairs that go down to the first floor. I think the wheelchair had been there, right outside the bathroom door.

"Holder, you know, can walk short distances. After she opened the door and we stepped inside—I didn't expect this—Constanza ordered me to wait outside. I asked her if she was sure . . . She said she was. She said she felt bad about dragging me into her problems. We argued a little, quietly, so Holder wouldn't hear us. She was adamant, so I stepped outside. She closed the door. I put my ear to the door and heard Constanza tap on the bathroom door and say, 'It's Constanza, Mr. Holder.' Maybe he was expecting her—to clean or whatever. He made no sound of alarm. It was hard to hear what he said, but I heard the bath door open. Constanza's voice was firm. She must have been right in his face: 'You owe me money, Mr. Holder.' "

Hero paused, recalling and replaying in her mind what came next.

"Holder laughed. He flopped down in his wheelchair. I know because the chair creaked. At first I thought someone had stepped on a small animal. Then he slapped his knee or something with his hand. I just heard the slap. He said, 'Sure, I'll pay you, honey. Git yer skinny brown ass over here.' There was silence for a minute, then Holder again. 'On yer knees.' He said something else, but I couldn't understand.

"There was another pause. I was afraid for Constanza, so I pushed on the door. She had re-locked it or the door had locked by itself. Holder's voice grew louder. The asshole started taunting her and talking smack: 'You want a little riiide, honey?" That's the last thing I heard Holder say: 'You want a little riiide, honey?' It was creepy how he said it. Made me sick."

More customers filed by. Magnus and Hero watched and waited for them to pass.

"The Holders." Magnus hoped the anger didn't show. "They're bad people. Nobody's a hundred percent bad. But these guys—"

"The next thing I heard was Holder yell. 'Who the hell—' was all I got. The rest was cut off. There was a gasp and the sound of him and the chair crashing down the stairs. Then this scary silence. I pounded on the door. Constanza yelled back. 'Un momencito. One minute!'

"Eventually she came to the door. Maybe a minute or two after the crash. It was like forever. I had started down the stairs, one or two steps, when the door opened. She was flushed. Her blouse and hair were messed up. I saw scratches and blood on her forearms. She swore: 'Puto culo' or something. She raced by me and down the back stairs. I don't know how she got home."

"Had you given her a ride there?"

"I had."

"Any sign of Félix?"

"None. I suppose he could have been hiding inside, but I don't think so."

"What did you do next?"

"I rushed inside and there was Holder, tangled up in the fucking wheelchair at the bottom of the stairs. He was a contorted mess, not breathing, and the wheelchair was on top of him. There were parts of the chair on the stairs and floor. His arms and legs stuck out. It was fucking grotesque. A big metal spike or something stuck out of his eye."

"Did you try to help him or call for help?"

"Well, yeah. I would have, but he was gone, Magnus. His head was all cockeyed, flopped over sideways. Neck broken. And there was that thing sticking out of his eye. It went deep. I'm sure all the way through. A metal tube or something. The first thing I thought was that Constanza must have done it. I couldn't imagine how something that weird could have happened by accident."

"I can't believe you didn't freak! This is not good, Hero."

"Yeah, but then, what the fuck? I was in shock I suppose."

"You're really sure Félix wasn't there?"

"Like I said: If he was, I didn't see him."

Hero was silent for a minute, eerily calm. She hadn't touched her chowder.

"I found one of Constanza's bracelets. You know, the Swiftie ones."

"Yeah. Those were a gift from Félix. Or it belonged to him."

An image of Swiftie carnage popped into his head, of fans being stabbed in the eye for their bracelets. Magnus shivered.

"I put the bracelet in my pocket and spent a minute thinking about anything else that would have identified Constanza's having been there. I thought: How would Mom handle this. And I wanted to wait a minute and see if by some miracle Holder would spontaneously come around, wondering if he truly was dead the first time I examined him or if I had imagined the whole thing. I double-checked for pulse and breathing. Nothing but a shitload of blood. A bones stuck out from his knee. I cleaned my shoes and threw them away later."

"What a horror show. Christ, I can't imagine being there with Holder's bloody corpse. Fuck."

Hero moved her head in circles. To loosen up her neck, or it was nerves. She held her head in her hands with elbows on the table, tilting it from side-to-side the way a chiropractor would release the cervical spine. Then she leaned back in the chair, head skyward and hands cradling the chai.

"So you were going down the back stairs when Miss Angel saw you. But that must have been quite a while after he had fallen down the stairs. I mean they were wheeling him out of there when I drove by and Miss Angel saw you."

She nodded to confirm what he had said.

"I thought about wiping the door handles and the railing on the landing. But then I remembered Constanza had worked there and that her prints would be all over the place. I worried about my prints and cleaned the door handle and where I had touched the railing."

This, Magnus thought, sounded so unlike anything he might have considered in the same situation. "That it? That's still—"

"Not quite."

The parents and their children, drinks and snacks in hand, walked by a second time. Again, Hero and Magnus waited for them to pass. Magnus took advantage of the break and ate, the 'not quite' remark tolling in his head. The chowder had cooled.

"There was blood on her hands. And I've got this sick image I can't shake."

"Sick image of what? Her hands?"

"No. Of Constanza, of someone jamming that piece of wheelchair tubing or metal—or whatever it was—into Holder's eye. I can't shake it."

Hero tried to eat. The spoon shook and she gave up. "I understand being blinded by hatred." She took a moment to breathe and settled down before continuing. "I wiped down the part of that tube, where Constanza might have held it. Then I squeezed Holder's bony dead hand around it. Like he might have tried to pull it out. One of his hands was next to the tube. Maybe he did try. I was holding his hand there when I heard someone outside walk up to the front door. They rang the doorbell and knocked."

"Jesus fucking Christ!" Magnus didn't know how to respond. He immediately thought about securing an alternative identity for Hero. He could talk to the Twins. It would take a week. Or Peggy could help.

"I ran back upstairs. There's a closet between the bathroom and the back door. I hid in the closet and waited. It must have been a friend or acquaintance of Holder's at the front door because they opened the unlocked door and walked in. They saw Holder, crumpled up, the bloody mess, and screamed for help. People outside rushed in."

"You hid in the closet? The whole time when the EMTs were there and did their thing, and took him away? And no one saw you?"

She bit her lower lip and nodded yes.

"I didn't come out until I heard them wheel him out the door. There was a brief period when no one was there. About pissed my pants waiting, shaking."

"That's really fucked, Hero."

"You're right. It's fucked and I fucked up. The thing with Holder and Constanza could ruin everything. And I wasn't thinking straight and wanted everything to go away. The dead body and the blood brought up all this awful shit. You don't know, Magnus, you really, really don't know. And Constanza! How that asshole treated her. If it *was* her, I couldn't let her go down for it."

"Do you want to talk about that awful shit?"

"No."

"Okay, yeah. I get you wanted to protect Constanza. But Christ, you can't go around murdering jerks who offend you."

"Fuck you! How'd you like that prick's dick up your ass!"

Hero knew she had been too loud. She turned around and smiled an apology to people who had overheard.

A nearby customer moved to a different table. Hero again put her head in her hands, letting the hair fall and hide her face. A braid fell into the chowder. Magnus carefully removed the braid and wiped it with a napkin, a tender act that seemed to defuse the condemning gaze from another upset customer.

Careful to keep the tone mild and his voice low, Magnus continued. "If Constanza was in fact responsible for Holder's death, then something ought to be done about it."

They sat quietly, Magnus working on the now tepid chowder.

"What you did may or may not help Constanza. But it sure as hell put you in jeopardy."

Hero leaned against Magnus's shoulder. She wrapped her hands around his forearm.

"I did do something about it. I accepted the risk. Second, Magnus, I really don't know if she pushed him or if it was an accident. And last, if Félix had been there, he easily could have hidden in the same closet I hid in and quietly slipped out while I was down with Holder at the bottom of the stairs . . . I made a mistake. I know I made a mistake."

"You didn't hear anything else? Did you hear a man's footsteps going down and up the stairs inside? Or the back door opening? If Félix had been there, he would have been with Constanza. Do you think she saw him and that's why she wanted you to wait outside?"

"Unlikely. Remember, I drove her there. I guess he could have been inside already."

"How is Constanza?" he asked. "Have you seen her?"

"No idea. I called later. She was fine, but she's whatever. I never got a straight answer about her age, but she's young enough to be in denial. I would be."

"Why didn't you call me sooner?" He was upset with Hero but didn't want to make her feel worse. She sensed what he was thinking. They were getting better at that.

"I didn't want to ruin things for us. For Mom. Shit, how would she deal with it. And I'm selfish. I don't have space for any more drama. Or trauma. No more fucking dark clouds, thank you."

"Did you talk to Peggy?"

"Sort of. She's worse health-wise. I told her that I heard a rumor that Constanza might have pushed Holder down the stairs. Mom said 'Karma, baby, Karma. No great loss.' She can be one cold-hearted bitch. You have no idea."

Hero's body involuntarily shuddered, a violent twitch of the shoulders. He wondered if she was about to explode into tears or have a panic attack. Unsure about what to do, he stood up and helped her stand. He put his arms around her and held her tightly and waited for the tension to subside.

"Did she say anything else?"

"Who?"

"Your mom."

"Oh yeah. I got an earful. Implored me to tell you everything. Every fucking little detail that I could possibly remember or imagined I remembered. I told her 'No way.' She's been asking over and over 'Have you talked to Magnus?' So, there you have it." Hero gazed upward. Magnus did the same. A lonely, immobile white cloud hung pinned to the sky. "Happy Mom?"

Her head leaned into his shoulder. "I'm so screwed up, Magnus. I'm sorry." The words physically moved through his body.

His watch said it was mid-tide. "Hero, I don't need to know every fucking detail about Holder or anything else. That's what I told Peggy. Are you working today?"

"God no."

"Where's the bracelet?"

Hero reached into her fanny pack and extracted an envelope containing the bracelet. She handed the envelope to Magnus as if presenting evidence to the judge.

"Can I hang onto it?" he asked.

"Happy to be rid of it, thank you. I don't know why I saved it. I guess I thought about showing it to Constanza. To see if she'd explain what really happened."

The conversation and the mood had grown glummer by the minute. He wanted to get Hero to think about something else. "Up for a wet sand survey? See how our little Plover friends are doing. Toes in sand, you know. Toes in sand always helps."

"I'm totally exhausted. No, no survey. Maybe a short walk, a half-hour. That's all I got in me." She hadn't touched her chowder.

"I love you." The expression had become natural; he no longer had second thoughts. "It's gonna be okay. We're gonna be okay."

"Thank you, Magnus. I love you, too." Her heartbeat had steadied. Magnus folded the envelope and shoved it in his pocket.

The Threat

They held hands as they walked to and from the boulder field at the north end of the beach, stopping briefly a hundred yards from where Lee's head had bobbled ashore. Magnus regretted the walk-on-the-beach suggestion. He'd been so focused on Shortley senior's demise that he had forgotten about Junior's beheading.

They managed the walk without mention of *the head*, but it was there, the thought floating in the background. When back in town, Magnus gave Hero a lift home. He was still hungry, almost ravenous. He ascribed the hunger to nerves. This is what it was like, he thought, to fear being ambushed by a saber-toothed tiger and needing all the energy one could muster to defend oneself. Then again, he had that geek mentality about eating being an annoyance. A trope, but sometimes true. On the way back from Hero's he settled the issue with a turkey and Swiss from the Little Apple. At home, he topped off the sandwich off with a beer from the fridge, then plopped down on the Beast and cracked open his laptop. It was time to think about and process what he had learned, to give it context. Often, often enough to be wary of this propensity, Magnus thought better of people than he should have. Some would have called this tendency a weakness. Mari and Ari would have called it a sign of good character.

Multiple layers of protection, including one layer solely to detect login attempts, guarded the video Lee had made of Constanza. As far as he could tell, the folder with the video had been undisturbed. Next, Magnus did exactly what he had promised he would not do. Circumstances had changed, he rationalized, and in the process of opening the file he realized that his reluctance to see the video had been as much a fear of what he would discover as his respect for Constanza's privacy.

People had all sorts of preconceptions and opinions about pornography. One of Magnus's colleagues had commented that porn was a tool in her armamentarium, describing porn as misunderstood and addictive. She commented that for some people, it could lead to sexual violence. Magnus, a boringly straight guy, had zero personal experience with porn. Whenever the topic came up in conversations at home in Detroit, he shrugged it off, accepting the obvious fact that a heck of a lot of people enjoyed porn. He'd heard that half of X's business was porn related.

In a prior conversation, Hero told Magnus that she had been openly curious and several years ago had attended an amateur porn film event. The five-minute submissions, as she described them, ran the gamut: hilarious and artistic to really out there and kinky. The attendees in the audience had been super nice, supportive of the filmmakers, never derisive, and fun to hang with. Nothing violent or hurtful appeared in any of the videos she had seen. It would be naïve, Magnus reflected, to generalize from one relatively benign experience. Regardless, the normality of her experience was, in a way, a relief.

Miss Angel was firmly in the "porn as art" camp. During one of their book sessions, he and Miss Angel had argued about Lolita. She had claimed the work was a brilliantly written commentary on Americana and the nature of obsession. Magnus had countered that Humbert Humbert might have been a butterfly collector instead of a creepy perv. At least lepidoptery was a hobby and passion for which Nabokov had earned much recognition. Miss Angel argued that a lepidopterist would never have resonated or challenged societal convictions and beliefs as deeply as a man who was sexually obsessed with an underaged girl for whom her care and well-being should have been his first concern.

From the first frame of the video of Constanza, Magnus realized they had been played. Constanza, as the demure, underage maid, ate up the role. The beginning of the video matched the story she had told Riley, the sexual assault nurse: A scene with a naif discovering her own sexuality, giving it expression by using a titillating array of props and offering low-def close-ups of a scantily dressed Constanza. The movie's low-budget look made it real.

Constanza, obviously not a professional and possible more effective because of it, moaned and groaned unconvincingly. The sound track recorded Lee's direction, meaning that the video and sound were to be edited later and separately synced. When the maid set piece had concluded, Lee turned off the camera but left the audio in record mode. This error was, quite possibly, what had cost him his life. Lee made demands on Constanza that were not dissimilar from what she had initially told Magnus. The cries and anger in this post-video recording had not been an act. The sound of Lee slapping Constanza and forcing himself upon her would have been enough to convince any judge or jury to put him behind bars.

Magnus couldn't watch or listen to more. The turkey and Swiss had disappeared. He didn't remember eating it. He'd finished the beer and didn't remember drinking it. Unwelcomed curiosity, guilty-about-it arousal, and profound anger about both Constanza's complicity and Lee's egregiously wrong behavior made for a toxic emotional cocktail. Weird, he thought, to be the normal guy in the room. He walked to the fridge, got a second beer, and returned to the recording, thinking there would be little more to be learned.

The quality of the audio improved after the video had stopped recording. Or, Magnus thought, it could be the case that the audio received his undivided attention. Constanza's words were venomous and delivered in English that belied her usual hesitation to assert herself in English.

She spat out the words between sobs and then stopped abruptly. He heard her clear her nose and sniffle. Then she cleared her throat. "Cabrón—" she slapped him—"I will make you pay."

Magnus listened to bed springs squeak and Constanza moving about, and a flurry of background sounds—clinks, cables being unplugged, Velcro ripping, fabric brushing the mic. These sounds must have been Lee packing up the recording equipment. Then this from Constanza: "If you don't pay me ten thousand dollars, I will tell the police everything about you and your father and your business. I can do it without giving them my name."

Another silence. "Good luck with that," Lee scoffed. "You and your precious family will be on the next bus to Mexico."

"If you don't pay the money," Constanza demanded, "I promise I will tell police."

"You don't get it, do you, chica? You go down or you go South. That's the deal."

"If I tell mamá, you are a dead man."

Magnus imagined Lee's figure towering over Constanza, mocking her. Lee was enjoying himself, enjoying being the big man with the derisive laugh.

"You try that, chica, and see what happens."

"I will! You will be the one who will see what happens."

Lee slapped her. Magnus knew how hard Lee could hit. He heard the thwack of flesh on flesh. It had to hurt. Constanza didn't cry, not a whimper.

Lee had had enough. "Go fuck yourself. You're good at it!"

Magnus heard Constanza take in quick, choppy breaths, the way a small animal would pant. In the background was the noisy clatter of objects being gathered, then things bumping into the mic. A harsh "Shit" from Lee punctuated the end of the recording. That must have been the point at which Lee had realized that the audio had been on.

Magnus sat for an hour and sipped room-temperature beer. Hero's revelations and the video and soundtrack had transformed his perception of Constanza. Peggy's prescient warning about Constanza haunted him. He put off any decisions until morning. A part of him wanted to publish all of it in the *BBQ*. And then leave Manzanita and never come back.

Bracelet

Panda Bakery had opened for the early-to-rise weekend summer crowd. José sweated over the stove and dished out orders of huevos rancheros. The aroma of home-made salsa and refried beans filled the air. Constanza was serving and saw Magnus approach. She walked up to him. They stood inside the entryway. She appeared fresh, happy, without a care in the world. Not so Magnus. He was a hundred-years old, an unwilling cast member in a Mexican soap opera.

"Hola," Constanza cheerfully greeting him. "Quieres desayuno?"

"El desayuno es lo último que quiero hacer ahora mismo."

"Okay." She matched his serious tone and switched to English. "What *do* you want? We are very, very busy."

He held open the envelope flap so she could see the contents. "Recognize this?"

Constanza took his hand and walked him outside.

"It is not mine."

"Constanza, it's yours . . ."

The last time Magnus had seen Constanza, he thought she had had three Swiftie bracelets on her wrist. But he wasn't sure. Today, there were two. Magnus gently reached for her wrist. She quickly withdrew her arm and covered the bracelets with her other hand. José, watching from the kitchen and through the window, caught her movement. Magnus had wanted to inspect her bracelets for blood stains.

"Or it belonged to Félix," he continued. "Which is it? That's Shortley Holder's blood."

"Where did you get it?" she asked.

"Hero found it next to the wheelchair. I don't think you're gonna get away with this."

"She helped. Dámelo!"

"Hero helped you? I don't think so."

"Give it to me!"

"If I say no?"

"I will ask Papá. Or Tio Fe."

"Félix is gone. Don't pretend you don't know. You blew your chance for the ten thousand. It's too late now."

She was tough, way tougher than he had ever imagined. There had been little emotional reaction when he showed her the bracelet, the same as when he had mentioned the money. He was certain she had understood.

"Ten thousand what?"

"Constanza, please don't play dumb. I watched the video. Lee left the audio on after the video ended. I heard it all. Maybe not all, but I heard enough."

"You promised you would not watch!"

"Yeah, well, my feelings changed after Hero described what happened."

That got a reaction. Was it anger, or the pain of betrayal? She tempered the bravado. "Then you know what he did."

"Does it justify murder? You know, trying to squeeze money from the Holders doesn't help your case." As he listened to his own words, Magnus asked himself the same question. Something inside told him the answer might be "sure" and that he should get off his high horse.

"Mr. Shortley, he paid girls. Lee did bad things to me and the other girls. And boys, boys too." Constanza was shifting from one leg to the other and repeatedly looking up at him and then back to her shoes. "He bragged. He showed me other videos, for ideas. 'I am important man,' he said. 'I would be his little star.' He knew the Spanish word: 'Estrellita.' "

Constanza's mother walked from the pastry counter to the front door and eyed Magnus and Constanza. Several customers were waiting to pay. Maternal instinct, reading her daughter's body language—whatever it was—made her stand still and watch.

"I have to work." Constanza turned toward her mother.

Magnus grabbed Constanza's arm, spun her around, and put the envelope in her hand. She started, as if shocked. Carmen stepped toward her as the envelope and its contents disappeared into a pocket. Constanza's face was feral.

On the drive home Magnus thought about that fierce demeanor, and about Félix. Like niece, like uncle? Got to give them credit, they don't go half-way. Constanza's threats were anything but idle and Félix was, well, whatever Félix was. And what had "She helped" meant? Hero had admitted to cleaning up, but nothing more. But what if there was something more? Hero could swing a machete, that was for fucking sure.

Peggy Wheelwright's words refused to go away. *She's wanted for murder, and there's a mountain of incriminating evidence.* Hero's behavior at the farm had been a violent, uncontrollable reaction to a horror-filled memory. Could Hero have delivered the coup de grâce to Shortley Holder? Had the shared horror of Hero's and Constanza's experiences driven them to kill Holder? There was not one passive molecule in Hero's psyche. In that respect, she was like her mother. She was physically strong, as strong or stronger than Magnus. Or, he reflected, maybe it was the three of them together? Hero, Constanza, and Félix. He visualized them gleefully launching Shortley and his chair down the stairs. And Félix smiling at the top of the stairs and sipping his horchata. Crazy improbable, but not impossible. That closet hid the story. And possibly evidence. Would anybody look?

Toes in Sand

The next day, after a surprisingly good night's sleep, a refreshed Magnus awoke ready to take on the world but at a loss about how to go about it. The first thing he did was copy the video recording of Constanza and Lee to a thumb drive and deleted the online original. Then, with thumb drive in pocket, he headed to the News, wisely reasoning that taking on the world would require at least a double espresso.

A USB stick, flash drive, memory stick—whatever name one called it —was nothing more than a fiberglass composite and epoxy circuit board, a trace of copper and gold plating, silicon chip, plastic case and a USB steel connector. It didn't have a soul or heart or mind; it didn't eat or defecate, but—in a way—it had a story to tell, a story had destroyed two lives. The question to Magnus was this: would it destroy others? He rolled the drive around in his fingers, a tactile coming to terms.

Magnus was a physical guy, a mechanic and computer nerd. It was how he understood things. And this "thing" had become more a sacred relic than a thing. It possessed powers to affect the natural world, to save, or condemn. A kind of *virtus*, he thought. But then virtus had dual meanings. The cardinal *virtus* referred to practical wisdom, justice, self-control, courage. Rational tools that never adequately explained the underlying animistic understanding Magnus had for inanimate things.

He ordered the usual from Morgan. As he waited, he imagined Jock walking in the door, extending an open palm and ready—as if he had been waiting for Magnus to come around of his own accord—to receive Magnus's offering.

Alas, there was no Jock, no car parked at the Police Station, no need to test the urge to come clean. Coffee in one hand, his other hand in a fist and wrapped around the memory stick in his pocket, Magnus walked home. Passersby probably thought he needed the bathroom. The weathered turned—as it can on the coast, turn on dime—and threatened.

Once home, he glanced at *The New York Times* puzzle but couldn't concentrate. Random words surfaced and fled, took shape and dissolved like a 10X time-lapse video of clouds. After a directionless hour, he decided to go for a run. He changed quickly and headed to the beach.

It was not the best day to run, especially barefoot. A nor'wester blew cold, relentless, and raw. Magnus ignored it; he had to move. He needed—to quote Hero—"Toes in sand."

Ruffled cat's paws skittered across the water, moving in ways no cat ever would. The hard sea merged with a melancholy sky; both a gun-metal grey. He transitioned from walk to jog at the Laneda beach access. The turnaround point would be the jetty.

The shore changes. Some changes are dramatic, as when big waves notch out the base of a dune and transform the dune into a cliff. Some changes are gradual and familiar dunes assume an unfamiliar aspect. Magnus was a mile into his run before he figured out what was different. Seagrass leaves and blades normally grew in clusters, erupting out from rhizome nodes that anchored them to the sand. Overnight, the steady onshore breeze had piled sand around the nodes, burying the nodes but leaving the stiff upper stalks exposed and poking out the sand like mohawk dos, upright in places and some at bizarre directions. The dunes with bed head.

The heady wind continued and chafed and numbed the backs of Magnus's legs and arms. At the jetty he found relative shelter and sat on a boulder with a scalloped, bench-shaped top. Curled up, legs tucked up and arms wrapped around the legs, he waited for feeling to return to the numbed areas of his body.

Pelicans tunneled gracefully through parallel throughs of waves. Magnus imagined pelican life, thinking it good: the uncomplicated diet of fish. No concerns about a lover, an adolescent, and a mysterious stranger—any of whom, or in combination, might have murdered an old grouch in a wheelchair. Pelicans didn't give a damn about men who extorted the disadvantaged, nor people for whom heads and coconuts were all the same, thank you.

He argued with himself about being so distrustful. What if Félix was who he had said he was, a friend who had offered to help the Reyes family and had made a road trip from Chihuahua to Manzanita, visiting old friends along the way, arriving in Manzanita with nothing nefarious on the agenda? And what of Peggy Wheelwright? What if she was a caring wife and mother, and all that cold-war warrior talk the stuff of fantasy? And maybe Magnus was an alien.

Magnus digressed further. Would Carolina find the same fate as Peggy as the demands of *her* career tested her commitment to truth and decency? Magnus hoped to hell she would become a Foreign Service analyst and not some death-dealing drone jockey. Carolina was hopeless at Mario Cart, giving Magnus another kind of hope.

He inventoried his own family. Ari, the umpire—he'd be alright. Mari was in the maybe camp. A threat to anyone who crossed her family and, as sure as she made the best tres leches on the planet, she would cross the line. Then there's Vinnie, who, under the charade of humility, got away with crimes that put other people in Rikers for life. Except for Ari, was there anybody among those he loved who was incapable of doing serious harm to his fellow man?

Had he, Magnus, unintentionally cultivated relationships with people inclined to wrongdoing? What of his own weakness of character, fear of confrontation, and his impulsive and futile acts in the name of justice, acts that had been small at inception, and then, for lack of forethought, had exploded out of control upon execution? Was his righteous desire to aid the underdog a misguided compensation for his own diminished relevance in the world? Had he been hiding, long before becoming Magnus Krum, under layers of self-deception? Was he a snowy plover, a threatened species whose only defense was camouflage or, in extreme cases, feigning a broken wing? Magnus had assured Miss Angel that he was no longer afraid. He had meant it. But there's a debt to pay for courage and he had only made the first few installments.

"Fuck it! Enough!" Magnus screamed at the wind, spooking the skirling gulls, and flushing the stolid eagle from his habitual perch on a massive log jutting out of the spine of the jetty. This endorphin-laden moment, Magnus *chose* to believe that everyone had some good, some kindness inside.

He clamored over boulders and debris and neared the endpoint of the jetty. This, he knew, was folly. A sneaker wave, or even a slightly larger than normal wave, were it to wash over the jetty, could sweep him out to sea. But he was fit. He was alert. He bent forward and crawled on numbed hands and numbed feet through the last wet section. At the last possible stance Magnus braced himself, stood up, and teetered above the dizzying ocean swirl.

He removed the thumb drive from his running shorts pocket—having much difficulty because of popsicle fingers and the drive snagging on the fishnet lining. He stared at it, fixated, as if its contents had been a dream. *Don't kill yourself,* an annoyingly sane conscience screamed. Magnus Krum Omar Adil Papadopoulos—he was all these —took a deep, salty breath. He brought his arm back and threw the drive as hard and as far as he could, committing it—and almost his life —to the wind, the water, and the abyss. It would have been a hell of a lot easier, he soberly reflected, to have just erased the fucking thing. Crawling first, then stepping with care, Magnus wove his way through the boulders and back to the safety of the beach.

He was thirsty and shivering. The wind freshened. As to the fear, he had expunged the fear, and replaced it with a stiff, numbed, blue-lipped smile. He started back, head leaning into the wind and arms across his chest to block the nor'wester's sting.

Despite—as Miss Angel had put it—the "unkindness of dark possibilities," Magnus thought of Hero, his "lark at break of day arising," and all the rest fell aside. That was the jetty's lesson. He was grateful for so much, grateful at this instant of existence, for "toes in sand."

Magnus: Weather had delayed

Weather had delayed our flight. We walked through the door two hours late and the party—a welcome home party for me and an opportunity for the family to meet Hero—was underway. Salsa music competed with whatever it was my father watched from his La-Z-Boy. The Twins were explaining something incomprehensible to a couple of friends from Mom's backup band. The musicians nodded obediently, as if they understood or were waiting for a treat. Tia Alejandra and her son, who was my age and whom I had not seen in years, cleared appetizers off the table in preparation for dinner.

I warned Hero that people at the party knew me as Omar, not Magnus. Though close family had learned that I had used the Magnus Krum alias since I'd left Detroit.

Mom buried Hero in besitos. This was a challenge because Hero was a foot taller. Still, Mom couldn't stop kissing her or yammering away in Spanish. Hero understood fragments that were common phrases or Italian cognates. She accepted and absorbed my mother's clingy attention, not at all embarrassed by the display of affection. When Hero spoke, she auto responded in Italian, prompting Zio Vinnie to join the party, bombarding her with a dialect that added to the linguistic chaos. The words didn't matter. My family was prepared to love and adore Hero. It's how we were.

Mom asked Hero if there was anything she wanted to do in Detroit —other than meet the family—Hero responded: "Yes, the museum. I'd like to go to the art museum."

"We'll go tomorrow!" Mari clapped her hands. "You've never been there?"

"No. But there's a painting, Artemisia Gentileschi's painting of Judith beheading Holofernes. There's a second painting of the same subject and by the same artist at the Uffizi in Firenze, where I studied. Gentileschi's work is brilliant. She was a strong woman and a brilliant artist."

A chill ran down my back. Enough with the beheadings. Hero picked up on my reaction.

"It's a kind of closure, Magnus—I mean Omar. I do love her work."

Mom missed our exchange. She was scanning the room, thinking about what was next. She returned to the conversation and addressed Hero: "Did Omar tell you, Hero, that he and I met at *Judith and Her Maidservant* the day he left Detroit?"

That coincidence was not the biggest surprise of the evening. The knock-out punch, the woman my mother had conveniently forgotten to mention would be there, had spotted me. I moved away from Mom and Hero and thought about bolting for the back door. My stalker's expression switched from quizzical and amused, to caring and tinged with jealousy.

Carolina, the ex, stood erect, immobile, and oozing D.C. sophistication. Mounted beside her in suit but no tie and equally refined, was a handsome man as well-postured as she. The heir to her affections, the replacement fiancé (or was it husband?), cut an imposing figure. He was older, quiet, confident, and watchful.

Ari froze the frame of a golf ball mid-flight and oomphed out of the recliner. As he got up—doing so in stages—his eyes locked onto mine. My father, four inches taller and eighty pounds heavier, lifted me off the ground the same way he had when he had been a head taller and a hundred pounds heavier. We separated but continued to hold and squeeze each other's shoulders. A tear worked its way down his fleshy cheek. What a big softy. I thought, not for the first time, about how fortunate I was.

"Dad, did you—"

"I have good news." Ari cut me short, using a tamped down version of the umpire voice, this time loud enough to carry across the infield but not reach the stands in center field.

Hero and I had dreaded the possibility of arriving in Detroit and being met by ICE and/or Detroit's Finest as we stepped off the plane. Ari had assured us that wouldn't happen. But he hadn't explained why.

"Immigration backed off. Out of the blue, no explanation given. One minute, I was a nobody. The next, I was their long-lost best friend. Never seen nothing like it, guys bending over backwards to be nice to a schmuck. Scared the crap out of me, let me tell you, to jinx it. I shut my big mouth and listened. 'We want to make things right,' they said. And 'Anything we can do for you, Mr. Papadopoulos. Can't thank you enough for your son's service.' Now what the hell was that about? I figure they screwed up and got you mixed up with some poor schmuck they put in the can, or maybe your friends—we won't say who—got you off the hook."

Ari winked and nodded toward the Twins. "Whadda I know?" He put his hands up in the air. "I'm the ambulance chaser—"

Mom's musician friends walked over to say hello and shake my hand. I had missed part of what Dad had said and hoped that he hadn't made new enemies in exchange for saving my ass. I didn't want that. My personal track record with trying to right wrongs invariably boomeranged. But Dad was smarter; he followed the rules.

I replayed what Ari had intimated about Harry and Charlie. The inference didn't add up. The Twins wouldn't mess with ICE, not unless they got the green light from a higher authority.

Ari continued: "Funny, huh? I honestly got no clue what caused the change of heart. I tell you I had nothing to do with it." Ari threw in a little Detroit attitude: "Nobody asked for nothin', Omar. Nothin'."

Somewhere behind me Hero wove a path through the jungle of people, weaving her story through the non-stop barrage of questions. I had lost track of her.

I wanted to look for her, but Ari wasn't ready to let go. He was keen to deliver yet more good news: "We got a plea deal with the D.A. Small potatoes—five thousand fine and six months community service. Translating or something for Latinx Housing Services. Pled the charge to a misdemeanor. I agreed to the deal on your behalf. You live with that?"

"Yeah, of course! Holy shit! That's fabulous." I was thrilled. "Thank you, thank you so much." I hugged Dad, truly grateful.

"You can stay with us. Your old room. Gotta move the pool table. You gotta help."

Ari searched for and found Hero. He nodded in her direction. "Her too."

Hero had planned to stay for the weekend and was here only because her mother had insisted that she take a vacay from the caregiving. Peggy promised she wouldn't die before Hero returned. I had explained none of this to my parents and, in fact, I had not planned to be in Detroit for more than a week. Then again, there wouldn't be a second chance to address the charges. Hero and I would work it out—we were adults. I could explain to the court that I would need to return to Manzanita from time to time.

"You're the best Dad ever. Six months, I can manage six months. And I want to spend time with you and Mom. Leave the table where it is. I'll find a place. I need closet space."

"She got a lot of clothes? Nah, she's not the type with a lotta clothes. Your mother, Jesus. She got a lotta clothes. You remember?"

"I remember."

I took a minute to remember and reflect on more than Mom's clothes, asking myself how Omar, surrounded by so much giving and emotional richness, had been so shallow and unreceptive. Why did Omar have to become Magnus to discover the authentic me, the me who didn't take the people in this room for granted? And what of love flourishing? I had let go reason and judgment to love a woman without a past, a woman for whom I would die a thousand deaths. Had I been drugged the first twenty-six years of my life? Apparently so. Manzanita had been a kind of halfway house, and I, the recovering addict, had gained insight into what it meant to be normal. To say "recovered" would be bullshit. We never fully recover from ourselves.

Ari waited for me to say something.

"I've not been gone that long. But it feels really long." I remembered we had been talking about Mom's outlandish outfits. It was true; she was a fashion firecracker. "We don't have a lot of clothes." I light-heartedly added, "Got plenty skeletons though."

Ari laughed, and then the laugh morphed into an expression of concern. His efforts on my behalf had gone well, but, being a lawyer, he worried that there was more to the story, things I hadn't told him, specifically things that might derail the compromise he had engineered.

My aunt, standing nearby, had picked up bits and pieces of our conversation. Alejandra finished her mojito and leaned on my shoulder. "Esqueletos! Verdad?"

"Yes, they live with us. We've gotten used to it."

She punched me in the shoulder and switched to English. "You are keedding me." Something from afar caught her attention. She branded my cheek with a sloppy kiss and moved on.

"I'll find something in Mexicantown. But thank you. Thank you for all the help, and for offering us a place and everything." I hugged my father once more. "I should rescue Hero before she suffocates."

Mari saw me coming and initiated a prisoner exchange: Hero for me. She bombarded me with a million besos interspersed with as many questions, all in bullet-hard Cuban. My cheeks bloomed with rosy, lip-shaped impressions.

"I love her! She is so pretty! But she looks so much like you! You are brother and sister. It is little strange, don't you think?" Mom flipped back and forth between Hero and me, she being in performance mode and thrilled for an excuse to be so animated. I half-expected her to announce that Hero and I were engaged and the wedding would be next week and that we planned to move next door and have six children and start our own mariachi band. Hero picked up on my embarrassment and sidled up to Mari.

"He's perfect!" Hero, looking down, winked at Mom. Mom, looking up, winked back as Alejandra arrived to drag her away.

Hero had to be exhausted. Yet something made her smile. "Are you going to introduce me to her or hide behind my skirt?"

"You're not wearing a skirt."

"You're screwed," Hero laughed. She was looking past my shoulder. "Incoming."

Carolina, like the shark in Jaws, approached. The hair on the back of my neck tingled. She closed in and wrapped not just her arms but her whole body around me, fitting it like an old shoe. A thousand hours of partner dancing did that. Competition dance partners know each other's bodies better than lovers do. I raised my arms and spun around within hers. We hugged, excited not from sexual intimacy, but comforted by the physical familiarity. Our conversation, conducted hip-to-hip, faces inches apart, reminded me of the many conversations we had had in closed hold. Too, I thought about what, out of my immature fear of commitment, I had lost. I'd sort of gotten over the loss; but the echo of shame and embarrassment over my cowardly behavior lingered. Hero watched and, I hoped, understood.

Carolina had matured more than aged. There was no adequate measure of our months apart. She paused to think before she spoke: "This time it'll work, Omar. I feel it in my bones."

"Me too! Thank you for saying that. I mean it."

Openly curious, Carolina turned to Hero. "Is that really your name? Hero?"

Hero nodded back yes.

"I love it. Are you a dancer?"

Hero played shy. The nod swayed side to side. "God no. I have, maybe, one-and-a-half left feet."

I thought about mentioning parkour and that Hero could probably slackline across the Grand Canyon, but didn't want to get into one of those dumb, conversational pissing contests.

Carolina, dancer and diplomat, continued: "What a wonderful name! Women are heroes. So, he has taken you out for a spin!" Hero raised a hand, finger and thumb pinched together. "Well," Carolina continued, "as they say, we were all beginners once. Expect a cowbell for your birthday!"

Hero smiled and leaned a shoulder against Carolina's and quoted the timeless SNL line, "You can't have too much cowbell!"

Carolina took Hero's hand, still keeping her focus on me. She did that same thing Mom had done, going back and forth between us. I expected the usual comment. It didn't happen. "Omar, you're a lucky guy. Hero, I'm happy for you."

"Omar told me about you." Hero had remembered to use Omar. "I mean, not personal stuff, but about dancing with you. He loved dancing with you."

"Still does, I hope. We'll dance tonight. That's a given, because this is Mari's home and her ground rules. You walk in that door, you dance!"

"I'm happy to learn." Hero sounded more enthusiastic than she was; we had gotten up early and she'd not slept well the night before or on the flight. "But maybe not tonight. Love to watch. Does your husband dance?"

Mister Handsome, with red curly hair and tortoiseshell glasses and pasty white skin, introduced himself. The British accent was a surprise. "I'm afraid not." He then qualified the statement. "Not like Ginger Rogers, here. Survived the usual preparatory drills, girls on this side, boys on that. Ready? On one!" He raised his arms in closed dance position hold, but—to make it goofy—shrugged his shoulders toward his ears. Carolina elbowed him.

She laughed. "Spare us!"

We ran through the usual introductory small talk. His name was Brian. He was an okay guy.

Carolina, comfortable with the answer she expected, laid it on me: "What do you think, Omar?"

"About?"

"Brian, of course."

I gave Brian a once-over and tried to appear stern. "Got a job?"

"I do," he cheerfully responded. "For the lads at Legoland."

"Legoland?" I hadn't understood. "Must be serious work."

Carolina connected the dots. "It is. That's the MI6 building."

"Well then, after much deep reflection, and reservations about his license to kill, I give him two thumbs up."

"We British might say," Brian laid on the accent, "cracking!"

"Excellent," Carolina hugged me again. "I was worried about you. You're a brother to me, Omar. I hope you feel that way about me."

Hero and I finished the conversation with the two happy, foreign-service-spies-made-for-each-other couple, and continued the rounds. She sparkled around the Twins, Harry and Charlie. I had described them to Hero, but her meeting them in person for the first time got an electric reaction. One sensed the Twins were quantum entangled. If they were in different rooms, different houses, different planets; if you said something to Harry, Charlie heard it real time.

"Been a while." Harry delivered the greeting in his usual deadpan way.

Charlie followed. "Have you officially changed your name to Krum?"

I responded with honest surprise: "No such intention."

"You should," Charlie opined. "Easy to spell. Anyway, I set up an encrypted email account with the new name. For work. In case."

I didn't bother asking, but I think that meant IBM still had a place for me. Harry updated me, but not about the job. "They remodeled our corner at Zingerman's. The tables are twenty percent smaller than the old ones; there are more tables but less privacy. They're the same height, but the chairs are two centimeters taller."

"Great, good to know. So, how's work going?"

"Same old, same old. We're slammed. China's a shit-show. All the new tariffs and workarounds. Chinese are going batshit. A great deal of cat and mouse."

"A regular zoo."

He didn't smile. I changed the subject. "Thanks, for that thing you did."

"Ecuador and Venezuela are bonkers. The gang wants you back." As he spoke, Charlie's gaze drifted around the room and recorded the changes since his last visit.

Neither Harry nor Charlie had acknowledged my comment, so I rephrased the statement. "I meant for the life ring with ICE. Don't know what you did, but I fucking appreciate it."

"Sorry, dude." Charlie was genuinely confused. "No thing done, no life ring from yours truly."

Harry piled on another metaphor. "Crossed your wires, Omar."

After Dad had recounted the ICE news, I repeated to Hero what he had implied, that the fix must have originated with the Twins. Apparently, Dad had been mistaken. I didn't bother to ask the Twins a second time. Hero smiled, an aha! expression on her face.

"Mom."

Of course it was Peggy. Se had shown no interest in arm-twisting ICE to help the Reyes family. If anything, the opposite. That she had made a deal with ICE on my behalf could have meant that Peggy had had only so many favors to cash in. Her intervention was the only explanation for why I had transitioned from pariah one to patriot. God knows what she told them. Hopefully not a tale as crazy as the one Miss Angel had fabricated.

We moved on. Vinnie, too, was thrilled to meet Hero. He quickly got to business. Half the reason I was willing to return to Detroit was because Vinnie had cut a deal with Zaidu and the Chaldeans. Per Vinnie's orders, I had transferred two-hundred-fifty thousand out of Vinnie's offshore account to a new offshore account in Zaidu's name. Vinnie implied that the cachet of having offshore money qualified for a deep discount to the million I had ripped off. That, and the positive status, notoriety, and new business opportunities Zaidu had received as a side benefit of the "charitable giving" that he'd had nothing to do with but got all the credit for. Oh vanity, all praise vanity. I promised Vinnie I would pay him back. He gave me a warm hug and thickly accented "Fuhgeddaboudit."

The bullshit aspect of Vinnie's explanation didn't sink in until we had finished and I had replayed our conversation. A Chaldean mobster would never go soft. I'm sure Vinnie threatened to break the guys's legs.

I was going to press him for more, but Mari clanged the cowbell and announced it was time to eat. Guests milled about and fussed over who would sit where. There was a gentle tap-tap-tap at the door. Hero and I were the nearest.

I eased the door open and recognize a familiar grin. One tooth hung like a half-open peephole cover. We exchanged hellos in Spanish. I introduced Hero. Rafael modestly and gently took her hand in his strong, calloused, mason's fingers. Mom saw us. She hit the cowbell again, loudly this time, playing a cáscara pattern. "Quiet! Quiet everyone!" When the talking and shuffling subsided, she announced: "This is my friend, Rafael. He's come to eat and wait until you see him dance!"

Rafael flashed a toothy, shy smile and introduced me to the woman standing beside him. His wife, a tall beautiful Latina woman, had arrived dressed in the showy bling-wear dancers adore. I led him them to chairs next to Mom and Ari.

Mom's declining physical and mental health meant that she needed 24-hour care. Riley, the same nurse who had seen Constanza after the incident with Lee Holder, managed one of the care shifts. Riley and I never discussed Constanza, at least not beyond a "have you seen Constanza, how's she doing, fine." Dad and I covered the other two shifts. I realized the end was near when Peggy stopped bossing us around.

The month before we lost her, right after I had returned from Detroit, I tried to find out how Mom had turned around the problem Magnus had had with ICE. Mom went mum, implying it was no big deal and not to worry. I wasn't going to argue with her. The back-room dealings had kept her alive the last few months. She was obsessed with the man to whom we had given the name "Avocado," a play on the Italian word "avvocato," meaning "lawyer."

Avocado was not the mystery man whose reflection I had seen in the mirror in the bathroom. Him, we had named "Looker." Avocado was, however, the only link we had to Looker. Avocado represented the prosecutor's office with such zealotry and righteous indignation that it was inconceivable to us that he was not on the take or living under some dark threat. Mom's theory was that Looker was pulling the strings and that he was the one who, ironically, was demanding justice, specifically my extradition from the States and trial in Italy for the double murder.

After the initial publicity, interest in my extradition waned. Mom explained that this was to be expected because Looker wanted to maintain a healthy, neck-preserving distance from both the up-ended drug deal and the two murders. He pushed, but not enough to generate unwanted attention. A burglary of Avocado's office uncovered a dozen companies listing Avocado as a board member or founder. Mom had been running these to ground and hunting for a link to Luca and Looker. This taxing work had been unsuccessful, and Peggy was running out of time. On a separate front, she was challenging the extradition request. There, as well, she'd made little progress. Statements by witnesses, the video of me clubbing the sbirro, and the phone falling out of my pocket constituted an overwhelming amount of damning evidence. A requirement of the US-Italy Extradition Treaty was Dual Criminality. To fulfill this requirement, Avocado had partnered with another firm and proceeded with filing charges in the U.S. Fortunately, the wheels of injustice moved just as slowly as the wheels of justice. Our attorney, a friend of Mom's in D.C., was doing his best to stall proceedings.

Our last actual conversation—one in which she had been sufficiently awake and cognitively with it—had been to warn me that I would soon be on my own and that she had done all she could do to keep me safe.

"My little Hero." It was always my little Hero. "I have failed you. Your father, the dear man, he loves you but there's little he can do." Her head turned back and forth, a loving acceptance on her face. "Or worse," she laughed, "he'll make suggestions. . . . He cares though; he really cares."

This was harsh on Dad, but we both knew it was true. We loved him anyway. But the poor man had gone to pieces—something I'd not expected from a guy who had spent months in impoverished communities in Africa with Médecins Sans Frontières and witnessed genocide and mass starvation. Maybe he'd get his shit together, but I couldn't count on him.

"If you go back to Italy—as you—you'll spend much of your life in prison. Worse, you may be murdered. We can't let that happen." She coughed and spit into a tissue. The fucking cough was new and it weakened her voice. "You can't let that happen. Magnus can procure false identification documents. I'll try but I can't promise anything. The rest is up to you, or the both of you. He's a clever boy. You memorized the account numbers and codes?"

"C'mon, Mom. Months ago." Peggy had deposited funds at several banks in the Caribbean and Panama. I had access via various codes and phrases, online or in person. She had schooled about how much I could draw down and when. The withdrawals needed to appear legit. Apparently, I owned a little import gift shop in Martinique. The ownership papers were in a lockbox in the Caymans.

"Plan B is now Plan A. Do you understand? Am I talking nonsense?"

"B is A. Got it. You're not talking nonsense."

"Good. The drugs, you know. And the fucking tumor. I drift in and out. I feel good right now."

It pained me, pained me so much to have this conversation. Most girls, young women, if I imagined that last conversation with their mothers, it would be about family, grandchildren, the garden, what a lovely day it was. Not hidden funds and avoiding extradition.

The following day, the exact date that six months ago she had drawn a red circle around, Mom stopped speaking. Her eyes followed me around. I sat next to her on the bed and held her hand. At dusk she lifted one arm toward me, to hold me. I put my head on her chest to listen to her breathing. The odor of death hung over her.

I'd slept beside her long enough for the sun to have set and the room to have gone dark. Her hand twitched. I think that's what woke me. When I opened my eyes, she was watching, like she was watching over me.

In a voice that was barely a voice, she said her last words. "It's going be okay. I love you. I have to go to sleep now." She closed her eyes. I closed mine and fell asleep.

Next time, when I awoke, her hand that I had been holding had cooled. The brittle rise and fall of her chest had unceremoniously ceased. I squeezed her limp hand and sobbed. Dad's warm hand rested on my shoulder.

Drop the mic

Magnus caught a red-eye connecting through Chicago. He picked up Subi at the lot in Seattle where he had originally purchased the car and where, for a modest monthly fee, he had been storing Subi. On the by-now-familiar four-hour drive from Seattle to Manzanita, memories of the last six months flooded his mind. He stopped at the rocky promontory overlooking Manzanita and its seven-mile-long beach, and took stock of himself now vis-à-vis the directionless and self-destructive man who had stood in that very spot some calendar months earlier, but a lifetime ago emotionally.

By the time Magnus had scheduled his travel to Manzanita, Peggy had died. Leonard had arranged for Peggy's body to be taken from the Wheelwright's Neah-Kah-Nie home to a cremation service in Seaside. Post cremation, a befuddled Leonard had fretted over the ashes, this residue of the woman who had been the emotional centerpiece of his life for so many years.

Sometime earlier, Leonard had asked Peggy about a memorial service or burial, and she had told him she didn't want a fuss. "Flush me down the crapper," had been her exact words. She followed that with a warning about clogging the pipes. An alternative, a second thought if the plumbing were subpar, was to fling the urn off the Devil's Caldron viewpoint in Oswald West State Park. In this case, she advised, don't even try to toss the ashes by themselves because of the updraft. Only a few bones and teeth would be dense enough to make the descent. Peggy liked the name, "Devil's Caldron," a name befitting a spy. "I gave the Devil a run for his money," she reminded Leonard multiple times. Another directive: secure the top of the urn with duct tape. And then she fretted—as much as someone at the border of life and death could fret—about Leonard's heart condition. She had suggested that he start cardio conditioning on a Stairmaster in advance of the half-mile Elk Flats trail hike. Don't miss the Tiger Lilies, avoid the Himalayan Blackberries—Peggy's final parting advice was an endless list of to-dos and not-to-dos. Leonard listened and loved every word that came out of her mouth.

Peggy fretted as well about Leonard being near the grassy edge because heights made him dizzy and the ground was unstable. She expounded on what a hilarious goddamned mess it would be if he were to slip on the wet grass and, urn in arms, plummet to his death in the rock-strewn roiling waters below. Romantic though, she had opined.

And then she obsessed about the urn, or "the pot," as she called it. The pot had to be bio-degradable because she didn't want a posse of rabid Oregon environmentalist chasing after Leonard. Assuming he survived the tossing event. They'd gone back and forth about how many years it took duct tape to degrade and finally the four of them—Magnus had been visiting and present for this discussion—fell into riotous, uncontrollable laughter and tears.

In the end, Magnus later learned, Leonard got his wits about him and did what *he* had wanted. He found a simple plot of earth tucked in a shady, wind protected corner of Manzanita/Nehalem's modest, picture perfect, small-town cemetery. There, he could sit at her gravesite, tend the adjacent garden, and share with her little things of little importance. There, in that pacific sanctuary for all manner of apparitions and wildlife, she would no longer need a voice to speak to him.

The drive from the airport had given Magnus a chance to prepare and calm himself for Peggy's memorial, an informal gathering sans speeches and taking place at the Wheelwright's home. He pulled into the driveway and stopped, waiting in Subi, the engine off. Subi's heat shield rattled; the car made other creaky, cool-down noises. The surf rumbled and reverberated off the ribs of the U-shaped draw that wound uphill from the beach to upper Neah-Kah-Nie Meadows.

Magnus didn't bother to knock. He introduced himself to a half-dozen friends and neighbors. Snacks and drinks covered the dining room table. Several attendees were from the church Leonard attended. Three people were work colleagues of Peggy's and blended into the crowd too well.

One of the three—the youngest of the triumvirate—introduced himself as Harvey Jameson. He stood next to Hero. With no prompting, Jameson spoke to Magnus in Spanish. Magnus detected a Slavic accent. Jameson described himself as working for an international head-hunting firm. When asked where he was based, Jameson laughed. "A suitcase." He qualified the response and added, "Mexico City, until mid-next year." They enjoyed a cordial conversation. Harvey gave Magnus his card and asked if he might call sometime. Better yet, Magnus and Hero should come for a visit and he'd show them around CDMX, i.e. Mexico City. A watchdog, Magnus wondered. Hero promised Harvey she would keep in touch.

A suitcase, duffle, and travel pack with a skateboard strapped to it sat neatly stacked by the door. Hero made her goodbyes, using as an excuse that she needed to depart with Magnus directly. They planned to drop off Subi at Henry's family's place in Portland and then Lyft to PDX. In truth, they had time to spare. When the socializing had concluded and father and daughter had had their special time, Leonard stood at the door, friends at his side, and waved and watched as Subi carried his daughter and Magnus up the hill toward Highway 101.

Hero and Magnus didn't speak until they had passed Cannon Beach and turned onto the Sunset Highway. They had been listening to a rebroadcasting of *The Ship Report's* calming, mesmerizing account of maritime traffic on the Columbia. Magnus turned off the radio shortly after the turnoff. The reception would be patchy until Vernonia.

"They're gone. Did you know?"

"Who's gone?"

"Constanza. Her mother and father."

"They left? Did Constanza talk to you?"

"No chance. Nobody knows the real story. Except maybe your buddy, Jock.

"Jock's a smart guy. What did he say."

"I heard the rumor first. Day before yesterday, I ran into Jock at the News."

"He's there more than the station!"

"Could be." Hero didn't smile; she continued in the same sober tone. "Anyway, he said it was ICE. He didn't learn about it until after the fact. I could tell he was pissed about not being in the loop. And that the ICE agents had dressed like local police. They came in the middle of the night. Like the fucking Gestapo."

Magnus visualized the scene. Black vans pulling up to the trailer. Someone pushing in the flimsy door. Agents man-handling José and

Carmen. Constanza fighting back. She wouldn't go without a vicious fight—a fight that could turn deadly in a flash.

"Fuck. They must have been terrified! Christ, the whole family. For once I wish Félix would have been around."

"Jock was pretty upset. I think he felt guilty about not protecting them."

"Jock's not only a smart guy. He's a good guy. He should be upset. I'm mad as hell but I don't think there's shit we can do about it."

"Someone spread a story that the family left because of money they owed. Locals aren't buying it. Jock figured they'd been deported to Mexico, not Ecuador. I don't know how he would know this but he seemed to know."

"Wishful thinking, Hero. Remember? José had a record, and there's the Félix connection. I have no way to reach Félix. But he's got to be a target. Weird timing, don't you think—"

"I don't know. It was right before she died. I'm sorry now, that I didn't tell you right away. I was so preoccupied with things on the home front—"

Magnus realized he was strangling the steering wheel. He tried to relax and put his hand on Hero's lap. She rubbed his fingers, and he tried to not obsess about the deportation. The reality was that no amount of obsessing could change what had happened.

What he couldn't shake was the memory of Peggy grilling him about Félix. At the time he hadn't thought her behavior unusual. She'd asked for Félix's physical description; the year, make, and model of the car he had been driving—even little things like the "wash me" sign had seemed important. She had asked for every personal detail Magnus had learned during the conversation at Trio Loco. Magnus only now realized that he had been intentionally and professionally debriefed.

"A package arrived last week, destined for Port Hero."

Magnus announced the news in a Ship Report voice. He had locked away the ICE raid.

Hero was adrift. Tears streamed down her face. She ignored them. They flowed as unchecked as the loss ravaging her heart.

"Wha—?" She choked on the word. Her voice tried to find itself.

"The passport. The one Peggy said she was going to arrange. It arrived by snail mail a few days ago. To my PO box. No markings on the envelope. I could feel it was a passport. I waited to tell you. That okay?"

Bars of light broke through the passing trees and flashed across her vacant, tear-streaked features.

"Yeah, sure. You didn't open it?"

"I did." He had been curious about the quality, the name. "It's good. Chipped even. I scanned it. Real, I think. Better than anything I could have gotten from the Chinese. Do you want to know your new name?"

"Sure. Yeah." Hero was only half-there.

Magnus waited before saying the name, curious about her reaction and slightly embarrassed to be excited about the new identity.

"Beatrice." He pronounced the name as one would in English. Then, widening his lips, he smiled and repeated the name in Italian, lingering on the vowels, making the "c" a "ch" sound, and rolling the "r," sounding the "e" at the end.

Hero shook her head, joining him in sharing Peggy's post-mortem joke.

"That's so Mom."

" 'Beatrice Amaroso.' It's her gift to you, Hero. A loving gift. They were cousins, you know."

"Hero and Beatrice, I know."

The tears stopped. A wintry sparkle returned, a wonderment about —Magnus surmised—how she might inhabit this new identity. Or maybe it was a reaction to Peggy's post-death gesture.

She didn't speak for twenty minutes, then punched in directions on her phone to Insomnia, a coffee shop in Hillsboro and a convenient stop along their route to the airport.

Magnus drove there, not asking why until after they had ordered and taken seats at an outdoor table. The clouds that had covered the coast had not made it to Hillsboro. Magnus removed his glasses and stretched. He hadn't run for a couple of days and his athlete's body wanted to move.

"Another 'it' arrived," Hero announced.

Magnus had no idea what she was referring to. He shrugged.

Hero explained: "Sorry to report that we are not kissin' cousins. Mail came yesterday with the Red Cross results. Not even close to a twenty-four percent match. That's what the DNA test would have shown had we been related."

"Relieved?" he asked.

"Not really."

This surprised Magnus.

Hero continued. "There was something about being cousins that's kinda cool. A secret intimacy. And I'm okay with not having kids. So, I guess I'm both disappointed and relieved." She teased him. "It would have made it naughty, the sex. And it would have explained our—"

She fished for the word. Magnus supplied it. "Connection."

They didn't speak for a minute.

"It can still be naughty!" Magnus offered, and then berated himself for being a dumb male.

"Do you think I can use this passport for a ticket? What about facial recognition."

"The Mom never fucked around. She probably tweaked the data base. You got plans I don't know about?"

"Maaaybe."

" . . ."

"Italy. I'm thinking about Italy."

"You're fucking kidding, right!?"

"No. It's the last place they'd expect to find me. And I want to find that bastard who killed Luca."

"Your mom said—?"

"—No, the guy in the mirror."

"And how do you plan to do that?"

"Unlock Subi."

Magnus reached into his pocket and unlocked Subi with the remote. Hero retrieved her daypack from Subi and returned. As she took her seat she unzipped the pack, placed it on her lap, and extracted a spiral bound sketchbook. She opened the sketchbook to a portrait she had drawn, placed the book on the table, and flipped the image around for Magnus to view.

"That's him."

" . . ."

"See that?" She pointed to a thin line just under the chin on the portrait's right side. "His face was at an angle to the mirror. He was looking up, looking at his chin. Maybe he'd just shaved. That's an old scar. I'd recognize him if I saw him. And he's left-handed. I saw him gesturing with his left hand when he was standing at the window."

The drawing gave him chills. So did Hero's expression. He wiped the lenses of his eyeglasses with the bottom of his tee.

"I'd kinda planned to buy a sailboat and rescue immigrants at sea."

"We could live on the boat, my love. Keep it on some island in the Med: Corsica, Majorca. Not in Italy, but easy to go back and forth."

"Or live here—I mean in Manzanita. Buy a modest lot, build the house you drew. I can build it. I can do all that stuff."

"Maybe. In time. I'd really like that. I love Manzanita."

"You know, I still have to complete the community service gig in Detroit."

"Fine. I can teach you Italian. Before we go. And you can teach me salsa!"

"I speak Italian!"

"Uh huh. Let me rephrase. We'll brush up on *our* Italian."

She was being polite. Hero's Italian, after living in Italy for so many years, was native fluent.

"Sure."

The 'sure' upset her: "Magnus. Don't fucking 'sure' me if you don't mean it! 'Sure' is what you said to Carolina."

"I mean it, Hero. Totally, in my heart, I'm committed. Italian, the boat. We find the bad guy. But . . ."

A wooden swizzle stick had come with Hero's chai. Magnus picked it up and spun it around with the tips of his fingers. He could do the same thing with a pencil or a drumstick, and in either hand.

"Couple things—" Magnus used a swizzle stick to fan away imaginary distractions. "—re justice for this dude. No matter how big an asshole he is, I don't want to kill anybody. I want to be clear about that."

"I'm good with plain old justice, the legal sort."

"And I don't want to lose my job. I can figure out a way to work remotely. Truth is, I love what I do. Is that weird?"

"Good again. A remote work visa is easy. I was working on an independent project when I left ETH. I might continue under a different name. Cover, as Mom would call it."

"We agree, then." Magnus extended a hand; they shook on it. "I'm not messing around, Hero."

"I love you."

"I love you too." Magnus checked his watch. "Yikes! We gotta go."

Hero gathered their cups from the table and dropped them in the waste bin. It was close enough for her to lean back in her chair and reach it. Suddenly, her expression brightened; the ice-grey eyes sparkled. She leaned across the table and, using a finger and thumb of each hand, carefully removed Magnus's glasses. She folded the temples and held the glasses over the opening in the waste bin.

"You don't need these."

Magnus signaled Hero to stop. He rose and stretched to his full height, twisting right and left to work out the kinks from driving and sitting. He stood beside Hero and put out his hand. The glasses migrated from her hands to his. The handoff complete, Magnus opened and closed the temples a few times, testing the hinges. He looked up and again turned right and left, seeing beyond the coffee shop, the strip mall and parking lot, the well-tended landscape, and this moment in time.

Hero watched as Magnus let go the glasses, their final act a faint rustle as they landed in the trash.

"You're right, I don't."